J
U
M
N
A
Sacred
River

An American Childhood in India

J
U
M
N
A

A Memoir by
Charlotte
Gould Warren

Sacred
River

An American Childhood in India

STEPHEN F. AUSTIN STATE UNIVERSITY PRESS

Permissions
Stephen F. Austin State University Press,
1936 North Street, LAN 203,
Nacogdoches, Texas, 75962.
sfapress@sfasu.edu
sfasu.edu/sfapress

Cover Artwork: Monica Setziol Phillips
Book Design: Brittany O'Sullivan
Cover Design: Brittany O'Sullivan
Copy Editor: Kristi Warren

LIBRARY OF CONGRESS CATALOGING-IN-PUBLICATION DATA

Warren, Charlotte Gould
Jumna: Sacred River / Charlotte Gould Warren - 1st ed.
p.cm.

ISBN-978-1-936205-29-5

I. Title

First Edition: May 2012

Many of the old place names in India were restored after the country won its independence from Great Britain in 1947. The river that ran by our house called the *Jumna* when I was a child ("Jum" as in "jump" and "na" as in "not"), is now known as *Yamuna* or *Jamuna*.

ACKNOWLEDGEMENTS

My heart-felt thanks to poet, Alice Derry, for her years of encouragement and editorial wisdom. Her friendship and unfailing
belief in the work kept me writing. Thanks, too, to author Mary
Clearman Blew, whose illuminating ideas helped shape the manuscript. To Stan and Mary Case, among *Jumna's* first readers, for
their love and insights, and for Mary's probing questions. To my
brother, Bill Gould, and my cousins, Betsy Hearne and Tamara
Matthews, for sharing stories and affirming family history. To
daughter-in-law, Annjanette Warren, who risked learning more
than she might want to about me, and for her help in catching
errors. To Bella Halstead, college classmate, for her detailed notes
and generous reading of the manuscript. To writer friends, Shelly
Cook and Michele Leavitt, for their ongoing support. To Margaret McHugh, whose compassionate years of counsel allowed me
to walk through the pain and find the words to free it. To George,
whose love continues to steady me, and to our children and their
families for sharing their lives with us.

Special thanks to Monica Setziol Phillips for her superb art
work and her life-long advocacy of the arts. To Laurie Tanguay,
wizard of technology, for her big heart. To SFA Press Director,
Kimberly Verhines, and assistant, Brittany O'Sullivan, for steering
Jumna through to publication.

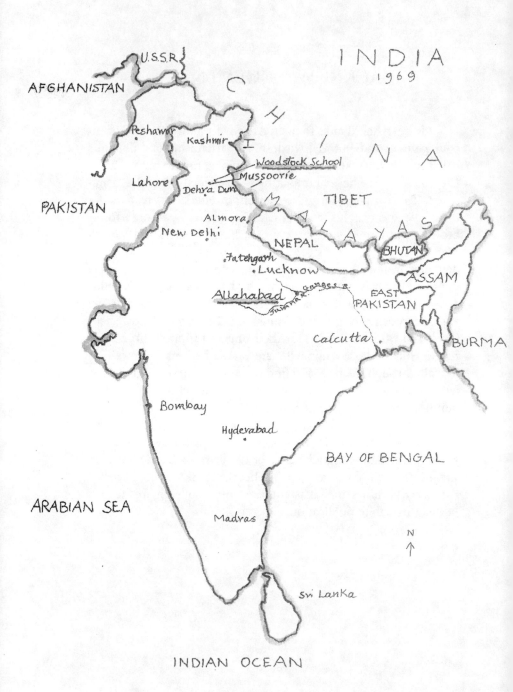

Hooves strike long sparks on the cobblestones of memory.
—Tess Gallagher
Dear Ghosts

Introspection is subversive here, and memory treasonable. And yet it is the brink on which we all live, the blade of the knife pressed against tomorrow.
—Mary Clearman Blew
Bone Deep in Landscape

1

LIGHTS DIM AND FLICKER as we leave Seattle, then Narita, Japan, then Bangkok for New Delhi. Thirty-two hours travel time. Before long, I pace the crowded aisles of the Boeing 747, stand at the back to flex my aching joints, or peer through the small cold windows to the turning world with its flock of clouds. Once more, I buckle myself in but can't settle down, read and shift about, finally lift the arm rest to wedge myself into the length of two seats, my head in George's lap, easing a painful back while he manages the endless hours of travel sitting up.

It's not until we're in New Delhi's vast arrival hall, waiting in line for customs, that the tears I've succeeded in holding back, or not feeling at all, begin to surface. They blur the colors of *saris*; the fatigued profile of an old man in his Kashmiri shawl; the impeccably turbaned Sikhs; the Punjabi women wearing bright green and orange *salwar kameez*, long silk over-shirts and loose pants fastened at the ankles; the Indian flight attendants with bodies fuller and more sensuous than those of their counterparts from Thailand. Like a kaleidoscope, whose bright pieces fall into place, India sparkles all around me. It's been forty-two years since I left this country I was born in. By the time India gained its independence from Great Britain in 1947, and our family decided to move to the United States, I was eleven years old.

Now, waiting in line for our bags, trying to calm the turbulence of my heart, I survey the signs in Hindi, Urdu and English, to find myself looking at an overhead walk-way with curving glass sides. When I shade my eyes, I see a figure waving. It's our guide, Bob Fleming, who arrived on an earlier flight. Bob was a former student from Woodstock, the missionary boarding school we attended in the Himalayas. He and I met again by chance forty years later when my husband signed up for a trek in the Himalayas. "Fleming," I said to my mom on the phone, "that's the trek leader's name. It sounds so familiar."

"Bob's mother," she said, "Bethel Harris, was the doctor who delivered you into the world."

What *Karma!* Now Bob was helping to make my return to India a reality!

Not only fluent in Hindi and other Asian languages, Bob is an astute student and teacher of the continent's diverse culture and history, an exuberant ornithologist and naturalist. His buoyant spirit will inform our travels. Now he raises two clasped hands in a victory wave and soon greets me with a bear hug. Because he, too, grew up in India, he knows, as none of the other trekkers in our small group can, the deep joy I feel, returning to the land I first called home.

October. The country is in the throes of festivals and an upcoming election. Mob scenes and mayhem are easy to imagine, but in fact we find people busy and well, less impoverished than in 1947, more able to feed themselves, once-dry lands now irrigated and productive, women better educated and more visible, a much larger middle class.

Over-population remains a crushing problem, one which is not being addressed, but somehow the country manages, even thrives. It is, as always, full of contradictions. Hindus and Muslims often live side by side peaceably, only to attack each other brutally during times of crisis. Culturally rich in all of the arts, India is responsible for some of the world's greatest epic poetry, music, dance and architecture, but its movie industry gluts the market with more than its share of the gaudiest, most violent films in the world. So, too, corrupt government, squalor and murder walk the same path as altruism and generosity, and in the midst of poor sanitation and killer diseases, one of the world's great cuisines flourishes.

New Delhi, a beautiful city with wide avenues lined in hardwoods, is nevertheless so murky with dust, diesel and gas fumes, I cover my face with a wet scarf to keep from choking. Two days after our arrival, we're on our way to the Gandhi Memorial. Its earth-bermed exterior is draped with scarlet and burgundy bougainvillea, the interior an oasis of quiet within the roar of traffic. Encircling sandstone slabs hold beautifully incised messages of tolerance, justice and non-violent political solutions to conflict— this one in Punjabi, that one in Hindi, yet another in Russian or Chinese, French, English or Urdu—languages from around the world.

In an open area of lawn, a wide, black marble slab marks the Mahatma's grave. Its polished surface reflects the sky and the faces of those who lean over it in passing. At the head of the stone, the everlasting flame burns in its bronze, lotus-like holder. Nearby, stand two crudely painted, black metal trunks slotted on top to receive money for the *Harijans*, the untouchables. Ironically, the trunks are chained to the ground so that no one will steal them. "Protecting" the grave site is a silly, low, white picket fence, its spiked tops looking puritanical and incongruous.

But I am moved, as most visitors are, by the hush that greets us, by the immensity of mankind's collective hope to eradicate violence from the world. Moved, also, by Gandhi's vision and example in leading the way. I had sat on his lap as a child and felt safe. By the time I reached adulthood, his commitment to non-violent resistance felt essential to our survival as a species. It led not only to India's independence from British rule but to peaceful protests by Martin Luther King and dissenters around the world.

Besides exploring a few sites in northern India, our band of twelve has gathered to trek in the Himalayas. We leave New Delhi's markets and monuments to climb aboard a battered, dust-ridden bus and head into the countryside. On the way, thumping over archaic roads, past ancient villages, we visit the red forts whose sandstone arches and walled towns Mogul emperors built four centuries ago. The artists themselves are dead, but the latticed walls still frame a timeless sky, the pillars—chiseled and inlaid with jeweled wildflowers, leaves, birds and dancing gods—still spiral into view, their energy intact. Iridescent bee-eaters and vivid parakeets sail through canopies of leaves that shade us in this tropical extravaganza.

At one of our stops we're aggressively pursued by men whose arms dangle fake stone necklaces and gaudy trinkets they insist we buy. We don't; we have been asked by our Indian guide not to encourage sales' pressures or begging. At other times we're expected to enjoy watching a trained bear dance, a chained mongoose, a painted elephant prodded behind the ears. Snakes in baskets perform while their keepers beg for *bakhshish*. I suffer for the animals as well as their poverty-stricken owners.

During our travels, we drink water laced with iodine, and eat hot, cooked food, tea boiled with milk and sugar, no fresh fruits or vegetables other than occasional oranges and bananas in their protective jackets. Besides these precautions, our western drugs remain at the ready. Each day, if we're on the bus, at around noon we open a box lunch of dull white sandwiches and hardboiled eggs, which our Indian coordinator must deem a traditional Western favorite. At rest stops, we walk and stretch, relieving ourselves in a cane field or grove of eucalyptus. On one occasion, we try a public bathroom, but the stench in the dark stalls is so overpowering, the hole in the filthy floor to squat over so sickening, we're glad to escape. Before I find the exit, a wizened woman grabs me from the shadows, clearly scolding me for something. I finally figure out that she must be the care-taker, sloshing water on the floor from time to time, and understandably, expects to be paid. Handing her a rupee, I ask myself how I would feel with no other choice but to spend my old age in such a foul place.

Throughout the journey, the land unfolds in the rhythms of work. Women in faded cotton saris bend over smoky fires, kneading *chapatis* or grinding fresh cardamom. They carry well water in clay jugs on their heads, gather cow dung to shape into patties stacked and dried for kindling or mixed with water to plaster the walls and floors of their homes.

Men balance bundles of sugar cane on their heads, women loads of firewood. In spite of their labor, they walk with the timeless grace we in the west have lost to high heels and hurry. Whether in cities or villages, we notice hundreds of men for every woman. A few women might be seen peering from roof tops or crowded on wooden carts moving along the road, but mostly they're hidden.

As our bus flings dust and fumes along the way, we catch sight of a man cutting hair beside the road, scissors glinting. Another irons a plaid shirt. Several lean over the blackened metal of a small machine shop, pounding out bent axles, bicycle frames, sheet metal. Others stack fire wood and lumber, always scarce, or fold fabric and ready-made garments in cobbled-together stalls. Vendors arrange fruits, vegetables, roasted peanuts, sweets on a cloth spread over the ground.

While we pass by, my own life watches the lives of others as if to unravel the mystery. Sometimes no one seems to be working, just hanging out, men waiting. Or a neighbor will have pulled a webbed, wood-framed bed into the shade for an old man to lie on his side, a young one with an arm flung over his face. A *darzi* sits cross-legged on a worn rug, his hand-turned Singer machine surrounded by shirts and *kameezes*; in a nearby field, a man breaks hard earth with a pick axe, an old woman carries bricks on her head to a skeletal building.

Such familiar scenes! I feel comforted by them in spite of the poverty they speak of, because the people, their gestures, the animals, the shade trees and heat, the very air, locate a part of myself I'd lost. Months ago, with memory as guide, I wondered if I would regret the return, but find it, instead, affirming, connecting me to my past, bringing back the world I had missed all these years. For no matter how conflicted it was, childhood introduced me to the life lived here—the walking pace of animals and people, the fragrance of cardamom and lime, wood smoke, temple bells, the brilliant colors of *saris* and flowering shrubs, trees shifting with parrots, mynas, monkeys—to arms that hold, to the taste of milk and tears, to the pungence of rain, to the moon that drifts like a blossom in the dark, to the train's wail and the nicker of a horse.

In the house where I grew up in Allahabad, light and shadow patterned the cement floors, a brown leather strop hung from its nail in the bathroom where a little tin-sided mirror glinted. Each morning Daddy daubed his face with a soapy brush, whisking a bit of foam onto our noses and chins if we were watching, whistling over the speckled cold-water sink. I delighted in the clownlike transformation—lather masking the countenance I loved, and how the lips drew to one side and then to the other as the neat tracks of the razor pushed through the suds to reveal, little by little, the familiar person underneath. Certainty was restored, no longer subject to a disguise that felt both teasingly playful and scary.

Shaving, especially in the bazaar, where skilled barbers drew their long narrow blades across a man's throat, shadowed my fears: fears of pain, of decay and ugliness I didn't know how to handle— the blotched skin and chin hairs of old age, the ravaged bodies of lepers, poverty's flies crawling over children's faces. I first sympathized with their misery and then was glad it wasn't mine, which left me ashamed of my feelings. Why do people favor smooth skin? Why does hair grow here and not there? I can't believe I, too, now shave, standing at the mirror like a man, an electric razor buzzing over my chin in the name of beauty, and how surfaces matter deeply to me, my mother's daughter, our love for color and form leading us sometimes to veer past uncomfortable truths. But back then, Daddy pulled his razor up and down a length of brown leather as he whistled *Shave and a Haircut, Two Bits!* or *Yankee Doodle*, the way any father does, and that was the start of our day.

Light and shadow sharpened each other in the tropical brightness, a brightness so blinding it seared the whitewashed walls, and we squinted our eyes for protection. Magenta bougainvillea tumbled over roofs, honeysuckle and jasmine releasing their scent, while the dry ropey vines that nurtured them hid lizards and spiders under a maze of layering leaves.

At the front of our house, a veranda or covered porch with a cool, cement floor sheltered us from the sun's heat and the monsoon rains. We ate on the veranda early mornings before it turned hot, catching a glimpse of the Jumna river with its hard-packed mud and clay banks on this side, its blindingly white sand dunes, seducing us, on the other. A double-decker steel bridge spanned the river. Its upper level shuddered with trains carrying coal, grain and hardware, as well as passengers, the lower level bustled with foot traffic—women walking goats, bicycles heaped with produce, families sitting cross-legged on bullock carts with slowly creaking wooden wheels, carriages drawn by bony horses clopping along at a brisk pace, bells braided into their harnesses. Later, during the war, when I was nine and ten, camouflaged lorries in convoys thumped over the cross-ties. But before that, each morning we woke to temple bells from nearby shrines, and the distant onrushing thunder of the train with its soulful whistle trailing into the future.

2

OFTEN, FOR MORNING EXERCISE, when the air was crisp and sweet, and the sun had not yet fired up its cauldron, Daddy, Billy and I walked in our pajamas and brown-striped woolen bathrobes to the bridge and back. Each of us towheaded children wanted to be loved best by our parents, Billy's eyes a rich brown like Mummy's, mine blue like Daddy's, Billy, two years older. The morning walk placated our jealousies. We loved these times together, Daddy holding our hands as we peered down at the dazzling blue of the river, the bridge connecting us to the busy world of commerce.

Back home for *chotha hazri,* "little breakfast," we sat in the shade of the veranda while one of the servants brought us hot, sweet tea with milk, crisp toast we buttered and sprinkled with sugar, plump grapefruit from the garden, ripened under the unrelenting sun.

When Daddy pushed back his rattan chair, he'd swing first one and then the other of us into his arms and kiss us goodbye, telling us to be good until he came back. If he wasn't in a hurry, he let us wind his pocket watch. In that easy manner of his, a book clasped like a discus in his hand, he'd stroll down the driveway in his good shirt, slacks and *chuppals,* sandals, stepping into the sunlight to pass under the *gulmohar* and *neem* trees, the one with its lacy leaves and pink to orange flowers, the other with its long curving pods lined with tart-tasting seeds we liked to suck on. Along with the chatter of mynas and the crooning of doves, saurus cranes called back and forth across the river. Daddy passed the brick posts at the end of the entryway, traveling the grass and cinder road to

Ewing Christian College's massive colonial-style stone walls where students in their bright *saris* and white *kurtas* were beginning to gather. Fluent in Hindi as well as English, he'd chat with them as he climbed the curving cement steps, turning at the landing and heading up to his second-story classroom where he taught English and literature. From his window he could catch a glimpse of the river, blue as a *sari* dropped in a field of grain.

Daddy felt at home in India, just as Billy and I did, fourth generation American missionary children born on the subcontinent. Doctors, teachers, preachers, they all came to spread the word of Christ, to help the poor, the sick, the needy. They came with high ideals and a sense of purpose. They came, too, for adventure, and because they felt more at home where they'd been born than in the faster-paced, structured atmosphere of the States.

As DARKNESS FLOWED INTO the sky, huts without electricity lit lanterns and tiny oil lamps, and under the trees the tips of hand-rolled cigarettes glowed as men chatted quietly after a hard day's work. On someone's veranda a *hooka's* bubbling released the pungent smell of tobacco. Jackals called. A *sitar's* strumming carried through the heart-shaped leaves of the peeple tree, mixed with the songs of mosquitoes and frogs, their contrapuntal tunes.

By morning, bits of light tagged a leaf and coaxed its shadow onto the white-washed wall. Light bounced off the nose rings of women carrying well water on their heads, lustered over brass bells tied to the halters of horses, the ankles of camels. It pooled in children's eyes, snagged on the wings of dragonflies, sharpened the metal blades of knives, the long straight razor drawn across the stubble of a villager's jaw. Light danced in my own hands, soaping themselves at the cold-water sink of home.

If we woke up early, Billy and I loved climbing into bed with Mummy and Daddy out on their screened sleeping porch when the air was cool and the frogs still sang, when the shapes of the world were starting to emerge. Currents of air came in to touch our faces, crickets sang with the frogs, and blurred stars sat in the nearby trees. Snuggling up to our parents gave us a sense of safety and of once more being together.

But one morning, when I was about four or five, Billy still

asleep in the back room, Mummy off somewhere, I woke and climbed into bed with Daddy. We listened to the train rushing across the river, and the day waking up. He called me his sleepy-head, and I leaned contentedly against his warm body. Then his hand pulled mine down onto something large and pulsing. It frightened me. I withdrew, but he brought my hand back, telling me not to be afraid, just to stroke it. His voice was wobbly and strange, as if he was somebody else. I felt myself slipping into a cold dark place.

Like a snake's tongue flickering in and out of our daily activities, the experience tagged me so that, without my knowledge, I became wary—a wariness of knowing and not-knowing that quickened my senses and kept me on guard.

In the daytime Daddy still whistled when he shaved, still helped me tie my shoelaces or read a book, still arm-wrestled with Billy, and laughed at his jokes. And many nights, many weeks of them, he kissed me good night without turning into a stranger, brought me a sip of water without scolding, tucked the mosquito netting carefully around my mattress.

As the years passed by, however, other nights were there too, just before dawn, when Daddy walked through the sleeping rooms barefoot to slip under my covers, caressing me awake, whispering words to his little sweetheart, his Goldilocks, his hands roving everywhere, mouth hungry and nibbling. He told me he loved me and that I must know that—I did—that this was another way of showing it, that I shouldn't tell other grown-ups because they twisted things and didn't understand, that only God really did, and God was inside me. He'd know if I told.

A year or two later I started putting myself to sleep by banging my head rhythmically again and again on the mattress. Mother asked why I did that; I didn't know and couldn't stop. Once, Daddy tried breaking me of the habit by holding my head, but I resisted, straining against him, and as soon as he left, went on with my thumping. The repetitious drumming somehow soothed me.

3

BILLY, I BEGGED, HELP *me bring these chairs together. If you do, you can play with me.* I knew, of course, that Billy played with Sally who was his age, or her two brothers, Chuck and Tom, who were only a few years older. But they were away, so he picked up one chair and then another, hauling them to a clearing in the largest room at the back of the house, and I tipped them over, pushing their high backs towards each other. I liked these cane chairs the color of dry summer grass, and carefully draped them with an Indian bedspread while Billy pulled up the heavier wool blanket that kept slipping away to let in patches of light. We sat in our cave like sparrows whose bits of conversation scattered in the shade.

Inevitably, once we'd irritated each other, Billy pushed one of the chairs aside as he left the tent, and I crawled out to set things straight and look for my doll. Trailing it back to the shelter, I scolded it, tucked it into bed, pulled my sweater around it. Then, in that shadowy refuge, as a bird might in a hedgerow, I sang to myself, one made-up song after another.

In the stillness outside, time moved slowly. Our cook, Shunkar, rested under a tree on a hemp bed strung between sturdy wooden legs—the same beds we slept on. He might smoke or read the paper or take a nap while a butterfly sailed past, its yellow and white wings rowing a leisurely and erratic course, shadows lacing the plain ground. As the day heated up, so did the fragrance of jasmine and nasturtium, sweet pea and lily, dried leaves and dust. Its brass worn to a silver sheen beneath the weight of sky, the metal handle of the outdoor tap grew too hot to touch.

Home from teaching by tea time, Daddy shared afternoons with the family, running errands for Mummy, playing outside with us children or sprawled in the living room over tiddly winks or pick up sticks, listening to our small victories and complaints. After dinner, he moved to his desk to work on student papers, opening a pocket knife to sharpen his pencil, red at one end, blue at the other.

Mummy liked to read to us before bedtime, but Daddy took us with him wherever he went—on errands, or to explore the bazaar, stopping along the way to show us a swallowtail, or a crested *hoopoe* wearing its orange and brown head-feathers like a fancy hairdo. We'd step aside for a horse and cart, the harness bells and clopping hooves soon swallowed by the calls of beggars, vendors, squawking parakeets, barking dogs and bargaining shoppers.

In the market, chickens hung upsidedown by their feet. I imagined the soft clucking of the hens, their many-colored feathers, the strutting sharp-toed roosters whose crowing mixed with the tolling of temple bells. In the shadow of stalls, burlap sacks with their tops rolled down held rice, lentils, split peas, wheat flour, salt and sugar. Nearby, shiny purple eggplants leaned against tomatoes, squash and every vegetable of the season. Another ground cloth held papayas, coconuts, lychees, mangoes, limes and, overhead, hanging clusters of upside down bananas.

When a street vendor dipped his slotted spoon into the spitting oil and pulled out *jalebis*, Daddy paid him a few *annas* in exchange for a half dozen held out in some leaves or on a twist of newspaper. After they cooled, I mouthed them the way bears eat honeycombs, sucking at the sweet, warm syrup, crunching the pretzel-shaped pastries, my lips lusciously glossed with their flavors.

Sometimes we'd answer to a distant drum-beat and join others around a traveling entertainer who chanted as he flipped his little hour-glass-shaped drum back and forth in one hand. Tied to the drum were two lengths of string weighted at the ends. As they flew against the taut heads, the weights tapped out a series of notes sounding like gravel flung against leaves. In the man's other hand was a rope tethered to a small *bhalu* or Himalayan black bear. It stood on its hind legs, danced slowly in a circle, swinging its head from side to side, eyes filmed, mouth partially open. Its coat was dulled by dust and inactivity, its forearms extended as if to beg or bless. The bear's long claws, curving and awkward on the hard-packed ground, dragged as it turned. I worried about that bear.

What must it feel like here in the hot plains crowded with barefoot people in bright clothes munching salted peanuts and sweets soaked in honey? Kept alive to dance, to earn its owner a meager living, moved from village to village, the bear must have wondered what became of its life in the steep pine forests where rhododendron grew as tall as trees, where boulders resisted the turbulent streams? The bear stood nearly eye to eye with me. Every now and then one paw extended for *bakshish* and Daddy dropped a few coins in the cloth at its feet.

Daddy never seemed rushed. He seldom scolded. He didn't mind getting dirty or wet. He stood in the warm rain with us children or walked us through the teeming streets, carrying us when we were too tired. He'd sit on the ground to tie a shoelace or mend a kite, let us ride sideways on the handlebars of his bike, show us how to split a blade of grass and then hold it taut between two thumbs, blowing to create a piercing medley of whistles. He smelled of cigarette smoke and shaving soap, and seemed to like everyone. The world out-of-doors held him, always, and so he shared it with us—bees and their habits, hummingbirds, grasses, rocks, beetles and birds' eggs, rivers, mountains, stars, twigs, feathers. He taught us to read the prints of passage, to hold what we saw with great care, to honor and look deeply. Although we ached to be good enough for Mummy, Daddy was our protector and companion.

For Mummy, beauty was what mattered. Not vultures, but songbirds; not cocoons, but butterflies; not snakes or turtles or lizards; and nothing in the house, please, but flowers. Ever alert to danger, needing order and progress, and busy controlling what she could, her thirst was for attention and applause.

4

MY FIRST FRIEND, SAVITRI, was the cook's daughter who sat on the shady kitchen steps with me and chattered away or shared imaginary tea in the little tin cups and saucers that had come from America, their rims painted with tiny flowers. The cups were just the right size for our hands, and the thin saucers, when we gathered them up, collided with each other in a chinking, gossipy, sing-song way. We wove garlands out of marigolds and jasmine, invented families and stories, gave directions in strict tones to imaginary children or sang them to sleep with Indian lullabies:

> Nin-nee ba-ba, nin-nee,
> Muck-an, roti, chin-nee.
> Sleep, baby, sleep.
> Butter, bread and sugar.

YEARS LATER I REMEMBER how I often watched from a distance as Savitri sat cross-legged under the lacy leaves of the *gulmohar* tree, her back to her mother; how her mother dabbed warm oil into her hands and rubbed it over her daughter's body, still cool from its bath under the outdoor tap, massaging rhythmically—face, arms, torso, legs, feet, fingers, scalp, hair. She loosened the mass of Savitri's tangled locks with the wide-toothed side of a sandalwood comb that fit neatly in her palm. After drawing the heavy strands into one hand, she turned the comb over, this time pulling the fine teeth through. Neatly, she parted the hair from front to back, braiding each handful, then lengthening the braids by weaving into them a three-stranded black cotton string brightened at the ends by silver, orange and red tassels.

How at ease Savitri seemed! Straight-backed while her mother tended her. How comfortably they changed places so that the daughter could comb out the mother's hair. Heavy and longer, once it was thoroughly oiled and combed, it was tucked up in a bun at the nape of her neck, and the sari drawn back over her head. Bits of sunlight floated over the beaten ground. The mother's ankle bracelets of hollowed-out silver jingled as she walked, accompanying her like a covey of finches.

It was clear from Shunkar's darker skin that he was a native of Southern India where the heat and humidity were even more intense than in Allahabad. A big man with an uncomplaining nature, his steady presence comforted us children. He worked in our cramped, sooty kitchen with its cast iron stove, and in the pantry where a screened cabinet, fitted with a block of ice, kept the flies out and the perishables cool. As he stoked and tended the fire, coaxing the heat to stay even, he clanged the heavy metal doors that latched and unlatched various compartments. Over one shoulder a large *jahran* or dish towel stayed always at the ready. Bunched up, it protected his hands from the heat of the stove doors or allowed him to carry a dishpan of boiling water through the house for the family's baths. Only cold water ran in the taps. Mother taught Shunkar to make mashed potatoes and other Western dishes, and he in turn, made wonderful chicken, fish and lamb curries for our meals. For Christmas dinner he and Mother made English plum pudding, a bit like steamed fruit cake topped with a delicious hard sauce. Whoever found the coin baked in the pudding was counted lucky.

When Shunkar wasn't too busy, he peeled back the tough outer bark of sugarcane and cut it into chunks for me to chew. I sucked the sweet juice from the pulp while he told me outrageous stories about man-eating tigers and poisonous snakes, or showed me how to blow through a metal pipe, or one made with my own hands, to bring the coals alive.

Once I watched in shock as Shunkar, sitting on the kitchen step, twisted the neck of a chicken before laying it across a board and chopping off its head. Even so, the chicken somehow got away, running headless and frantic, blood spattering everywhere, startlingly red, feathers like bandages in tatters on the ground.

When it slumped over, Shunkar grasped its scaly reptilian legs and bright yellow toes, and dunked it upside down into boiling water. The smell of wet feathers and newsprint made my nostrils flare as his powerful, dark hands plucked the wet bird, leaving it loose-skinned and goose-bumped, pink and white as I was.

Shunkar and his family lived in a one-room clay and tile house at the edge of our yard, sharing the same trees. Shunkar's wife swept the floors of her home, and kept them and the walls refreshed with a slurry of mud and cow dung that she applied skill-fully with the flat of her hands. The thin glaze hardened quickly in the heat. She tended the children, the family's laundry, the shop-ping for food and supplies, and meal preparation. But what was her name? In all those years, did we ever know it? Was it Kamala?

Hard-working, quiet and shy, she ground *massala* for the eve-ning meal or dipped her fingers in water as she kneaded the dough for *chappatis*, expertly flattening and turning them under her thumb until they were paper thin, then laying them, one by one, on the curving cast iron *chulla* heated over the coals of her small fire. Often on a quiet morning, Savitri and I would sit outside with her, listening to the rhythmical sounds of rice being caught and thrown, chattering as it fell back into her shallow, fan-shaped bas-ket before again becoming airborne, letting the chaff blow away. We helped her pick out tiny dark bits of stone.

In each Hindu home, whether a hut or a palace, at least one ledge on a wall held a small altar with its image of Ganesh, the ele-phant god, or Krishna, god of creation. Garlanded in marigolds, or offered tiny dishes of rice and sweets, the gods were carefully tend-ed and prayed to. To me, their images always seemed garish and out of place inside the quiet rooms with their classically-shaped brass and clay urns holding water, oil and grains, or their shallow, elegantly-curved iron *chullas* for cooking *chapatis*. And yet I could see that these deities were more intimate and accessible than ours, and were acknowledged many times a day, not just on Sundays.

After preparing the mid-day meal for the *sahibs*, Shunkar walked back to his own house for lunch—a bowl of fresh tomatoes cut up with raw onion and red chili peppers and their seeds. He relished the fiery feast that caused his face to break out in a sweat.

When I was three or four, I remember sitting on my haunches at the entrance to his small house, lured by the fragrance of curry. Peering into the dark interior, I said nothing but looked longingly at the food the family was eating. Shunkar's wife turned to her husband, and at his faint nod, rose to fetch me a little rice, a little curry and *dhal*, a piece of *chapati*. How delicious it tasted! Much better, I thought, than our food.

When Daddy found out, he explained firmly that I must never approach Shunkar's family for food, that it was expensive and precious and that they had just enough of it for themselves.

The local milk we drank looked blueish and thin after being watered down by the villagers to bring in a few more desperately needed *annas*. Before serving it to us, Shunkar saw that it was well boiled. In between meals, I often looked for a box of KLIM. I'd lick a finger and pull out the powdery white substance that stuck to it just as it stuck to the roof of my mouth when I dug it from the box with a spoon for bigger helpings. Eventually I learned it had kept me alive as an infant, a powdered milk formula from the States, rich in iron and protein. When the KLIM ran out, Billy and I turned to cans of sweetened condensed milk. With an ice pick, we punched a single vent hole on one side of the lid, and on the other made a cluster of holes we enlarged in order to drink the milk. First the smell of metal as I brought my mouth to the opening, then the honeyed fragrance, the rich, thick sweetness.

SHUNKAR AND HIS WIFE also had a son, Bulwanth, who played with Billy sometimes, as Savitri did with me. If Bulwanth disobeyed him, Shunkar caught him by the ear and hauled him around until his tears and their shouts subsided. Once, while Bulwanth was playing, he fell and broke his arm but was too frightened to see the doctor. After Daddy's gentle coaxing and Shunkar's orders, Balwanth gave in. He came home in a cast, subdued but no longer terrified of the doctor.

For sores and cuts that grew infected, we'd visit the Mission clinic. A doctor would open a little white envelope and tap out over the wound some of its yellow powder. Sulfa—the magic cure-all. Mother, however, was allergic to sulfa so had to rely on Mercurochrome and other remedies. She seldom needed to go to the clinic, but a couple times a year suffered from strep throats which left her barely able to swallow, and painfully fretful. On those occasions she begged Daddy to take us outside to give her some peace and quiet.

At least twice during her stay in India, she also came down with malaria. It was quinine that saved her. Moaning and flailing about in bed, sweat running down her face, for days she carried on wildly delirious conversations, and once, when a deathly cold started creeping up her legs, called out for whiskey. We kept a bottle for Christmas plum pudding, and Daddy brought her a dollop in a glass, propping her in his arms so she could swallow it. At other times, when she called out for a washcloth, I could bring it to her, wiping down her forehead, crooning to her to get well. It frightened me to see her suffering, the doctor coming and going. As a young girl, she, too, must have felt that fear, visiting the asylum her mother was confined in, and not being able to save her.

While Daddy taught English and coached basketball, swimming, hurdles, javelin, or worked on the following Sunday's sermon, Mother wrote letters, arranged flowers, chose fabric for curtains, and patterns for clothes the *darzi* sewed on his hand-turned Singer. She supervised the servants, planned meals—telling Shunkar what to cook, Kishan how to clean—worked on committees, attended conferences and visited art centers. For our birthdays she made chocolate cake from scratch, sifting the flour three or four times, creaming the butter and sugar with a fork, turning the egg-beater by hand before combining all the ingredients. When she asked what kind of icing we'd like, we always clamored for the creamy, mint-green frosting she swirled around the cake.

In the garden, Mother planned, and the *mali* planted, nasturtiums, sweet peas, marigolds, larkspur, hollyhocks, phlox, poinsettias, fruit trees and vegetables. She supervised, and he did all the digging, the sweat-work. As I played, moving about the yard, I especially loved bumping into the surprise fragrance of sweet peas, the head-high flourish of their little bonnets on stiffly-upright stems, the grip of their thready tendrils. On the other hand, the intensity of color in the larkspurs and marigolds drew me to them. Color and fragrance buzzed with life in Allahabad.

MOTHER ESPECIALLY LOVED TO entertain, on occasion inviting as many as thirty people to a sit-down dinner. Indians of all faiths, British R.A.F. Boys and American G.I.'s desperately homesick, political leaders like the Nehrus who lived nearby in Ananbawhan, and anyone who "counted" came to these affairs. After the house was cleaned down to its remotest corners, the best glassware and linens were brought out, fresh flowers decorated the front rooms, mirrors were polished, and children admonished not to touch anything, to stay outdoors.

Mother also liked to travel. When we were nine and eleven, she petitioned the Board of Foreign Missions to pay for her solo trip to South India for three months to study the arts and crafts of that region, and to visit Shantinakaten, a retreat for Indian poets and artists founded by Rabindranath Tagore.

While she was away, Billy came down with a fever of 105 degrees and was not expected to live. A telegram urged her to return, but when another followed to say he was recovering, she continued visiting the Maharaja of Jaipur who had invited her to be his guest. By the time she came home several weeks later, the three of us had decorated the living room with streamers, made cut-out cards and stuck flowers in little jars, running to meet her carriage when we heard the harness bells and hoof beats of the *tonga*'s approach in the driveway. How lovely she looked in her *sari*, her smiles and hugs, the softness of her face next to ours at last. She said she always treasured our exuberant welcome.

Once when Billy was little, he disappeared. The story became part of family legend. He was two or three, as sturdy and adventuresome as any child, padding about the house one minute, gone the next. His *aya* looked for him, Shunkar looked for him, they told the *memsahib*, and she looked for him. Not a trace. Not in the house, not on the veranda, not in the front yard or the garden out back, not by the outdoor spigot or the cook's house or at the gate.

After an hour or two of searching, anxiety mounted, and one of the servants—or was it Mummy? I've forgotten that part of the story—hurried to the college, barged into Daddy's upstairs classroom as the words tumbled out. Did Daddy open his window to scan the campus below? Probably. Did his students help in the search? I think so. But at some point, one of them heard the sound. It broke through the daily—the train's receding whistle, the howl of a dog, peacock cries—a distant, persistent wail, pitched high by fear.

The sound seemed to come from over the bank, and the searchers quickly followed it, taking shortcuts across the slope and through a field. Rounding a stand of shrubby trees, they came to a clearing. There, in the middle of a small fenced yard, stood Billy, platinum hair blazing in the sun, fists clenched, mouth open and bawling, closely hemmed in by wall-to-wall pigs.

DURING ANOTHER, QUIETER TIME, Mummy brings home a brown paper bag heavy with seeds. The seeds are a Chinese-lacquer-red, round and smooth as lentils. Slipping against each other in silky handfuls, they tug at me to scoop them up, play them through my fingers, listen to the slush and whisper of their telling me who they are.

Touch! How can a child not touch! I must run my hands over the body of the world to read it as if it were Braille. When Mummy and Daddy spend an evening with friends, and Billy and I have the cook to ourselves, we ask for our favorite dish, dip our fingers into the mashed potatoes, stuccoing them with peas and soft-cooked eggs. Before licking our hands clean, we grin at each other.

Now, as I reach for a handful of seeds, Mummy's sharp voice stops me. She sweeps the seeds into a bowl and carries them to a circular, Kashmiri table whose outer edge has been carved into lotus blossoms and leaves but whose center is of smooth, polished wood. With her palm and the tips of her fingers, she pats the seeds into the same paisley design imprinted on our Indian bedspreads. The low table is just my height, but I'm not to touch.

Thinking back, I wonder, Why not give a child her own table, own seeds, side by side, the pleasure shared? How could a child not touch, not feel the body of a mother's tenderness or menace? But who knows what beauty meant to my mother, what desperate ledge of survival it offered her, that she would deny it to me, or how, as her daughter, I, too, would be ensnared by her past, a past I still feel shifting under my feet?

IN A YOUNG GIRL'S day, monsoons cut a stream across her path. A bright leaf sails into view, and she reaches out to catch it, the way she reaches for her father, but the leaf is swept away, and her own bed no longer safe, her own body no longer pulled towards but pushing away from him.

Outside, barefoot in the yard one afternoon, she discovers that the ground tucked under the shelter of leaves feels cooler than ground in the open. When it's time to go inside, she rinses at the spigot, water, still hot from the sun, unwinding its silver braids across her legs, glittering and splashing onto the cement square to snake across the dirt, soon staining it dark.

ONE DAY, AFTER MY own children are grown and Mother has died, I sort through the last of her belongings. In the corner of a shelf is a small, worn, unmarked cardboard box whose lid resists my tug. Bunched inside the crumpled tissue paper are the red, lentil-shaped seeds. They have crossed the Pacific and been carried down the years as if waiting for me to find them, less bright but undiminished.

5

FROM AS FAR BACK as I can remember, Mother told me stories about her own childhood. Hearing them, I longed to protect her and make up for the pain she had suffered. I never could. Both of her parents grew up in Sweden. When her father, Franz Oscar Petterson, graduated from high school, he enlisted as a merchant seaman, lying about his age in order to qualify, eager to escape his father's beatings and their strict Protestant home in Kalmar. Several years later, when his ship docked in America, young Oscar collected his severance pay and stepped ashore. He applied for citizenship, changed the spelling of his name from Oskar Petterson to Oscar Peterson, and worked wherever he was needed. Once settled, he begged his Swedish girlfriend to book passage and marry him. After many courtship letters and assurances that he could make a good living, he persuaded her parents to let her go. Eager and hopeful, Maria Sophia Olson arrived at Ellis Island with a carefully-packed trunk of tailored wool clothes, a few keepsakes, and a Bible.

Almost immediately she became pregnant. Jobs were not nearly as plentiful as promised. The young family moved several times from one small town to another looking for work, always on the edge of poverty. Eventually they settled in Katona, New York, Maria by then the mother of five, her last child still-born. She never learned English, and grew desperately homesick for Sweden, but didn't have the money to return. I have always been haunted by Maria's story, one of two grandmothers I never met. Her children longed for the family to be seen as American, but they had to speak Swedish at home so that she could understand them.

Sigrid, my mother, as the eldest daughter, was responsible for the younger children's welfare, and was often scolded for whatever trouble they stirred up. At school, classmates teased her for her accent. She never brought friends home to play because of her family's foreignness. Once, in a fit of anger, she lit the living room curtains on fire to watch the beautiful burning. Her already over-worked parents hauled water from the well to put out the flames. Bucket by bucket Mother felt herself drown in their labor and despair.

Maria, an excellent cook and housekeeper, baked bread to sell, and took in ironing to supplement the family income. Mother remembered the endless piles of shirts and dresses her mother toiled over. Isolated, Maria grew ever-more depressed until, after the loss of her fifth child, she ended up wandering the streets, weeping and tearing off her clothes. As a nine- or ten-year-old, Mother was forced to find her and bring her home, mortified by the shame of it.

Mother's father, Oscar, worked as a carpenter and handyman, made deliveries of coal by horse and cart to peoples' homes, hefting huge loads on his back to empty into the chutes that opened into their basements. After a long day's work, he tended the vegetable garden he'd planted and took pride in. A good craftsman and gifted woodworker, he nevertheless lost jobs because of his fiery temper and stubbornness. At times his frustrations erupted at home. He broke a treasured platter, hit a child, pushed over a just-decorated Christmas tree. At other times, he carved wonderful toys for the children and took them sledding.

Mother told me she remembered feeling happy when she walked with her brother to a nearby field to pick fresh bunches of violets for their mom; happy, when the family ice skated on the river; or when she sledded with other children. But she said most of her memories were painful. Her youngest sister, Martha, a curly-headed toddler full of joy and doted on by the family, contracted polio at the age of two, and spent the rest of her life in a wheelchair. Eventually, she did marry and had children, presiding over a family of her own. But for Mother, the polio came as another blow. She saw Martha receiving all the attention she wanted for herself.

Speaking Swedish at home and English at school, Mother often became confused about what was expected of her in the classroom. Because she hadn't yet grasped the use of local idioms, she couldn't make sense of a poem the class was once expected to memorize in grade school. Called on to recite, she stood in front of her peers, trying again and again while the students made fun of her. The teacher had her sit in the corner. Even though Mother felt ashamed and angry, the tears unstoppable, she knew she wasn't stupid. Her father's fighting spirit came to her rescue.

Fortunately, other teachers in elementary and secondary school were kind to her. She told me they wore pretty dresses and smelled good. She wanted to be like them and like the girl in class who tied her hair in a beautiful ribbon. Even at eighty-nine, Mother remembered each of her teachers' names.

As Maria's depression deepened, life at home became more difficult. One evening at dinner, another sister, Gertie, wondered aloud why her mother hadn't come to the table. She went looking for her and found her sitting on the edge of the bathtub having just slashed her wrists and ankles with a razor, blood everywhere. *Does it hurt?* she asked. *No,* her mother said. Then her father arrived and shooed Gertie away. Later, men in dark suits drove up in a long black car and carried Maria out. She never came home.

Institutionalized at forty-eight, still unable to speak English, and with no one to communicate with, her loneliness deepened. Mother was eleven when she made her only visit, her hands clutching a jar of homemade blackberry jam. The grim-faced matron who led her through the halls stopped to unlock Maria's door. There she was, pale-faced, wearing a long white gown. When Mother reached out to give her the jar, it somehow slipped between their hands, crashing to the floor, splattering bits of glass and jam that looked like blood across Maria's gown. The matron, furious, yanked Mother away. That was the last time she ever saw her mother.

Mother's sister, Gertie, visited Maria more often, vowing that when she was eighteen, she'd take her home and care for her. But just before Gertie's eighteenth birthday, Maria died of pneumonia and complications of the heart. She was fifty-four. Years later, when I begged Gertie to share memories of those early years, she said they were too painful, but added that she continued to miss her mother, deeply regretting that she hadn't been able to rescue her.

Without Maria to help him, Oscar couldn't take care of the children, and farmed them out to relatives. When he ran out of family members, Mother was forced to live with a stranger from the church, a spinster named Aunt Jessie. Jessie meant well but knew nothing about Mother's needs or the pain she suffered. At thirteen, Mother arrived by train with one small suitcase, and was driven to a large Victorian house where her room was in the attic. In return for meals and lodging, she was to get up at four to empty chamber pots, bake bread, scrub the floors, beat the rugs, hang the spinach out to dry, weed the walkways. Eventually she escaped to Northfield, an excellent boarding school in Massachusetts that her best friend's mother helped her apply to. From there, she was accepted by Wooster College in Ohio where she earned her B.A., but her life was always lived precariously over the abyss of the past. If people asked about her parents, even in high school when they were still alive, she simply said they were dead.

MOTHER AND DAD MET as students at Wooster. She had fallen in love with a senior named Red who went on to become a brilliant attorney. But he chose someone else. For solace, she turned to Dad. He was the gentlest, most loved of their classmates and, having grown up in India, was given the Hindi nickname for dove. He could whistle birds from the trees and had a naturalist's keen interest in the world. After graduating, they decided to marry. A simple ceremony on the 22nd of February, 1930, took place at a friend's house. They then moved to Chicago where Dad completed Divinity School at McCormick Seminary and became an ordained minister.

In the photograph, brightness bounces off the rim of his glasses and the small gold band of her wedding ring. Young and in love, they sail from New York on the *Conte Grande*, leaning over the rail to wave goodbye to well-wishers, alive with hope for their new adventure, and no doubt expecting to escape their own childhoods. On board, much to Mother's delight, they are taken for movie stars.

August,1932. She hasn't the faintest idea what she is getting into, but for Dad this is a home-coming. Born in India, where he lived until he was eleven, he's fulfilling his father's dream by continuing the work of the mission, returning with his bride as his treasure. For the next thirteen years, India is their home, the place in which they raise their two children and hone their own talents.

But the tensions, which were to surface later in their relationship, must already have been evident. Just before they were married, Dad was given permission to spend a rare and coveted evening with Mother. No chaperone. Excited, she wore her prettiest dress, washed and set her hair, picked flowers for the table, cooked Dad's favorite meal, lit a fire, and waited. She wanted to enjoy their precious time together, wanted to be hugged and kissed and talked to about the future. He arrived hours late with a hitchhiker whose car had broken down, invited the man to stay for dinner and visited with him long after the meal was over, in spite of her signals to let him go. He seemed oblivious of her needs, content in her presence and in conversation with his new friend, while her disappointment and frustration deepened.

NEVERTHELESS, THOSE EARLY YEARS FOR my parents were happy ones. Energized by the politically tumultuous events surrounding them, they participated by supporting the Quit-India movement which culminated in the overthrow of British colonial rule.

At the same time, they lost people who were important to them. Two of their Wooster classmates, Florence, a nurse, and George Carruthers, a doctor, who had married each other and sailed to India to work in the Mission, lost their two-year-old daughter to sunstroke. Years later, when her husband transferred to a military hospital and fell in love with another woman, Florence shut herself in a car with the engine running and committed suicide.

In 1935, when Mother was six months pregnant with me, Dad's only and beloved sister died suddenly of leukemia. Still in her twenties, she had been working as a nurse in a Chicago hospital, assisting in surgery, when the surgeon noticed a mark on her arm and asked how long it had been there. A few months, she thought. He suggested she have it looked at. Within weeks she was dead. Dad was stricken by the news.

Ready to deliver, Mother paced about in her doctor's garden, exclaiming miserably, *God, why have I gotten myself into this mess again!* When my brother was born, he had fair, silken hair and, soon enough, Mother's dark brown eyes. I arrived with a scrunched-up face, auburn hair in disarray, and milky blue eyes. I seemed utterly foreign. She scolded the nurse for bringing her the wrong baby, and sent me back. Mother's doctor, Bethel Harris, stepped in, insisting I was hers.

As a toddler, I followed Mummy into the garden's head-high flowers, stunned by the iridescent blue of larkspur, and the sudden, startling flight of one of its petals—not a petal, I learn, but a hummingbird, matching color for color the blossom it left behind.

Sunlight shifted through the *gulmohar* tree's lacey shadows, and the dust grew hot. The chattery myna, the crow with its nasal lament, its beak cruelly sewn through with a big white button, the snowy egret's silent discourse with the river, the bugeling saurus crane—each of them imprinted their lives on mine.

6

AT AGE SIX, I clung to Daddy's neck, sobbing, and he unwound my arms and told me to be a big girl, to be brave, so I was, and then he was gone. For the next five years, each February at the beginning of the school year, he would take Billy and me to the station where four or five other kids and someone's parents milled around waiting for the train. Like his preacher-grandfather and physician-mother before him—both of whom were also born in India and attended Woodstock as boarders—Daddy raised his family in the plains and sent them away to school in the mountains to escape the heat. We children experienced the same dorms and classrooms there, the cottages and mountain trails, the stars and rocks and grasses and tribulations he and generations before him had known. Once when I was alone with Daddy, we rolled out our bedding in the middle of the busy platform, the way the Indians did, to sleep the night before the steam engine with its shunting wheels and hello-goodbye whistle rushed into the station, stopping with a blast of white steam that escaped like a genie from its bottle.

Most of the people in the station were men. They wore white *dhotis* or hand-spun Nehru shirts. As the trains came and went, they jostled for position, scrambled onto the roof and the outside ledges of compartments, shouting to their friends, elbowing others out of the way, clinging precariously, their white garments fluttering like prayer flags as the train pulled out of the station.

From vendors' stalls, hundreds of delicate glass bracelets in every color glinted and chimed, lighting my imagination. Beside them stood sequined elephants, peacocks painted in brilliant hues, camels and inlaid boxes carved from fragrant sandalwood. Other stands held roasted *chunna* and unshelled peanuts, sweets in glittering piles, mangos, bananas, loose-skinned oranges, leaves tooth-picked together to hold hot, syrupy *jalebis*, silver-leafed *hulva* cut into fudge-like chunks.

Newsstands carried Hindu and Muslim papers, and magazines with movie stars on their covers. Cheap cloth dolls dressed in pleated *saris* with silver borders sat in a row on shelves, while real women in plain cotton *saris*, their backs perpetually bent over, swept the cement platforms with brooms of bundled sticks.

Occasionally, in a small clearing, women with oil-scented skin and glistening hair stood quietly while their husbands tended the luggage or scolded porters. The women wore nose rings and ankle and wrist bracelets that chimed when they moved, and their luminous eyes were rimmed in *kohl*, their sandaled feet painted with *henna*. The glow of their *saris* reminded me of how, when Mother was away, I would open her dresser drawer and stroke the heavy satin slips, one the color of nasturtiums, worn under a favorite *sari* on formal occasions.

A velvet-lined wooden tray slung from his neck, a vendor sold cigarettes and *pan*, hawking his wares in a high nasal voice that carried above the hubbub of porters, passengers and the coming and going of trains—*Pan, beeri, ciga-reeeeee-t*—he sang out, stopping often to measure a handful of tobacco or wrap some *betel* nuts and tart pastes in a green leaf for his customers to chew, the way we might chew gum to refresh our mouths. Farther away, with clay mugs stacked around him, and a great urn steaming, the tea vendor's voice rang out in answer—*Cha, cha, garam cha*! Daddy found some *annas* in his pocket, and soon my hands were warming around the narrow, clay container, my nose breathing in the hot, sweet cardamon-spiced tea laden with milk. I blew on it and sipped contentedly.

My legs soon grew long enough so that I could climb the steps of the train myself and clamber to find a window seat on the dark-green, cracked, faux leather upholstery stuffed with straw. Rhesus monkeys lined the railing on the other side of the platform, their red rumps embarrassingly turned toward me, whole families in a row, the females nursing or cradling their young while the males jumped nimbly into an open window. I watched one snatch a banana from a man's hand as he read a newspaper. Another tried to grab Billy's sugar cane as he chewed on it, but we yelled and waved our hands and scared it away, its brown eyes glossy and intelligent. Challenged, the monkeys shrieked with anger, jostling for position on the railing before quieting down.

I recognized a few older missionary children and their parents joining us as our second-class car grew crowded. Soon the train lurched forward, snorting and gathering itself to pull out of the station. Its wheels turned faster and faster, finding the rhythmic gallop they soon settled into.

When it was time to go to sleep, one of the parents unlatched the overhead bunks, letting them hang down from their chains. Then the boys pushed off from the lower seats and hauled themselves up, while we girls settled into the benches below them, glad to have less far to fall. Each of us brought a *bistar* or bedding roll consisting of wool blankets, and in no time, with the train rocking and rumbling, we were fast asleep.

Before going to bed, however, I had to face the bathroom. It might be in another car, which meant crossing the great metal floor gaps that clanged and shifted as fresh air slapped me awake. Sometimes cinders stung, and always the excitement of imminent death reached up from the racing-away ground glimpsed below. Even if the bathroom was in our own car, it remained a dark and frightening landscape, shifting ominously. Entering it alone, I had trouble closing the heavy door that shut out all but a shadowy light, and felt imprisoned by the din and racket of steel, and by unnamed fears that lurked closely. To squat over that smelly hole with its whistle of cold air, to keep the edge of a pant leg or skirt from grazing the shit, to hold my breath and bare my bottom to the breeze and not fall in, called on all the gumption I could muster.

Finally back under my blankets, I slept soundly until daylight blazed through the windows and the countryside re-appeared. Frame after frame swept by as if in a movie: gazelles with their elegant stripes bounced through dry grass; a villager waved; a boy herding goats stopped to lean on his staff and watch our bright windows race away; pigeons and parrots scattered out of trees. I grew to love the annual train rides, my window open to the rush of forward motion, the shunt and pulse of wheels quickening or slowing down. Sound bounced back to us through a tunnel, to be thrown away again by space. I liked the way that trees and shrubs near the tracks sped by in a blur, while those farther away moved slowly; that a village flashed by, light skipping over the scummy pond where a boy scrubbed a water buffalo's dark, looming form; that a woman holding a child looked up from a field; that rounding a curve, the very train I was on came into view, leaning into itself, its long, hitched compartments jostling and swaying behind the steam engine someone stoked with coal. I seemed to see myself in the landscape plunging forward.

IN TWO DAYS THE train had left the low country and climbed as far as it could go. We had reached the hill town of Dehra Dun where we hauled out bedding and trunks, oranges, bags of peanuts, sugarcane—whatever we'd brought with us—and piled into a bus, heavy gear loaded on the roof. After many delays in the heat and dust, the driver turned on the ignition, and we were off. If the train had needed several engines to help it climb into the hills, the bus now depended on switchbacks to grind its way up the ever-more-vertical slope cut into the mountainside. By the third or fourth corner, all of us children felt queasy. By the thirty-sixth switchback, many heads hung out the window, throwing up.

When the bus ran out of road, I climbed down with the others, dazed and seasick, blinking in the bright mountain air, milling around with the coolies, the pack animals, the bundles of bedding and small trunks stashed with sheets, towels, clothing, each piece sewn with a name tag.

I could still see Mummy's hands shining under the lamp light as she held each name tag, dipping the needle in and out with tiny stitches. She soon tired, and showed the two of us how to continue. Daddy's hands, large and patient over the bits of fabric, took up the work, then mine, eager but awkward, bunching the cloth in spite of my concentration.

When I was too young to hike the steep mile-and-a-half path to the school, I climbed into a *kundee*, a basket-seat hoisted onto a coolie's back, always surprised when he bent to the straps, tipping me forward before pushing himself upright from the stone wall. The stone itself had been worn smooth by people resting their loads on it over the centuries. Other flat-topped boulders, or hand-piled rock walls known to the coolies, marked way-stations throughout the mountains. Once stopped, a man might roll himself a *beerie*, smoke in the shade of a deodar or scoop water from a nearby stream to splash on his sweat-soaked face.

The basket squeaked agreeably as the coolie walked, its rhythmic motion soothing and freeing me to look at the passing world. Older children, whacking at weeds or taking shortcuts, straggled up the zig-zag path worn into the hillside by countless mule hooves, goats, ponies, bare feet and wild game.

At 7,500 feet, Woodstock school perched below a ridge in a stand of oak and pine. A dormitory housing six- and seven-year-old girls stretched above the quadrangle: two rows of beds, high windows, a glimpse of red metal roofs. Billy's dorm stood a half-mile down the steep *khud* along with housing for the older girls. At the clang of a bell he would trek with his schoolmates up to the quadrangle and beyond, to the sloping, covered walkway that led to classrooms and the assembly hall dug into the side of the mountain.

Miss Gasper was matron of the little girls' dorm. Grey-haired, large-boned, dour, she loomed over us quietly, as a great-horned owl shadows mice in the fields. Behind her back, we called her Skinny-Connected-Gas-Pipe.

She was probably kind enough, hired to enforce the rules and civilize us as best she could. Thick-waisted in her shapeless dress of plain wool, she moved methodically on heavy, lace-up shoes, saw to it that we put our underpants on right-side-out, remembered pinafores over frocks, made beds neatly, and lined up for the *ayas* to brush and braid sleep-rumpled hair. No talking after lights out, or in the morning before she appeared from her room next door.

Our beds, in rows, stood far enough apart to keep us from visiting with each other without her knowledge, but invariably someone had a secret to share or a story to tell that couldn't wait. We were six- and seven-year-olds, maybe two dozen of us in the eyrie that served as our home for most of the nine months of every year. School buildings were unheated and always slightly moldy. The walls were bare of pictures, and our blankets were grey and brown. No colorful curtains or cheerful pillows caught the eye. The floors were cement, and tin wash tubs sat on worn wooden planks. Only geraniums and nasturtiums in the few hanging baskets on the balcony outside provided intense and precious reminders of color's gift to the world, so abundant back home in Allahabad. We children comforted each other as best we could.

Sometimes at night I cried from homesickness, or threw up with a stomach ache, or wet my bed; sometimes I felt the covers move and lay in terrified stillness in case a snake was resting there. Once a bat got through the clerestory window, and shrieking, we stood on our beds flapping blankets to keep it from nesting in our hair. But when the commotion died down, I found the great swooping paths of the dark-winged creature lapping the length of the dorm beautiful and bewildering, and longed to set it free.

One morning, early, I was caught giggling with a friend, my back to Miss Gasper's door. When it opened, her voice turned me around. For punishment, I was to stand at attention until it was time for breakfast. But before long, I felt the world go black and fell to the floor, bumping my head on a storage cabinet on the way down. The commotion brought her out again, this time to reach into her pocket for a tiny sack of smelling salts which she broke under my nose, the sharp amonia-like fumes snapping me awake.

On a different occasion, several girls ended up in a fight, the buckle of a classmate's shoe caught in another girl's hair. Cries of pain. In the fray, I was accused of fueling the argument with a mean remark, but although I agreed with the remark, it had come from someone else. Unable to get at the truth, Miss Gasper lined us up, littlest ones in front, and brought out the long wooden hair brush we dreaded. Pants down, bent over, we each received a paddling. Anticipation and the sounds of others crying terrified us more than the thwack itself. I vowed never to hit children.

Before bedtime, each of us was given four pieces of toilet paper and told to have a bowel movement. If we couldn't, we were fed a spoonful of cod liver oil. We soon learned to lie. The toilet paper, a lifeless grey, was stiff and needed to be rubbed to soften it. It carried the imprint of the crown of His Majesty the King of England.

After Miss Gasper's morning inspection, we single-filed out of the dorm, along the balcony, down the corner stairs and into the breakfast hall beside the quadrangle. Prayers, the scraping of chairs, and then I gagged over the congealed skin of blueish, watered-down milk on our sticky oatmeal. Even though the toast was often burnt, I liked it and the occasional jam we were served along with small, hard apples. If the bananas were over-ripe, they made me gag too. In the plains, Daddy tried to teach me that the riper the fruit, the better for us, but I was never persuaded. I eventually acquired a taste for *dahi* or homemade yogurt sprinkled with brown sugar, but what I missed the most at school was Indian food. Why was it only served to celebrate the end of the year when we headed back down to the plains? Meat was apparently hard to come by. Years later I heard the story of a student who caught a very large snake and took it to science class where the teacher demonstrated how to skin and dissect it. After class, he took the meat to the kitchen to have it cooked, and the next day, offered it to his students without telling them what it was. They liked it, thinking it was chicken, until, with a collective shudder, they discovered the truth.

Dismissed from breakfast, we could run around in the quadrangle for a while or sit on the stairs and visit until the bell was struck. That was our signal to line up and pledge allegiance to the King. As the years passed, our pledge was to the Queen. Then we'd fan out to our separate classrooms and begin the task of studying.

I blanked out the long hours at my desk, the critical voices and dulling regimes, and only years later remembered my clutched pencil and how it formed overlapping circles and sloping fence lines for the teacher's inspection. One day it was capital letters, and weeks or maybe months later, we were issued long-handled wooden pens. Mine addressed the ink bottle in its hole at the top of the desk, dipping into the wobbly, light-stippled surface. When a word skidded into a smear on the page, the strict voice pelted me for not following directions, for clumsiness and wasting paper. But I liked the smell of ink, the lovely sky-blue marks on a colorless page.

Occasionally I saw Billy kneeling at marbles with his friends, or milling about during recess on the dirt playground with its metal pole and clanging grab-bars. Children took turns holding on as they ran around the circle, deepening the dusty track, pulling up their feet for a moment of flight. I could just reach the lowest two rungs, and tightened my grip as I gathered momentum for lift-off. Those brief, exhilarating moments linger, mixed with the raw smell of metal, sweat and dust.

But I knew not to rely on my brother, not to count on seeing him or being defended by him in a skirmish; he had his own survival to tend to, his own dangers, triumphs and challenges. Years later, he told me of the bully in his dorm who tormented him and the other boys, confiscating their weekend treats, threatening them at every turn unless they obeyed, a little Napoleon, holding sway for all of Billy's years at Woodstock. He had no wish to return.

On the playground, games of tag and kick the can churned with the shrieks of children hoping to run fast enough, to be chosen, to brave the gravel-skinned knee or forearm. I wanted to be the best, but other girls could run faster, jump higher and catch whatever was thrown more easily. During the end-of-year field day, when we competed with neighboring schools, one Catholic, another Protestant, I marched in proud formation with my class, and once ran furiously in a relay. But on the playground I was usually among the last to be chosen.

On rainy days, we girls played jacks or jump rope under the metal-roofed shed. Sometimes, as the rope turned, I could gauge my entries and exits without getting hurt, but at other times, hesitating too long, my legs smarted and my feet tangled in the rope's inexorable whomp: *Teddy bear, teddy bear, turn around. Teddy bear, teddy bear, touch the ground.* The chanting went on, sometimes in English, sometimes in Hindi, as my tears welled. All too soon, a whistle drew us scattered players into lines. Scuffed and breathless, we funneled back to class.

During cold or rainy weather, recess was in a room just off the quadrangle, a teacher supervising. We younger girls stood in a circle holding each others' hands high while we sang *In and Out the Windows*, one of us weaving, ducking under the openings—Until what? Were we caught?—Yes, whenever the song, mid-phrase, was stopped. My heart raced as I escaped the "windows" or ran around the circle formed during *A Tisket, A Tasket*, letting the handkerchief fall unnoticed behind someone's back. I loved the excitement, the suspense, the chiming words and musical cadences. When we paired up for *One Potato, Two Potato, Three Potato, Four*, my partner and I stacked fists on top of each other, higher and higher like Jack climbing the beanstalk into thin air. Everything imaginary seemed intensely real, and the real unknowable.

Charlene was my best friend. She had dark, serious eyes and

swinging hair that framed a delicate face often lit by mischief or laughter. Because her mother and father worked at the school, she in the kitchen, he in the dorms, Charlene boarded with us but could visit her parents every day, secure in the knowledge that she was an adored child. When the two of us met again decades later in the States, friendship intact, she reminded me of our singing voices, good enough to save us from being sent to the principal's office when we got into trouble—which was often—because few of our classmates could carry a tune, and the teacher needed our voices. Charlene reminded me that her father stopped by every few days to see us, his tweed jacket holding sugar-coated almonds, the pocket on one side for her, on the other for me. We reached in for a handful, said goodbye to our benefactor, and then skipped away to the heaved-up ground and shade of a deodar where we crammed the sweet morsels into our mouths, giggling and chattering, sticky-faced with contentment.

Another game we devised for ourselves was to bounce down the cement steps that fell steeply from the third floor infirmary to the quadrangle. Sliding over the rounded edges like otters over a mud bank, our bottoms thumped along, picking up speed. At first we could only manage three or four steps at a time, but before long we started at the top of each landing, careening all the way down. Once our feet touched the ground, we climbed back up and started over.

When we played jacks, my hands felt clumsy next to those of my Indian girl friends. Over and over, we threw the pieces onto a patch of cement where they landed sturdily on their many-pronged feet. Before the ball could make its second bounce, Tara's nimble fingers swept in, plucking up just the right jack, the way a hawk unerringly targets its prey, leaving the rest of the flock untouched. When the bell rang, whoever owned the set, scooped it up in a final handful, the pieces chiming like coins in Lord Shiva's pocket. A grown woman now, at home in my own kitchen, no longer so awkward, I sweep bits of onion and carrot into my palm with that same graceful gesture.

SATURDAYS AFTER BREAKFAST, WE lined up on the quadrangle with our hands out for a *paisa*, our tenth of a penny allowance. Later, crowded around the sweet *whallah*, we inspected the wooden tray slung from his neck. Cupcakes iced a faded pink and green, called piggies, were favorites. Mine were the wide twists of ribboned taffy, glass-clear and faintly pink- or yellow-striped. I could suck on one for a long time and hold it up to the light.

Sometimes after school, I joined the boys who played on a steep embankment. Mimicking them, I'd run down hill with the loose stones, and then, at just the right moment, grab the overhanging branch of an oak, letting the hillside roll away without me. At first I hung there until one of the older boys lifted me down, but soon I was strong enough to let go of the branch by myself, side-slipping across the shifting stones to the *khud's* safer ground.

After November's torrential monsoon rains, when the air had cleared, we waded through hip-high daisies, ferns and cosmos, the grass tender. By the time the ground was dry again and the oak leaves brittle, our play turned to bunching pine needles into clumps which we sat on like sleds to ride the mountain trails. The day inevitably came when a boy picked up too much speed to negotiate the turn, and skidded over the embankment to his death, his body caught far below us on a jutting rock ledge, eye glasses still unbroken. I hadn't known him, so the grief of losing a friend was absent, but that a body, including my own, could fall and break made a deep impression, and I still see him lying there.

Once a week in the dorms was strip and step into the round tin tub, steaming and dangerous, the *aya* on a stool beside me, scrubbing my face and ears, my back and front and bottom and toes with a bar of Lifeboy soap, two other *ayas* tending children on either side of us. Heads were inspected for lice or ringworm and periodically treated with lysol. The wooden platforms the tubs sat on soon slicked with water, and our bodies turned pink and crinkled. We were towelled and given clean clothes. The worn ones were added to a pile in the middle of a bed sheet later tied by its corners into a giant hobo's bundle and dragged off to the *dhobi's*.

Looking back, I think of the enormous burden of work those servants managed; the toll it took on their lives. And I think of my own children, Carl and Todd, how they loved their baths, how I didn't have to boil water and carry it to the tub but simply turned on faucets, how even the faucets were easy to use and sparkling. Having out-grown his plastic dishpan in the kitchen sink, Carl slid back and forth in the spacious tub as I knelt beside him, his hands patting the water as he squealed with pleasure. The first time water splashed on his face, clinging to his eyelashes, he stopped abruptly, held his breath and blinked. Soon he was back to kicking and chortling. Four years later, his younger brother, Todd, would again pour the always-escaping sparkle through spread-apart fingers as if light were solid and pliable, his hands a celebration of moves.

Slippery with water-light, the children's bird-like voices intertwined with mine as I washed them. How plump and sweet their bodies! When I lifted either of them, slick and dripping, over the side of the tub and onto the bath mat, to be wrapped in a towel, they could barely stand still, pranced on their toes, babbling and bright-eyed, leaning damply into me. However tired I was, I never tired of their lives. I was comforted, knowing how deeply I loved them, and how, whatever hardships they faced down the years, that bond would sustain them.

But on wash days at Woodstock, the *dhobi* stood in the cold water of a rectangular cement trough built into a mountain stream, scrubbing clothes by first light with other men of the village, chanting as they worked. After the clothes were spread on the ground to dry in the sun, or when it rained, draped over tall baskets indoors above smoldering coals, they came back fresh and folded. In the same way, we left our scuffed leather shoes outside the dorm each evening and found them polished and neatly lined up the next day. Servants. They were said to be grateful for their work, that it lifted them out of poverty. But how must it have felt to compare us with their own children who wore only ragged clothing and no shoes and couldn't afford to go to school?

Like other students, I visited the infirmary when I came down with chicken pox or a cough, dysentery or a fever, but for years I also suffered the shame of blisters on my legs and arms, the skin puffed here and there with clear fluid no one could diagnose. I felt like an untouchable. The British nurse who took care of us wore a stiff white cap, white dress carefully starched, white shoes and stockings, and if the weather was cold, a navy blue sweater. She was brisk but kind. Priding herself in neatly-made beds, she pulled the sheets tight, squaring their corners and the corners of blankets and counterpanes.

Mornings and evenings the nurse's hand bristled with thermometers. She carried them wedged between her fingers like rows of cigarettes, brandishing four or five at a time, warning us to keep them under our tongues, to hold our mouths closed. Once the temperatures registered, she again filled her hands with them, returned to her desk and wrote the numbers neatly in a ledger, remembering which one belonged beside each name.

In spite of my efforts to lie still, I sometimes leaned over the bed to chat with a friend, and my thermometer fell out. As it broke apart, mercury rolled away into delicate silver beads. One bead might latch onto others, pooling to form a mirror, or scatter to many tinier points like distant stars. We knew not to touch the mercury with our hands because it was poisonous, but pushed it around with pencils, combs, whatever we could find. The person whose bed it was under was sure to get into trouble, but I was too absorbed by how the beads bumped into each other, forming wobbly lakes, or scattering into galaxies, to care.

Once, confined to the infirmary, I was given a whispered message that at noon I should unreel a ball of string out the back window. I did so, peering over the edge to where some boys in shadow scuffed the gravel, laughing and punching each others' shoulders. They tied something to the end of the string, and as they ran off, called out for me to pull it up. I discovered a stick of chewing gum and a wadded-up, pencilled note. Not yet attracted to boys, I was nevertheless thrilled to be singled out, and even more excited by the danger of being caught, but didn't much like the sullen fellow who was asking in the note to be my boyfriend. Still, there was the chewing gum, a rare and delicious treat. My status rose noticeably in the eyes of my friends.

BY THE TIME I was in third grade, I felt proud to be allowed to walk from the dorm to the other end of the balcony and knock on a door that opened into a room crammed with rich carpets, flowering plants and pictures, and a piano flashing its ivories.

The woman with the broad face, husky voice and thick glasses who lived there was brusque but kind. She had everything ready—the brass candlesticks and bowls, the round clawed bell, ashtrays and vases, newspapers underneath all of them. Her thick black hair swung up at the edges just above her shoulders, green eyes

hidden in a pale, pock-marked face. I knelt, the prickly-soft oriental carpet pressing into my knees, tipped the narrow tin can with
its acrid smell onto a cloth, picked up an ashtray from the low table
in front of me, and began to scrub. How black the cloth became
as the brass filmed over with its chalky pink liquid, giving off a
pungent smell. The blacker the cloth, the brighter the brass. I liked
doing the work, and earned a few *annas* for sweets. The room had
a homey atmosphere, and I felt singled out and cared for, however
briefly.

Best of all were those times when the woman pulled out the
bench, stubbed her cigarette, and gave herself up to the piano. Her
strong, blunt hands stayed level, her sure thumbs and fingers fitted the keys like birds bedded down in their nests. Out of the rich
sounds, one or two phrases floated past the others and into my
keeping. Note by note, I would someday make them my own, practicing in the small cell where the students were given their lessons.
There, the music teacher rapped the backs of our hands with a
ruler if we forgot to hold our wrists flat. One time, after the smack
and cross voice, I fainted, sliding off the bench onto the floor. That
teacher didn't hit me again, but music opened its heart to me.

Each year, a judge from the London Philharmonic crossed the
ocean to test piano students from all over India. I was eight or
nine when he asked me to play, listened quietly, made a few notes.
Months later in the mail, my scores came back to the school. I had
won top honors and was chosen to give a recital. But the stage was
a lonely place. Even though I performed flawlessly, fear drenched
my body. I felt exposed and vulnerable. Although later I played in
front of others when I had to, I never learned to enjoy it. Fortunately, however, music continued to call out my deepest feelings,
giving them voice. I played to learn what each of us had to say, and
let the notes open me to their mysteries.

One winter, when I was back in Allahabad, a British soldier
named Eric stopped by for a visit. Like other G.I.'s and R.A.F. Boys
hungry for a home-cooked meal and the company of Westerners,
he had heard about our house, and felt welcome. After dinner, he
found the old upright in a corner of the living room, and his large
hands flew to the keys, hovering there until it was time to leave.
I had never heard such a torrent of music!—Beethoven, Mozart,
Chopin, Brahms tumbling out from the mysterious reservoirs of

the human heart. It changed me as surely as a bend in the land changes the river.

SUNDAYS IN THE MOUNTAINS, children and teachers dressed up and walked the mile and a-half uphill to the grey stone church. The sermons were a way to turn Bible stories into lessons: Think of yourself as a clean sheet of paper handed out by the Lord; every unkind thought or deed, each lie or lack of kindness leaves a crease in the paper that will never come out! There were sermons about not hiding your light under a basket, and others about the meek inheriting the earth.

My ears went to sleep, light slanting through the tall windows picking up a loose hair on someone's shoulder, adding a glow to the sloping brown wool hat that floated above the pews. How did the building's heavy wood, or the granite slabs, get there, if not hauled up narrow trails on someone's back? And why were white men's backs not used? Eventually, with a scraping of shoes and a sigh of clothing, everyone stood and sang *Glory, glory, glory, Lord God Almighty*, or *All Things Wise and Wonderful*.

As a teenager, I would play those same hymns for chapel at the all-girls' school in Pennsylvania, my fingers urgently seeking the right keys, too many flats or sharps throwing them off, even though I'd practiced during the week. But after church in the mountains, I loved running out into the sunshine or rain, down the switchback trails whose trees held the piercing colors of bird song and the hoots of black-faced monkeys traveling overhead.

Once I had it memorized, I could join the grown-up congregation's droning recitation of *The Lord's Prayer*, and feel myself less a child. But I always wondered about that phrase, *Our father*. My own father was at home, I was sure of that, and my heavenly father was everywhere, even inside me, but lived in the sky. Still, the two fathers weren't that easily separated. At every meal the family prayed to one while the other sat at the table (or on Sundays preached from behind a pulpit): *Do unto others as ye would have them do unto you. Suffer the little children to come unto me.* Did God condone a father's behavior? Were children offerings to the needs of others?

Sitting cross-legged on the floor at school, I sang *Jesus Loves*

Me, This I Know, For the Bible Tells Me So, careening into the chorus—*Yes, Jesus Loves Me!* Or I belted out *Onward Christian Soldiers Marching As To War*—never sure about the words *as to*. Nor did I question the war imagery I later realized mocked both Jesus' teachings and Gandhi's. But the musical beat, the beguiling rhythms of the hymns, and the King James version of the Bible stayed with me.

Before we went down to the plains for our three months of holiday, Joseph and Mary, the shepherds, baby Jesus, the camels and other animals— even the manger, the hills, a star and the wise men—all appeared in our classroom, cut out of brightly colored felt and placed on a felted board for the class to enjoy. I had never seen felt before, or touched it. It interested me that it stuck to itself, that it came in vivid colors, that its edges could be intricately cut into living shapes. Our soft-voiced Bible teacher was thin and awkward and had dark, woebegone hair, but as she told the story, she placed each figure thoughtfully on the felted background to accompany her words. Years later those camels still seemed to move across the horizon at a stately pace bearing wise men and gifts, and the family stayed holy.

When I was chosen to be Mary in the nativity play, I felt important and looked forward to cradling a baby or a child-sized doll, but instead was given a blanket wrapped around a light bulb. So that the audience would feel the radiance of the Christ child and not that of a fifteen-watt bulb, I was to look at it adoringly. It was then that I first felt betrayed by the church.

That Jesus had nails driven through his hands and feet, thorns pressed into his head also tormented me. Whenever I thought of such torture, my stomach constricted, and I felt the terrible weight of my own body hanging from those spikes. Why would people do that?

7

IN JUNE THE MOTHERS came up for a month to escape the heat of the plains, the fathers joining them later for a week or ten days' vacation. It was then that my brother and I lived with our parents in the little cottage called Zig Zag. As temporary day students, we could walk the mile down through the oak and pine forest to school and back again, hanging onto clumps of tough mountain grass to pull ourselves up shortcuts. We relished being a family once more, eating home-cooked meals, playing out of doors until dusk. One year, too homesick to wait until Mummy was unpacked and ready for us, Billy ran away from the school infirmary, his body feverish and itching with chicken pox as he trudged up the final hill to Zig Zag in pajamas and slippers. He begged Mummy not to send him back. Since there were no telephones, she had a servant carry her chit to the nurse, as was the custom, saying the patient was at home and could stay.

Zig Zag was one of a dozen cottages loaned out each year by the Mission, small shelters scattered across the hillside, hidden by trees and connected by a maze of crisscrossing trails. Billy and I slept in a tiny screened room at the rear of the house. Because it was during the monsoon season, rain thundered onto the tin roof overhead, drumming us to sleep. In the evenings, when the weather was clear, the four of us crowded onto the narrow back porch for dinner. Hung over the hillside, the porch offered a sweeping view of the world. The air was crisp and pure with a distant glint of rivers winding across the far plains. Once the sun had slipped below the horizon, the sky blazed with startling displays of color—

magenta, vermilion, peach, fiery gold—soon deepened to indigo.

After dinner, the family sometimes walked up to the *chukkar*, the gravel road at the top of the tallest ridge, its stone wall wide enough to sit on. Flanked by deodar and pine, we could gaze out over the Himalayan Gharwahl rising steeply from its valleys. In the distance, glistening white, the perpetual snows of the Tibetan peaks. I had no way of knowing I would return after forty-two years to sit on this very spot with a narrow piece of watercolor paper, dipping a brush into a small tray of paints, trying to catch the spirit of the mountains I had loved as a child. That little painting went back home with me to America, eventually illustrating the cover of my first published book of poems, *Gandhi's Lap*. By then, my own children were grown, and the watercolor seemed to bring together the shattered past of my family's life in India, and mine in the U. S. filled with hope, the two intertwined on the page—deep shadow anchoring the light.

My book-title referred to the time Daddy took me to visit Gandhi-ji, whom he deeply admired. Wearing his *dhoti* and seated in the shade of a tree, Gandhi returned my father's *namaste*, palms joined in the traditional greeting. During those years—the mid-1940s—Indians determined to free themselves from British rule. Was there some way Daddy and other American missionaries could help in the fight for independence? With his funny ears, big smile and gentle voice, Gandhi coaxed me: *Come, child, sit in my lap while we talk; here, you can play with my pocket watch.* The watch, so like my father's, was just the right lure. I climbed into his lap and held it as carefully as if it were alive: a cricket, maybe, or a fledgling bird. Even now I can feel its weight, its warmth in my hand, the curving roundness of its silvered edge, its glass face tilted to catch or deflect the light, light that illuminated or overwhelmed the orderly numbers, its ticking heartbeat close to my own. Dimly reassuring, the men's voices ebbed and flowed around me.

On January 30th, 1948, Gandhi was shot and killed. His beloved country had been divided into Pakistan and India, and millions of Muslims and Hindus turned against each other in a blood bath of slaughter that Gandhi had worked all his life to prevent.

IN THE MOUNTAINS, ON occasional weekends, Daddy took us children to the bazaar in Mussoorie to enjoy its bustle of shops, barking dogs, temples, hotels and theater. We bought a black puppy there once, each of us taking turns carrying it home, Billy and I beside ourselves with joy. But what would mother say? Before long, the puppy's needle-sharp teeth tore the family's hands and clothes. A Tibetan guard dog, or *bhutia*, it had to be taken back.

Kicking small stones, running down the trail, we children were also easily side-tracked on our way to school, stopping to gather handfuls of vibrant moss greening branches after a few days of rain. Billy picked off a rhinoceros beetle that reared its glossy, mahogany back when he stroked it, teasing me with it, its prickly feet catching in the soft hairs of my arm. It didn't hurt. He and his friends liked to put two stag beetles face to face, then stroke their backs, irritating them to rear up and fight each other with their long, branched pincers. The narrow-bodied bamboo beetles were harder to find and much more aggressive. Their pincers drew blood or left a painful bruise. Were we often late for school? I don't know. I stopped for butterflies, their vibrant colors and erratic flights writing musical scores in the sky. Sometimes one would land on my sleeve or sail fearlessly over a cliff. I wanted to be like that.

How determinedly the ant at my feet carried its log of straw across the rocky path; how giddily a leaf floated last night's torrent only to be left high and dry in today's gully. Rain bent the grasses, gouged new paths, deepened old ones, rushed headlong beside us, spilling over edges to catch the sprawl of light. Perhaps I'd meet the *dhudh wallah* and his horse on Tehri, a wide dirt road that looped past one side of the school. Slung from rope harnesses across the animal's back, two tall cans of milk were on their way to market. The horse had a quiet, steady gait, its halter tied with bells, its long straight eyelashes visible under the leather guards. It smelled good, knew the way, and gave no hint of hurry. I liked the soft colors of the *dhudh wallah*'s clothes, layered and quilted as autumn leaves, our shy exchange of smiles, his tireless stride. Mountain people were different from those in the plains.

AT THE FIRST HINT of dawn, the silvery notes of the whistling thrush floated up to announce the coming of light. Quiet throughout the day, its song rang out again at dusk as if for my soul's sake, praising a world that ran too deep to name. But much as I loved the mountains, home was in the plains.

MOTHER RESENTED MEN'S EARNING power and status, and refused what she considered the menial jobs traditionally available to women—secretarial work, nursing, lower school teaching. Dad, however, wasn't interested in power, wasn't ambitious, enjoyed his simple life style. Time remained dreamily unstructured for him, and even though he taught English for thirteen years at an Indian college, he was more pal than professor, loved by the students for his patience, his good sportsmanship and his having been born and raised in their country. He was on their side, and clearly at home in their language and customs.

When Dad was at his desk correcting papers, our pet mongoose, Riki Tiki Tavi, liked to crawl into his shirt to sleep against the warmth of his back where the tucked-in fabric formed a sort of hammock. If he couldn't wake Riki before class, he simply took him along. He liked re-telling the story of how his students' faces froze once when a pair of beady eyes and a narrow snout peered out at them from between his shirt buttons.

The Indian principal resented Dad's popularity, scolded him if he was late, and considered him negligent for not being authoritarian or British enough for the good of the students. But Dad went on being himself. When he praised Gandhi-ji and Mohammed in his classroom as equal to Christ, or said the Virgin birth didn't make sense, the Board of Foreign Missions sent him a serious reprimand. Besides being an English teacher, he was an ordained minister and missionary and had a duty to uphold the teachings of the church and show it more respect. Mother urged him to keep his unorthodox ideas to himself. In an attempt to smooth things over, she invited the principal and his wife to our house for tea. We children always sided with Dad, who seemed in every way sane to us and pleasantly unflappable. Mother, the realist, fretted about, others' opinions, money and survival: somebody had to.

When we were children, the distant scufflings of adults went largely unheeded, but the fights at home, more and more frequent, upset us. Mother was often irritated or angry; Dad, the peace-maker, refused to engage. Dad would lose the keys or be late for class. He'd forget a dinner date or not wipe his shoes before coming inside. Always something. We could see both parents' points of view but didn't know how to reconcile them.

Once in a while Mr. Ralaram, one of Daddy's colleagues, stopped by to entertain us with raucous imitations of a braying donkey. Other visitors arrived on bicycles, by horse and carriage or on foot, including students, teachers, soldiers from the States or Great Britain, and the occasional dignitary like Nehru or his sister, Vijaya Lakshmi Pundit, whom we knew as Aunt Nan. She and her three daughters lived near by and were our friends. Spirited dis-cussions invariably took place about India's fight for independence and whether Gandhi or Nehru, or both, should lead the country.

On the other side of campus, in a basement with its high win-dows, a "worm-specialist" worked. Mr. Higgenbottom was world-renowned, a title that impressed both parents. Taken to visit, I was shocked by the brownish yellow formaldehyde-filled jars of float-ing worms in their miniature and terrible sizes. Shocked, too, by my first sight of a human fetus. It hung, suspended in that curled, clench-fisted stance, its head too big, its eyes dark points forever sheathed. The man himself loomed heavily, grey-haired and jowly, frightening as the room with its cavernous sights and smells.

I WOULD MUCH RATHER have been on the Jumna's clay bank, head-ing for a wobbly boat, a slip of dark water between us. Daddy handed me over to the boatman who knew just how to stand to keep us steady. He'd lead me to one of the planks I'd sit on before bracing my feet against the wooden floorboards. When all of us were in and settled, along with the picnic baskets Shunkar, Kishan and Mummy had packed, and the thin wool blankets to be spread on the sand, the boatman leaned into the great oars, and we glided like a floating island onto the sparkle and yaw of another world.

Like others, our boat was fitted with curved metal rods that arched overhead to support a cloth or thatch as protection from the sun. On festive occasions the canopy was strung with mari-golds. Boatmen and their families often lived on the open boats, wife and children left on shore when the vessel was for hire.

The boat's heavy timbers creaked, and the oars rose and fell, sheathed in a silver run-off of water. Each stroke unleashed a string of whirlpools I tried to catch as they passed. The bridge, now far above us, boomed with traffic, and its vast cement pillars stood planted in the water like the legs of a mythical elephant.

As the boatman pulled steadily on his oars, the bridge grew smaller, and the river widened into view. The bit of shore we'd left, stretched out, tilting into new shapes before gradually slipping away. Little by little the distant white sand banks of the other side came toward us, edges widely-scalloped and darkened by the lapping water.

We waded ashore, sand giving way underfoot to more sand, bits of mica sticking to our ankles. Even on a bright moonlit night, the sand was warm, only slightly cooler as we pushed below the surface. I could run my hands through its endless weight and texture, or shape it with a bucket of water into imaginary castles with real sides.

The distant wail of a whistle announced the train hurrying over the bridge. Passengers pushed up windows to toss coins and marigolds into the river. Below them, clinging to a ledge on the pillars and hidden from view, six-year-old boys dove for the bright flickering coins as they sank through the water.

Moonlit nights when the sun's heat had eased, the family picnicked with Indian and American friends on the river's fine, white sand. Daddy found a stick and drew a giant circle, then smaller circles at intervals inside it, and finally, a series of intersecting lines that formed a spider's web on which we played a favorite game. Adults and children raced along the lines to keep from being caught, all the while shrieking and gasping with excitement. Afterwards, to cool off, we'd paddle in the shallows, or open picnic baskets for the evening meal. My favorite food was something Mummy made, a dough each of us wrapped around a fat stick saved for the purpose, turning it over a beach fire until it was golden brown. As soon as it was baked enough to pull off, we'd stuff the cavity with creamed chicken or butter and jam.

Once, during a daytime picnic with friends, while the adults visited on their blankets, I played in the shallows and became engrossed in watching my toes magnified by the water. As I moved about, the sand beneath my feet shifted and began to slope away until I lost touch with it, finding myself unable to reach the bottom. Flailing about, I soon floated face down. The next thing I felt was Daddy's hand hauling me out. Until then, I had never been afraid of the river.

Few Indians, during those years, knew how to swim. When Daddy taught the college men who signed up for his classes, he often helped any of the villagers who came to watch. Sometimes Billy and I joined them. While students milled around, practicing their strokes, their breathing, pulling themselves, soaked, onto the wooden float, tipping it precariously as water sloshed overboard, shouting and laughing, white shirts and pants sticking to their bodies, Daddy had us hold our noses and jump in one at a time, even though we couldn't swim, assuring us he'd be there—the scary leap, the shock of cold and dark, the going-down that seemed to last forever, and then the explosion of breath, the search for his head—there it was, bobbing and wet, his laughing voice, *Shabash!* Well-done! as we flailed toward him, pride racing through us.

Before long, we learned to hold onto his shoulders, take a deep breath and let him pull us under for a few strokes until we rose to the surface, gasping. Daddy said lots of Indians threw their young children overboard, telling them to swim. If they thrashed about and survived, fine; if not, they drowned. I couldn't bear the thought of it. We both soon learned to be good swimmers. As a teenager, I took pride in mimicking Daddy's strong overhand crawl—fluid, effortless-looking—even though my own body always ached, and I worked hard. I rested by rolling over for the back stroke and again for the breast stroke.

The river itself, so light-struck and blue, kept moving but never disappeared. No wonder it was sacred to the Hindus, blessing the dry land and our hot, sun-baked bodies. It flowed from the Himalayas, plummeting over boulders the way Lord Shiva's hair streamed from his head, tumbling over his shoulders. By the time it reached the plains, the river had widened and quieted. But as I learned years later, the Jumna's sapphire glitter was even then deceptive, polluted with human waste and bodies scavenged by turtles, then with toxic chemicals and petroleum products. Today, more and more people wade in its waters and crowd its overworked banks.

Sometimes Daddy took us to the nearby town of Benares where the Jumna and Ganges rivers meet. During the annual *magh mela*, over a million pilgrims from all over India congregate at this sacred site to bathe and perform *puja*, or worship. We might walk across the top tier of the weathered cement steps stretching across a vast area and leading into the shallows as Daddy explained the pilgrimage. Women in *saris* and men in *dhotis* poured water over their heads, drinking from cupped hands and offering prayers as well as bits of food and flowers to the gods.

Off to one side, acrid smoke from the burning *ghats* still drifted on the air day and night. I learned that people's bodies were cremated there, bones and ashes carried away by the river. Daddy explained that this was a sensible measure, that the people were already dead, so it didn't hurt them, but I had touched fire, and the pain was instant and fierce. I couldn't imagine "being dead." In high school when I read about teenage wives forced to throw themselves on their husbands' funeral pyres, I felt the same electric shock I'd had over the crucifixion, too visceral not to comprehend.

On the outskirts of towns, wherever building projects were underway, women in *saris* tied at the waist carried baskets of rock on their heads up steep embankments, arms dusted white, slender bodies beautiful however long their labor, however short their lives in the pitiless heat of poverty. Men, too, balanced heavy loads on their heads: bricks or bundles of laundry, sheets and shirts beaten clean on river rocks and spread on the ground to dry. Carefully folded, edge to edge like our lives. Children carried other children on their hips.

8

THE WEATHER'S SULTRY. MUMMY wants me out from underfoot.
Even the cement floor is warm. I lie on it anyway, six-year-old
cheek burning, bare arms and legs sticky with heat, my hair like a
sweater I want to pull off. *Punkas* stir the air on the ceiling but no
breeze reaches me, only the flat squares of light from the distant
windows. Outside the *bulbul* calls and the *myna* answers. Evening
will offer imperceptible amounts of relief, but whatever cooler air
arrives will filter in on the wings of mosquitoes. We'll slap ourselves and get stung. The cement floor is even hotter now with the
heat of my body, darkening it with sweat. I've pushed my hair away
from my neck.

Mummy, what can I do? She suggests I sort a drawer, one with
its everyday mix of rubber bands, old pencil stubs, stray buttons,
a bicycle clip, string in various colors and lengths, matches, bits of
ribbon. All of it seems manageable now that it's neatly organized
by language. But at the time, I first felt an eagerness to please by
turning what was messy into something beautiful and orderly the
way Mummy did, and then, a hopelessness at not being able to do
so. It wasn't just that we didn't own the little boxes and divided
containers, the plastic bags we have today. It was that even as a
child—or especially then—nothing was trivial or useless, the mer-
est object took on a life.

When the drawer was closed, it blended in with the rest of
the wood. Who would guess what was hidden inside? When it
was opened, I could run my hands through an adventure of shapes

and textures, finding what was familiar and comforting, what was needed, or what seemed new and surprising.

Why does this particular occasion re-surface in the muddy currents of memory? And why, so long ago, did it gradually come to represent a chaotic and unmanageable part of life I had no words for as a child? Where was I to put this, and how could I throw that out? Eagerness was eroded by indecision in the same way that my own life dragged against the lives of my parents. No matter how I tried to rearrange myself, I was tattered and flawed. Billy and I drifted between wanting to be like Daddy and wanting Mummy to like us.

For Mummy, order and beauty steadied what could otherwise topple. Since life was precarious and unpredictable, to control anything, flowers or clothes, counters or dinner parties, allowed her to move forward. Appearances mattered. She was sure others were always judging us, so we had to measure up. At the time, her heroes were Lord and Lady Mountbatten because they looked so elegant, so able to rule the world. She, too, was ambitious. People had to be interesting if she was going to spend time with them. Children got in the way. At best, they were ornamental. They needed to grow up to be useful: to acquire good looks, expertise, public accolades. Then they deserved to gain her attention. I not only couldn't order the drawer, I saw no way to make sense of our lives.

Possessions were often shadowed by family sayings: *Waste not, want not. A stitch in time saves nine. This might come in handy. Remember the poor.* Besides, there was Gandhi's example of the tin cup and homespun. Were these the models by which I was to decide what to keep and what to throw away? And why? Weren't things saved because of their usefulness, or for future possibilities? Was that it? I could easily put the rubber bands together looping them onto a big safety pin, the wooden matches back in their little slide-in boxes, but what to do with a small piece of ribbon too bright to throw away, or an envelope where in one corner a white bird stood on one leg in a tiny blue pool? What to do with a spool of used typewriter ribbon still smudging the fingers, rippled at the edges by the imprints of letters tumbling brightly down its center?

The first memory I have of giving a present to someone, other than picking flowers for Mummy, was when I found a typewriter ribbon in the waste basket and wrapped it up for Daddy for Christmas. When he opened it and thanked me, my brother guffawed, *That's an old, used ribbon, not a present. It's been thrown away already!* Daddy pointed out that Billy shouldn't make fun of me, that I was too young to know the difference but had the spirit of giving, which was what mattered.

In India during the thirties and forties, a loaf of bread wasn't found on a shelf, didn't appear in a plastic bag, wasn't fastened at one end with a wire tie. If it had been, both bag and fastener would have been re-used until they wore out. Bread came as it was, either wrapped in a cloth unwound from the head of a man who otherwise wore it as a turban, or simply delivered by hand as he walked or traveled on his bicycle to knock on the front screen door and be paid by one of the *sahibs*. On that first delivery, Mummy sent the man back and told him to wrap the loaf in newspaper before returning, and then always to deliver it that way. Indians, quite sensibly, handled breads differently: *chapatis, purees* or *naan* were kneaded, hand-flattened and cooked on the spot just before being eaten. No need for expensive wrappings.

So, too, yogurt came in clay bowls that were broken after use and recycled. Milk from cows, goats or camels was carried to market in a lidded metal can, or brought to our back door where Shunkar poured it into cook pots kept for the purpose, making sure it was boiled and cooled before we drank it.

ALTHOUGH WE WERE RICH compared to beggars, we were poor compared to upper class Indians. Not that I felt poor, but like all missionaries, we were dependent on The Board of Foreign Missions for whatever we owned, which wasn't much. Besides, thrift was considered a virtue. Owning things was self-indulgent. Only our eyes could gorge on color, our ears stuff themselves on the music of birdsong or bracelets, and our hands and feet feast on the textures around us of leaves, homespun and silk. A piece of string securing a package wasn't cut away and dropped in the waste basket; it was carefully unknotted, rolled around one's fingers, cinched and saved for future use. A scrap of paper was smoothed out to be written on. If we were out of toilet paper, we rubbed pieces of newsprint together to soften them for that purpose. Indians didn't own toilet paper; they rinsed with water instead.

Watch where you step! A path through fields of flowering yellow mustard is splatted here and there with diarrhea, roadside ditches with urine. Wrapped around a branch of the banyan that's perfect for us children to climb, a well-camouflaged snake. These and the flies and mosquitoes that flourish in the tropics alarmed Mother, and by default, Billy and me, but Dad seemed simply to accept them as part of the world he had grown up in, rich in both beauty and squalor.

It was the sick, the hungry and the maimed who concerned him as he took me to visit a leper colony, saying they were ostracized and would welcome company. Through the tall link fence, I watched a man knitting with his toes. His pink and white skin was blotchy as a sycamore's, and he'd lost his fingers and part of his face. Some lepers were blind, some leaned on sticks or shuffled on bandaged feet; all were disfigured, dull-eyed, struggling to make something to sell, caged animals I was revolted by. I wanted to go home, but my feelings filled me with shame.

In the bazaar or along a village path, I learned that the person with trunk-huge, leathery legs suffered from elephantitis, that the one on the bus with a melon-sized bulge on her neck grew a goiter. Among the children who followed us, begging, many had only stubs for legs and arms. Parents cut them off, I was told, when they were babies so that they'd be pitied and given money to feed their otherwise destitute families. People too weak from hunger to sit up, lay along the sidewalk, hoping passersby would leave them a little rice, a few *annas*. In the busy crowds around them, many eyes looked red from the smoke of daily cooking fires, or were filmed over by cataracts. Some were blind: an elderly man or woman led by a child, or a child with arms extended, groping along a wall. I felt unprotected in my own life, a leper of sorts, vulnerable and open to others.

Moving along on the crowded street—but more like lotus blossoms floating on the surface of a darkened stream—two women in colorful *saris* and glowing skin chatted together; a cluster of young men stopped to buy *pan*, their thick, ebony hair catching the light; children pushed hoops or raced after kites. We, too, were part of the hubbub, apparent foreigners who felt ourselves at home.

Without a telephone, radio, television, microwave or electric stove and oven, without plastic bags, foil and wax paper, or hot, running water, not to mention computers or CD's and apps we rely on today, we made do with what we had, just as others did. Occasionally we'd hand-wind His Master's Voice, a portable Victrola or record player, whose heavy swing-arm was fitted with a replaceable needle. The needle, once secured, had to be carefully positioned onto a spinning outer groove of the shiny, black seventy-eight. Seconds later, music! But mostly we listened to the songs of birds and the braying of animals, the voice of the weather and the passing trains, the horse-drawn carriages and zinging bicycle wheels, the sounds of sweeping and of sandals slapping the hard, bare ground, of voices calling out, and others conversing quietly.

UNDER THE SHADE OF a *neem* tree, young boys—never girls—sitting cross-legged, recited lessons barked at them by a strict, stick-waving teacher. They wrote in the dirt with twigs, or memorized sacred texts, in unison sang out the alphabet, their numbers, the months of the year. No money was available for the simplest school books or for chalk and small slates.

As poor as missionaries were, we were unimaginably rich compared to our servants, who, in turn were richer than the villagers, day laborers or untouchables. Whose fault was this? Did our house, our food and clothing take away from theirs? I felt myself to blame. How could I walk in their shoes when the poor had no shoes? I didn't have words for these feelings, but they nagged at me. They still do. Besides, however much we came to help, we were also in the way.

In the meantime, Daddy kept posing questions for me to consider. How would I choose, for instance, which person to push off of a life raft if one-too-many threatened to sink all the others? The famous opera singer? The convict or surgeon? The leper? The policeman? The soldier or untouchable? The fisherman or mechanic? The child? And if, in a hospital, either a pregnant woman could be saved or her baby, but not both, which would I choose? I quickly choose the baby, but Daddy said, No, the mother, because she could have more babies. I knew that in India girl-children were often thrown away at birth. I was a girl-child too.

Billy wears khaki shorts, one hand gripping the base of the wooden sling shot, the other pulling against the Y, thumb and forefinger pressed on the fold of leather wrapping a pebble. It's hot out. Rows of sweat bead his upper lip as he squints against the sun.

The farther back he pulls, the more the elastic stretches. Zap! A commotion of snapping leaves, the wing beats of mynas and crows. Hours of practice. Accumulated power. Every boy's prize. One day he'll be given a gun.

For me, it's a rainbow of pastel shapes in a cellophane package. Carefully cutting open the crinkly wrap, I drop the tightly-packed wads of rice paper into a glass of water. The folded tidbits unpleat their wings and petals, stretch open and take form: a tiny lotus in cupped leaves, hyacinths with trailing stems, a drift of parasols and Japanese lanterns. When I tap the glass, the floating garden sways as if in a current, tugging at me to follow.

Only years later will I ask whose mind envisioned the shapes, gathered and dyed the paper, folded it, and cut with sharp scissors each intricate design. Was it a mother too poor to afford a toy, making one up to watch her child's eyes brighten as mine did? And why are boys armed with power and girls with dreams of beauty?

A broken shard of mirror catches the sky's blue and silver rivets. By edging the mirror with tufts of moss, I make a tiny lake, and the moss becomes encircling hills. A pinch of sand and some speckled stones form a beach, a fistful of leafy stems becomes a forest, half a walnut shell a boat, its mast a toothpick spearing a scrap of paper sail. Play becomes my spirit kingdom, rising from sources unknown. It comforts me and counteracts the everyday perils.

WHEN I HEAR THE noise, and step into the front yard to see what's happening, they are already at it—the servants and their wives and children, a few of their friends, bunched in a half circle with their backs to me. Pushing my way through, I take in the bare expanse of ground and the mangy dog tethered by a long rope to a post. A man with a bamboo pole in his hands swings at the dog as it runs the loop, racing out of reach and then, dazed, back into it, the crack of wood on bone triggering the animal's screams.

I lunge for the dog, *Stop! Please stop!* but hands pull me back and I'm told the stray has been caught while scavenging food, and innocent or guilty, will pay for the killing of our two pet rabbits torn, bloody, from their cage. Each time the bamboo strikes home, the dog staggers and wails. When it falls, it gets up, dragging its hind quarters, looking bewildered, its ribs showing, its long, rangy body patched with sores and pale brown and white hair. The women and children stare, and the men shout at each other, goading the animal as it yanks at the rope.

Hit again and again, it runs until time seems to blur, dragging us with it. The men argue about whether to let the animal go or to finish the job, but the one with the bamboo pole keeps hitting as if unable to stop, as if obliterating evil to save us all from its reach.

I stand shivering and sobbing as the dog's yelps keen into those high-pitched wails no human ear can bear. Violence—I'm a part of it, the one who caused it by loving two rabbits. Mummy and Daddy are visiting friends, and there's no one I can turn to. The dog will be killed, dragged off, left for the vultures, their hooked beaks, their bare heads bloodied as they feed their own hungers.

William Stanley
Gould and Sigrid
Peterson Gould on
their wedding day,
1930

Charlotte at birth
with nurse, 1935

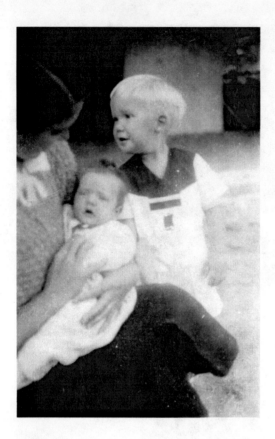

Charlotte with mother and brother Billy

Family house in Allahabad

Ewing Christian College - ALLAHABAD - - Published for the North India Christian Tract & Book Society. Allahabad.

Ewing Christian College

Playmates Kiran Caleb, Charlotte, Sally Hazlett, Savitri, Billy

Charlotte and Kiran

Allahabad, Mother and her towheads

Charlotte and Billy on tricycles

Leaving from San Francisco, September 26, 1939 on the SS President Cleveland: Sigrid, Stanley, Billy and Charlotte en route to India after a furlough in the USA.

Charlotte with pets, Allahabad

Family portrait with bikes

Billy during the
monsoons, Himalayas

9

CRACKLING SQUARES OF TISSUE paper not much bigger than a hand span but brilliantly dyed—red, green, yellow, magenta— lie flat on the ground, while neighborhood boys edge them with homemade paste and strips of bamboo carefully cut to size. After paper and wood dry to form a bond, two more ribs are added at right angles to each other and where they intersect are neatly tied with thread. Finally the harness is attached to the cross-piece, and string to the harness, tethering the kite. It's ready! A boy's hands hold it close to his chest while his quick strides walk it out like a thoroughbred into the ring.

Some kites buck and veer, crashing before they're head-high. A paper tail, or one of knotted cloth might be added for stability. Other kites, at first carried protectively, are given a short run before they're tugged back in, let farther out and then reined in again, finally released until they soar higher and higher into the great expanse like falcons born to take wing.

Circling, tumbling, drifting, playing the current, each bright bit of paper carries its owner's heartbeat, as if childhood itself could be given a voice. All over Asia, in the hands of countless children, string, reeled out from spindles, traces, in faint calligraphy, the biography of hope—the excited shouts, the breathless running, the jockeying for success. Later, in the stillness of dusk, trees and power lines will have snagged and grayed their colors.

Besides ordinary kites, there are those used in contests, drawing crowds as people cheer and bets are placed. For these, the string is run through glue embedded with bits of glass. When all the kites are up, a skillful player can cut his opponent's piece from the sky. Later, he'll bask in the shouts, the warmth of men's hands on his shoulders as he passes, the women's calls. He won't notice the blood on his palms or on that of other contestants, the fallen faces of children he's defeated.

I like our everyday kites better. The way they look like questions swimming up there in the sun, full of joy and promise, the way they wrap around a seamless sky, sending back vibrations from the universe, the immensity of the journey buzzing through our fingers, string so strong and worthy, it disappears, taking us with it. How could such a life-line slump in disarray at our feet when the kite falls?

It's boys who fly kites. But sometimes I'm allowed to hold one in the house, or run with it outside to get it started for Billy. Sometimes I'm offered the reel, Billy's or Daddy's hands over mine to keep it from spinning out of control. The higher the kite climbs, the more I feel it, like the tug of a King salmon I'll catch as a teenager at Neah Bay, the whole sky shuddering in the reel, as if each of us, in different worlds, is free, or fighting for our lives.

Besides kites, there are boats. But how could this have happened? Weren't we around seven and nine, no life jackets, though I suppose we could swim? Who owned the little duck boat?—the college, the Mission, a friend of Daddy's? And why was it never to appear again?

We were used to river boats built of heavy timbers. This boat bobbed like a toy beside them. Painted blue, and made entirely of metal—a double-ender—its two identical halves were fastened together, mid-section, by a long bolt. We each sat in a well on either side of the center bolt. Pulling in my arms so as not to touch the hot steel, I folded myself into the partial shade of the boat's inside edge where the slip-slap sounds of the water felt close. Bits of sun bangled and shimmied across the river. Billy's sun-darkened arms, with their golden hairs all flowing in one direction, pulled on the oars. We were free. Just the two of us on the Jumna.

Had the bolt been removed, two mini duck boats would have floated apart, each containing a covered hatch and a self-contained airspace for flotation, each with one end sheared off and the other swept into a roundish point. Billy informed me that the boat was used for hunting, and the hatches—where we dropped our *chuppals*, or sandals—were used for caching dead birds. Excited as I was about being on the river, I worried that he might undo the bolt and set me adrift. He didn't, of course, but saw us safely home, the slap of water-light, the pull of oars, dancing in my head.

Row boats, roller skates, even stilts intrigued me. To move in a new way, to stand taller, to feel the world change, especially under my own power, proved thrilling.

The roller skates I was given weren't new but I loved them. Just beyond our yard I found a piece of abandoned cement, perhaps once the floor of a shed, now covered with dirt, stones, leaves, tufts of grass. The space in the center was about the size of a ping-pong table. Gathering a few branches into a broom, I worked at clearing the surface, envisioning a rink. Every day I took to my sweeping, some days enlarging the center, only to find that the next day it was again blown over with grit and debris. A part of me believed in the possibilities; another part knew I was working as recklessly and futilely as when I banged my head on the mattress to rock myself to sleep.

Eventually I secured a small clearing, and skated, tipping the front rollers into the dirt to stop. I kept imagining a vast arena I would some day embrace, wind in my face, arms swinging freely, the rumbling sound of wheels underfoot proof of passage.

As for stilts, they taught me to re-think walking. I stepped from the veranda onto those homemade wooden blocks, soon lurching forward to fall into Daddy's arms. It was no longer sufficient to lift one leg and then the other. If I did, the stilt would fall away and I would too. Not the leg but the stilt must be lifted, the arm wrapped around it, the hand engaging both. Only then, with the mind's new way of thinking, could I walk in a leisurely way, like a stork above the little running sandpipers. Part of me registered that if I was able to do that, I was no longer a useless child. Another part was pure giggle and fall.

Aside from walking, our family's main form of transportation was bicycling. Each of us owned a bike. Only on special occasions, when we moved a trunk to the station, or welcomed a visitor, could we justify hiring a *tonga*. After running errands, or dropping in on a friend, we returned home and parked our bikes on the veranda. Daddy was strong enough to lift his over the veranda's two or three shallow steps, and helped the rest of us when he was at home, but otherwise Billy and I, as well as Mummy, devised our own ways of managing the heavy equipment. I tried pulling up on the handlebars, but either the front wheel turned sideways against the first step, refusing to budge, or the whole contraption leaned precariously, threatening to topple and squash me.

Already thinking like the engineer he would become, Billy decided to solve the problem and win Mummy's love. He knew there had been talk of building a ramp, and that the *mali*, the gardener, had bought a bag of cement for that purpose, so he hunted it down, read the directions, mixed in some water to make a sludge, and packed it between each step for the width of a yard or so. Seventy years later, that same brother sits at my table, telling me the story.

The ramp was a child's ramp, Billy explains—he must have been around eight—but he labored over it mightily. With great excitement, he drew Mummy out to admire his masterpiece. Praise would have cost her so little. Instead, it was *Oh, Billy, how could you! You've made such a mess!*

I asked him if she had him break it up and throw it away, but he said he thought it stayed there, crumbling over time. However awkward it looked, the ramp was a big help to us children.

But hearing my brother's words tore open my own heart for his child-bruised self.

ONE DAY MOTHER AND I talk about those years. She says she wishes she'd written down what Billy and I said when we were little. *Determined* is the word she uses for me. That's the way I'd ridden my first tricycle, a shiny red one brought back during a furlough in the States. Billy had already graduated to a two-wheeler.

By the time I'm finally old enough, at nine or ten, to be included, Daddy lets me join the men on their annual deer hunt. He lifts our bicycles onto the bus, and the next day, in the chilly dark, leaving our *bistars*, or bedding rolls, at the village, we start out on foot. I have promised not to break the silence. A local man acts as guide, along with two of Daddy's Indian friends, both of them crack shots, he the only novice. As we wait beside a tree, the rest of the woods come into focus, a maze of thickets, slender trunks and ragged grass. Time moves slowly before the doe appears. It turns its head towards us, its body cross-hatched with the shadows of leaves, its neck smooth and alert. For a moment its gaze meets mine, steadfast, and then my own body feels the shock of guns as it jerks once and buckles. When the men rush forward, shouting, the woods stay behind, stunned into silence. The next day I refuse to join the hunt, and Daddy leaves me in the care of the village wives.

Neither women nor children have ever seen a white person—my long hair light as straw, eyes blue as a kingfisher's wing: I might be a Hindu god come to bless them. Such sweet commotion! They draw me into the courtyard and onto a hemp bed, undo my braids, take turns to finger them, their chattering, musical laughter full of questions—Where have I come from? How old am I? What is my name? Who is my father? What is our house like? How many cows does my family own? They feed me sweets and draw dark crescents of *khol* under each eye and around my lids, dip a finger into red paste and center a dot on my forehead. They soften my hands in their own to draw on bracelets, while the children dance around, begging me to play.

That afternoon when Daddy returns, he visits at length with the villagers, thanking the women, asking the men about their crops and livestock, and the health of their families. By that time, we have missed the last bus. Besides, he has forgotten to bring enough money for both our fares. So the bicycles brought along for fun will be pedalled in earnest for ten miles on the way home.

As always, I like watching Daddy fasten the shiny bicycle clips around the cuffs of his trousers to keep them from catching in the spokes, and before long we settle into a steady rhythm. Looking over his shoulder, his front wheel wandering briefly before righting itself, he checks to make sure I am O.K. I, in turn, can call to him or thumb the lever of my bicycle bell to signal a stop. But the ride and my own thoughts engage me—the deer's eyes, wide and steady, the shock of blood, the men's shouts, the women's fluttering attentions, and how, as we pedal, the songs of birds and the trail itself lead us through the great expanse of land. I hear the close-up snap of my own tires crushing a leaf, the whir of spokes as they splash through sunlight like sparklers I'd one day wave on the fourth of July with my own children half way around the world. The springs under the leather bicycle seat chirp like crickets, and Daddy's shirt unfurls its sail.

If the track widened, we could ride together, but most of the time it snaked its way narrowly through the flat terrain. We stopped for water or to relieve ourselves, and sometimes walked our bikes through sand, but otherwise pushed down on those pedals and kept the wheels turning. Sun floated over the horizon as the pale, transparent moon grew brighter. The palms of my hands ached, my legs grew heavy, the ground harder to resist. I called out more and more often to ask when we'd be there, and Daddy answered that we were half way, or, again, that it wouldn't be long. He distracted me with stories, pointed out a hawk, a rabbit, a butterfly, reminded me of *The Little Engine That Could*.

Not having eaten for half a day, and fatigue weighing me down, I grew sleepy. He told me to whistle and sing songs, to talk to him, to keep on pedalling, sometimes reaching across to the middle of my handle bars, propelling my bike as well as his so that I could rest. The trail finally met a dirt road where we could ride together. But my head slumped forward, my eyes fixed on the rushing-away patch of road directly beneath me. It moved like a conveyor belt, unvarying and of the same dull color. Sometimes I swerved for a pothole. The first time the front wheel veered off the road, it jolted me awake as it bumped into some grass clumps. I cranked the handlebars around, pedalled some more and fell asleep again.

Finally, Daddy caught sight of a hut in the distance and told me we'd rest there. My legs shook as I lowered myself to the ground. He lifted both bicycles onto their stands and moved toward the door.

A wizened old man and his wife stepped outside, staring at us travelers as if we were ghosts. Daddy explained in Hindustani that he and I were hungry and tired; could they spare a bit of milk? The old woman left and soon came out with two fist-sized chunks of brown sugar, and then clay cups of hot sweet tea.

Years later I would remember that hard handful of blessed sweetness I gnawed on like a dog. The old couple stood quietly as we bowed and thanked them and ate, and I now wonder if Daddy had offered them money or some useful item like a pocket knife or scarf. In their soft brown, ragged clothes, the pair watched wide-eyed like two astonished owls, turning first to the tall, pale man and then to the girl with the platinum hair. I knew, even then, that if there *were* any, *they* were the gods.

Shortly after we left them, we neared a village and hired a ride home on the jouncing wooden platform of an *ekka*, its wheels old, the bony horse cursed by its threadbare driver as he brandished his whip. I was grateful not to be pedalling, and took comfort in the steady rhythm of the clop-cloppety hooves.

10

THE TEARS, THE TEARS! They don't even come to her eyes any
more. Not a drop of evidence.

By now, Mother is 84 and I am 55. We are having tea and English muffins, and talk about everything but what we most long for:
missed opportunities, time, age, death, love; the questions not yet
asked; the answers not yet haltingly given.

So I ask. Mother, this is what I need to hear. Not how adorable
we were as children, not the trips from India to America and back,
not the excitement of politics, not the great parties you gave, but
all the awful parts—the diseases, the separations, the losses, the
diarrhea, the knotted intestines and burnt heels, the deaths by sunstroke, and the deaths by suicide, the betrayal, the fear, the loneliness, the painful reaching for love.

Year by year, memory by memory. Tell me. Please. I need to
know. How else can we heal?

When I ask why she didn't intervene in Dad's incest, she says
she didn't know about it. And when I remind her of his extracting
my promise never to tell, she says, *I'm glad you didn't; it would
have ruined our family.* Shocked by her response—as if the family
weren't already ruined—I'm hurt, too, that she has sacrificed me
to her own needs. She makes no effort to comfort me or imagine
what my life has been like. She says she doesn't want to hear about
incest; she's old and wants to live in peace.

Mother goes on to tell about nearly losing both of us children
to dysentery when I was a year and Billy three. Of my whooping

cough at two. Two? But I remember the unending cough I had for over a year, and how Dad took me to the hospital by train to another city where I broke a glass and wet my bed, and we saw a white peacock dancing on a roof in the moonlight. How could I remember all that at two? I would have been six or seven. Mother says I had another terrible cough when I was older.

Her face is puffy with pain and her nose snuffles, and a few unstoppable tears slide a bright track down her ruddy little-girl, old-woman cheeks. It's nothing, she says, and she doesn't mind and, no, she won't be depressed. And I want to comfort her and also want her to stop evading, stop calling us such a wonderful family, or saying she remembers both of us children as only good and happy.

Look, I say, we didn't make it up, this pain. It comes from somewhere. And Mother says, I know where mine comes from, from childhood. I say, So does mine; I need to hear your memories of how things were. Mother tells about putting Billy's crib out on the porch at night so she wouldn't have to listen to his endless crying during those first weeks when no one knew he was starving. She tethered him by the ankle so he wouldn't fall out, but he did, and the milkman found him at dawn and knocked on the door to wake her up. Mother says she guesses he must have thought the *memsahib* was crazy.

Why is it, I wonder aloud, that I only vaguely remember any of the *ayas* who took care of me. Well, the first *aya* committed suicide, she says. Was that because of me? No. But that reminds her of other deaths. The beautiful, bright college student who lived in our house for several months also killed herself. Mother's close friend lost her baby when an *aya* left the child in its crib for too long in the sun. Years later, Bethel Harris, the doctor who delivered me, died when her neck was broken in a fall down the stairs. So many losses.

A mother busy with meetings, travel, talks, entertaining; a father teaching, parenting, as well as sexually abusing his daughter; both children in boarding school: no wonder the pain. I found ways to comfort myself.

In India stray dogs, often mangy, were as much a part of the landscape as sacred cows. They foraged for scraps, wary, trotting out in the open or sneaking past danger zones. If a child bent to pet one of the dogs or give it a piece of *chapati*, it skittered away, watchful, tail between legs, ready to run, anticipating a rock in the hidden fist. Bony-backed and ribby, a female dog often dug itself a tunnel, or used an abandoned one, as shelter for its pups. In this way, the newborns' eyes were shielded from the light, and their bodies from the intense heat of the plains.

When Mummy scolded me for slamming the screen door, or being in the way, sending me outside to play, I sometimes looked for a tunnel. Finding one, I'd lie down on the hard-packed dirt, breathing in its pungence as I reached an arm, full-length to the shoulder, into the cooling dark. As soon as I felt a warm body, I drew it out, cradling the heavy bundle, cooing and stroking its sweet ears, its snuffling head, soothed by its lapping tongue on my face and the milky smell that comforted me. The puppies were perfect in every way. Before leaving, I tucked each one back into its underground home.

A FEW STEPS LED up the veranda to a screen door opening into the living room of our house in Allahabad. Even though it felt spacious and welcoming, the house suffered from heat, humidity and the passage of time, its doors warped, its small windows as hard to clean as the cement floors and white-washed walls, the dark woodwork often riddled with silverfish. Sometimes a lizard dropped from the ceiling, startling us. A consoling *punka*, or ceiling fan, hummed as it stirred the air with whatever flies had managed to find their way inside. Although the house was old and worn, Mummy transformed each room into a cheerful, inviting space with framed pictures and colorful curtains, lightweight rattan furniture, an oriental carpet, a corner fireplace blocked by a Kashmiri screen intricately-latticed and carved of wood, and, in the front room, an old upright piano that belonged to the mission.

To one side of the living room, and also opening onto the veranda, our parents' study held a couple of desks, a few book cases and a Remington on which Daddy typed his sermons and Mummy wrote letters.

Beyond the living room was the dining room, the hub of the house, from which all the other rooms fanned out. It was Mother's domain. She loved to entertain, and the dining room held the only substantial furniture in the house, a mahogany table and six tall-backed chairs. My parents had bought them in Manila when their ship made a stop-over on its way to India. A cabinet against one wall held green glassware; against the other, a side-board for linens and everyday china. On top of the side-board, a pair of Siamese figures carved in wood seemed to go on dancing to the unheard music. Between them hung a round, bronze gong meant to announce dinner, but in our house it was decorative and was only struck when one of us wanted to hear its deep, melodious hum.

Billy and I shared the bedroom and play area directly behind the dining room. Brightened by windows, its shelves and drawers held the family's clothes, our games, extra bedding and household goods. Each of our beds was draped with a musty whitish mosquito netting hung from crossed bamboo poles at the ends of the bed, the loose netting tucked in around the mattress once we were kissed good night.

Attached to one side of our play room was a tiny storage space, more like a closet, which held a steamer trunk. We children were never supposed to open it because it hid Christmas presents from America. The one time I remember looking, so much guilt and fear swept over me that whatever I saw remained a blur. Beyond the closet, a narrow guest room and partial-bath waited neatly for company.

On the other side of the play area, two half-rooms shared space, one holding the baby's crib, the other a gloomy Indian-style bathroom with its hole in the floor by the corner, along with a brass jug of water that substituted for toilet paper. A low, weathered door at the back opened into the garden.

Just off the dining room stood a pantry where Shunkar and Kishan prepared fresh food for our meals, perishables cooling in a screened cabinet, or *dhooli*, over a block of ice. All day the ice melted, filling the drip pan, and the next day more ice arrived, carried in a burlap sack over the *ice-walla's* shoulder. Attached to the pantry, a small soot-blackened room housed the cast iron stove where Shunkar did the cooking.

On the other side of the dining area was a room which held our parents' dressers and a day bed. It was lit by high windows, and was spacious enough so that, when I was alone, I sang and danced there in bare feet, whirling about with outstretched arms in my own ecstatic universe.

Our small family bath with its cold-water tub, sink and toilet joined one end of this room and shared a wall with the screened porch where my parents slept.

DURING THE HOLIDAYS, WHEN I was nine or ten, we learned that an Indian dance master would be in Allahabad, giving classes near our house, so I was allowed to attend. An overbearing, shiny-skinned man with bulging eyes, he wore a *dhoti* and smelled of intensity, boredom and sweat. His accompanist sat cross-legged on the floor, tapping out rhythms on a *tabla* and singing in a nasal voice.

Classes took place in an upstairs room soon crowded with young girls in cotton *saris* and *salwar kamez*. Even though I was the only foreigner and wore a dress, I felt at home with these girls. We were all the same age, around nine or ten, spoke Hindi, and had been brought up to obey adults, especially men. The room itself was stiflingly hot.

THUP-a-THUP-a went the master's rhythmic voice as we girls slapped our feet on the floor, one arm forward, one back at right angles in the classical dancer's pose. While heels measured out rhythms, and torsos learned to sway, our hands practiced telling stories ancient and familiar to Indian audiences—back straight, head tilted, an imaginary flute for Lord Shiva; flowers scooped up and threaded into garlands for Vishnu. *THUP-a-THUP-a.*

Meanwhile the dance master barged into the crush of bodies, lifting this girl's elbow, that girl's chin, all the while shouting instruction. Often before the class ended, his impatience gave way, and he butted me with his knee. Sometimes, too, he praised one of the *khol*-eyed, bangled dancers. Clearly, their bodies were nimble and wonderfully expressive compared to mine, no matter how I wished otherwise.

Later, on leave in America, Mummy had me dance for the church ladies' tea. I'd shy in with bell-wrapped ankles, glittering bracelets, a silver-threaded, gauzy scarf and tunic, and explain the stories before positioning myself for the rhythmic *THUP-a-THUP-ing.* The women clucked and smiled, clapped and were charmed, leaving me pleasantly fussed over, a bit like a performing pony fed apples before being returned to the barn.

Forty-two years later, back in the Himalayas at Woodstock for the first time since I'd left as a child, I visited with the head of the music department, Doris Ditta. She could play all the instruments and dance the classical forms. When she asked me to demonstrate the hand movements I'd once learned, she quickly identified them as those of northern India. After our visit, she kindly presented me with a set of ankle bells that she had woven together. I keep them in a little basket now, their sound, when I lift them from one hand to another, calling out with stories.

11

EACH MISSIONARY FAMILY WAS granted a furlough every seven-and-a-half years to return to their country of origin for a couple of years of rest and study. During our first furlough in 1938, Billy was five and I was three. We left Bombay in April by ship to San Francisco where Mother stayed to visit friends, while Dad took us children to the east coast by train. The three of us apparently created quite a stir, charming the other passengers. I remember nothing except through photographs and family stories. Aunt Gertie, Mother's younger sister, who lived on Long Island and was always taking care of children and the elderly, made a home for Billy and me while Dad earned his Masters at Columbia University and Mother joined him for classes. When our time in the States was up, our family returned to India for another seven-and-a-half years' work until our second furlough.

That was in 1947, just before India gained its independence from Great Britain, before Gandhi was killed and the country went mad with bloodshed. I was now eleven and Billy thirteen. He and Dad crossed the Pacific by ship on the Queen Mary, Mother and I by plane because I was bleeding internally with amoebic and bacillary dysentery and needed medical attention not available in India. It was my first airplane ride. Both of us threw up in the little DC-3 that droned, without air-conditioning or a pressurized cabin, from Allahabad to New Delhi. Mother had to be taken off the plane on a stretcher. Once we were on the huge Pan American carrier, we felt safe, were thrilled by the plane's beautiful interior and the young, smartly-dressed stewardesses whose smiles welcomed us. Thirty-six travel hours later, we arrived rumpled and weary in Gander, Newfoundland, where the plane re-fueled. After landing safely—thanks to our seasoned pilot—we were told we had lost one of the plane's four engines while flying over the Atlantic. I stood outside in my sleeveless cotton dress—this, the first time I'd seen snow—and let its feathery coolness, its silence fall over me.

A family friend met us in New York and took us to lunch. Who was this man? Perhaps a "part-timer" who stayed with us in Allahabad. I had never ridden in a car and couldn't bear the fumes or the motion. He and Mother had a wonderful time, but I was grumpy and jealous of their pleasure. The meal seemed interminable. In spite of it all, however, I liked the dessert—chocolate ice cream, rich and flavorful, and the tall glass of sweet, fresh milk I drank with it. Eventually we said our good-byes, and Mother and I rode an elevator to the thirteenth floor of our hotel. The minute I saw the bed I fell across it and went to sleep. Mother did too. She woke up just enough to unlace my shoes and put a blanket over me. We slept for twenty-four hours, inert as boulders in a meadow.

The next few days were a blur. At some point I was admitted to a hospital, and soon had a handful of interns circling the bed, palpating my grossly enlarged liver, and discussing the seldom-seen pathogens so common in India. I loved the attention, the kindness shown me, the clean sheets and warm bed. In spite of the often-uncomfortable tests, the miracle drugs soon had me feeling well again.

We spent that first idyllic summer in the Alabama countryside with Dad's brother, Kenneth, known as K, his wife, Betty, and their three children, Edward, Lance and Betsy, thrilled to discover we had cousins and a new-found family. K and Betty had built a tiny six-bed hospital near their house to serve the medical needs of the community, and K performed his more demanding surgeries in Birmingham, about forty miles away. They'd built their house around a single pine tree, woods skirting one side and fields the other. Living in a cottage within sight of the main house were Grandfather Aylmer Gould and his second wife, Carrie, (his first wife had died in India of spinal cancer). Each week, all eleven of us crowded around their table for one of Carrie's wonderful *Hindustani khanas.*

I adored my new family. Lance was nine and Betsy five. Edward, who was my age, twelve, taught me to milk the family Holstein, Bessy, and led their patient horse around the yard with me on its back. Uncle K taught us kids how to set dynamite to blow up field stumps, and gave me my first driving lessons in the stickshift Jeep. I learned to feed his pet hawk whose curved beak and ferocious glare closed in on the pieces of raw meat we kids shoved through his cage. A raccoon shimmied down from its tree branch inside the screened porch to be fed, and an alligator in the slimy little pond at the edge of the yard liked to roll over and have its white belly scratched with a stick. Betty and K treated me more like a young adult than a child, letting me carry sterilized instruments to the metal table under the operating lights, and watch a baby being born in their tiny hospital. Once, mortified, I dropped the steaming instruments, but K didn't scold.

Afternoons, we children often jumped into the family's homemade pool, barely big enough for the five of us. Lance would hold his nose and cannonball in, sloshing waves onto the grass, surfacing brown and shiny as a seal. We were a raucous bunch. It was after one of these sessions that I contracted an ear infection that nearly killed me. Both Mother and Dad were in New York working toward their degrees at Columbia. In and out of consciousness for many days, with a fever hovering around 105 degrees, I was moved across the yard to a hospital bed where Betty and K took turns nursing me around the clock. They used a syringe to irrigate my ears with solutions of hot salt water. I remember floating up to the ceiling once, and looking down at the three of us, feeling how kind they were and how deeply I loved them. Years later, Betty told me K had infuriated her by letting us swim in the pool that day when she'd warned him to wait until the water was chlorinated.

Finally, a telegram was sent to my parents, warning them that I might not pull through, and at the same time K sent away for a new drug he had heard of: penicillin. It saved my life. My ear infection cured quickly but because dosages hadn't yet been standardized, my rear bore a lump the size of half a grapefruit that burned and itched for a week.

When they started the hospital, K needed an anesthesiologist, so he trained Betty to be one. She proved a steady help-mate, but confided, years later, that she'd never been comfortable with the sight of blood. Her real love was music. Having played the piano from childhood on, she then turned to the harp, studying in France with one of the great teachers in Fontainbleu who encouraged her to consider a concert career. She chose not to, but once her children were grown, she gave solo harp concerts and played in both the Birmingham and Chattanooga symphonies. When I knew her, it was the piano she was drawn to after cleaning up the kitchen or working outside. Her strong hands and tempered heart soon filled the house with Beethoven concertos, her favorite being the Pathetique. While washing dishes she memorized music from books propped up on the window sill, and taught me to practice scales and read music with a patience and kindness I was not used to. Whatever we children wanted to learn, she made possible: how to weave lanyards and colorful belts, how to tool leather, how to cut old bicycle tire inner tubes into thin circles for rubber bands.

Even though Mother was with us when I had my first period, it was Betty who explained what was happening, who reassured me and demonstrated matter-of-factly how to make a pad from gauze and cotton, and how to wear it. She gave me aspirin for cramps, and tucked me into her bed for a rest. Betty was the first level-headed, kind woman I'd encountered; she could sew up a son's scalp when he fell out of the barn, re-wire a lamp, teach piano and harp lessons, and surround children with a steadying sense of warmth and affection that allowed them to flourish.

That first week in Alabama, having just arrived from India, I drank at a fountain in Birmingham without noticing the sign marked *For Coloreds Only*. Yanked away by a Black woman who pointed at the lettering, I was startled to realize we had left one caste system to jump into another. My pride in America slipped a notch.

Later, at Betty and K's, I happened to glance out the window as two heavy, Black women wearing dresses, nylons and shoes walked the dirt road to the house, each carrying a large bundle of clean laundry on her head. I tried to imagine how it must feel to wash, starch and iron clothes in that humid, one hundred degree heat, and wondered if these were the linens for K and Betty's hospital. The women smiled at me but said nothing, their backs erect, whatever pain they felt, groomed into silence. They seemed mysterious as great vessels drifting by on a river.

Betty, who invited them in for a glass of lemonade, clearly

needed their help and appreciated their work, no doubt paying a fair wage, but, again, here in America, I found what looked like a servant class. Whites weren't washing and ironing for Blacks. Blacks weren't presidents of Princeton or Chase National or even of a country school. Colonialism. Slavery. Incest. The elite relied on subjugation and power over others. Over children, over women, over the poor.

Today as I write, I think of Degas' painting, *Woman Ironing*, the endless pile of wrinkled clothes beside her, her hair loosened by heat, shoulders slumped and weary, fatigue consuming her life. That figure, caught and transformed by the artist through gesture, line and color, defines—not just beauty—but the emotional accuracy of a life of labor. In her short stories, Tillie Olsen catches the weariness, as well as the resolve, to survive against those odds.

Women starched and ironed most of their clothes then, before the arrival of synthetic fabrics. Even I ironed blouses and skirts, men's shirts—father's, husband's, sons'—but enjoyed the luxury of quitting when easy-care fabrics surfaced. Now, when the iron glides under my hand, it's for my own pleasure, smoothing wrinkles from a dress I'll wear to town, flattening seams for a child's smock I'm making. While I nose the iron into corners, pressing and lifting with one hand, turning an edge with the other, I can think of how better to resolve an argument, or how to revise a poem. Ironing becomes a mantra, a mystery, marvelous and eccentric as any ordinary task—like peeling onions in their symmetry, their glossed and rosy skins—only because it's not forced on me, not the everyday labor of a sweat shop.

DURING ONE OF OUR summers in Alabama, Daddy, K, Betty, Billy and I, and our cousins drove to Florida where I had my first look at the ocean. It swept into view through the palm fronds, sparkling a deeper blue than the sky that balanced on it so effortlessly. Great stretches of sandy beach shifted at our approach in a rustle of fiddler crabs, while shells of every size in their rainbow colors littered the high tide line. The salty, turquoise water rushed up the sand and down again in a sound like breathing, buoying us as we splashed excitedly in the shallows. We learned to watch out for the dark shapes of small hammer head sharks, our itchy wool bathing suits drying out as we ran about in the sun. K delighted in driving the jeep along the water's edge while we shrieked encouragement, and Betty gathered clams for the evening's chowder.

Back in Wilsonville, we children continued to play inside and out, and in the evenings lay sprawled on the floor, listening with rapt attention to *The Lone Ranger* and *Uncle Remus Stories* on the radio. When Uncle K visited the hospital in Birmingham for surgery or meetings, he took us with him, leaving us at the movie theater to watch two or even three shows in a row. The only movie I'd seen up until then was a terrifying film Daddy had unwittingly taken me to in India in which the many-armed goddess, *Kali*, stabbed someone to death. In Birmingham we watched mostly Westerns, introduced by a newsreel and cartoons. The heroes were brave and handsome, and the women they fell in love with had lovely faces and slightly wind-blown hair. They wore long skirts cinched at the waist, and blouses that revealed just enough cleavage to make them enticing without losing their chaste reputation. I intended to be just like them, and to love and be loved forever.

When K picked us up after the movies and one by one we fell asleep in the old Hudson on the way home, I noticed that his thick hair was combed and still wet from a shower. I supposed he needed to clean up after surgery, and only learned, years later, he was having one of many affairs and would eventually leave Betty, breaking her heart and the children's. Even then, she knew, but went on playing the piano while we leaned against her, singing *Red River Valley, The Bells of Saint Mary's, Old Man River* with passionate intensity.

One afternoon I looked out the kitchen window and caught a glimpse of her beside a tree, sobbing. But when she came in, she gave me a hug and went back to work cutting open fresh lemons, squeezing the juice over ice, mixing sugar and water and pouring each of us children a glass of lemonade. Lives had hidden layers.

IN THE ROUGH DRAFT of Aunt Betty's family history, she describes the Woodstock school Grandfather Gould and Helen's children (including Dad) attended in the Himalayas during the early 1900's:

K travelled by train, then by cart and finally on foot. The boarding school was spartan in the extreme and the discipline based on the same philosophy found in Dickens' books. If lessons were not adequately learned, students were caned on the hand. If discipline was needed the cane was applied to the bottom. Food was adequate but that is all. For supper 5 slices of bread with milk or soup were provided with butter for only 3 pieces. One evening a week the boys were given liberty and Kenneth and his younger brother Lindsay, who had joined him by then, would take their bread out into the woods, build a fire and toast it. Building fires was forbidden so they had to be careful not to get caught. None of the children ever had a chance to grow up in a home. Even when small and still with their parents, they would be turned loose for the day with a lunch packed and left to roam while their mother was busy in the hospital. . . . It was not until after our marriage that K ever had a birthday cake and a Christmas tree. When he was fifteen, he had completed the English equivalent of a high school and came to Wooster to enter College, graduating when he was 19, intellectually on a par with the older students but socially out of place. At that point all the pent up rebellion of youth and his years in the English school [Woodstock] took over and he broke off all contact with his family and started bumming. He went to Chicago, where he lived on the street, slept over grills, warmed by air exhausts, washed dishes for meals in grubby places. He earned some money as a sparing partner in boxing gyms and finally got a job driving a taxi. He also took some art lessons at night in the Chicago Art Institute, being gifted in drawing. After several years of this, his uncle, Carrie's brother Edward, located him and offered to support him in one year at medical school in Louisville. He was ready to settle down by then and left for Louisville. During his freshman year his drawings so impressed the anatomy professor that he was hired to make anatomy drawings for the department for the rest of his four years. After completing residency he went to Pine Mountain, Kentucky, as a school doctor and rode the hills taking care of the mountain people along the Pine Mountain ridge that started at the little town called Hell-fer-certain and ended at another hamlet called Kingdom Come. A year after we were married he came to Berea for a year then took a position with a large coal company near Big Stone Gap, where I joined him after completing my contract with Berea College, and where Edward lived for the first ten months of his life. By saving all we could we made enough to start practice and moved to Wilsonville, Alabama to open a small hospital.

TALL AND LEAN WHEN I knew him, with a shock of dark hair, piercing eyes and a hawk-like nose, K served farmers and townsfolk in the surrounding community, as well as in the city of Birmingham, regardless of whether they could afford to pay. Patients often brought him corn or tomatoes, a chicken or eggs by way of thanks. Before he built his six-bed hospital, his first operating table was in the town's abandoned jailhouse where their eldest son, Edward, learned to walk. For years Edward thought he'd started life in prison. K served Blacks as well as whites at a time when segregation was strictly enforced.

Besides his gift for drawing, K was a good writer and photographer. He enjoyed tracking game with a bow and arrow, and, like his father, was an excellent marksman. Billy and I looked up to him, adoringly. His children, however, found their dad's attraction to danger frightening. Once he asked six-year-old Betsy, who was playing barefoot in the yard, to stand near a copperhead he'd just killed. It was still writhing, but he wanted to photograph her foot beside the snake to give the viewer a sense of scale.

On another occasion, K had all five of us kids carry glisteningly-damp sticks of dynamite and coils of fuses to stumps we blew up in the field. When he told us to run, we ran, thrilled by the excitement, unaware that our lives were also on the line. Sometimes, on especially hot days, he took us to the Coosa river where the boys would swing from a long, frayed rope to cannon ball into the lazy current. I wasn't brave enough. Nearby, a dilapidated houseboat leaned against the bank. We climbed onto its roof to jump into the water, whooping as we flung ourselves over the edge. Looking back as a parent, I shudder to think of the loose boards and rusty nails that could have impaled us.

On one occasion, K accidentally backed the Hudson over the family's beloved cocker spaniel, Sandy. Luckily the dog survived, but K showed little sympathy for his children's anguish or the dog's suffering. Perhaps because of the harshness of his own upbringing, he had lost the capacity to empathize.

When he gave me my first physical after our arrival from India, K proceeded the way any doctor does, tapping, listening, having me say ah or breathe deeply. But before I had put my shirt back on, he told me I had beautiful breasts. I blushed. His remark made me think of myself differently, more like a woman, but confused, shy, self-conscious. A few months later at the breakfast table with my brother, two boy cousins and little Betsy, I was further singled out when K announced with a grin that I had become a woman.

It wasn't until I met Betty again forty years later that we shared stories kept secret all those years. Now that I had written about incest in a published book of poems, and given many readings, I felt free to bring up the subject, especially with family members, even though I risked losing their friendships. Fortunately, Aunt Betty was outraged and sympathetic. Later, when I told her daughter, Betsy—by then a mother herself—Betsy, too, affirmed my experience: during one of our summers in Alabama, Dad had run his hands over her, and another time masturbated in front of her in the barn before she escaped to find shelter at her mother's side. How could a six-year-old child make sense of such shockingly bizarre behavior? If society hadn't considered sex a forbidden subject, and we girls had been able to talk to our mothers about it, our lives might have been different. Even though my own mother might not have taken action, Betty was an unusually strong woman used to defending her own and others' children. She would have confronted Dad forcefully.

Ironically, she, too, was being victimized by her husband's sexually destructive choices, the latent consequences of his own up-bringing. Family rumor had it that as a teenager in India, K often snuck out of the house at night to spend time with Indian prostitutes. The brothers' unmet needs followed them into adulthood.

When I visited Betty in her seventies, she shared a story with me that she found particularly humiliating and had seldom talked about. K once got a local teenage girl pregnant. When the baby was due, he asked Betty to help him with the delivery and to tend to the new mother in their little hospital. She did, but only because the girl was too poor and frightened to know where to turn.

K finally decided to marry a red-head he'd had an affair with, leaving Betty to raise their three children with little financial support. She taught school, gave harp lessons, played in the symphony, and saw that her sons and daughter finished their formal education. Once they were grown, she continued with her music, studied, and published books on the history of architecture in southern communities. She never re-married.

Although Mother denied knowing about the incest, I had told her sister, Gertie, about it shortly before Gertie's death. I apologized for bringing up such a painful subject when she herself was not well, but instead of being shocked, Gertie said it didn't surprise her. When she had taken care of Billy and me during our first furlough—Billy five and I three—she had informed Mother that Dad couldn't keep his hands off anyone. Mother's need not to know must have been compelling.

12

BEFORE BILLY AND I were born, three of our four grandparents were already dead. The last of them, Dad's father, Reverend Aylmer Brooks Gould—known to us as Grandfather Gould—still preached and carried out missionary work in the northern Indian town of Ambala. By the time I was six, he was sixty-six and seemed ancient. I found him portly and remote, if courteous, soft-spoken and methodical: he had been born in Louisville, Kentucky, in 1875, and brought up as a southern gentleman. A quiet man, he liked to smoke cigars and fish, pull chairs out for the ladies, and tell stories about hunting. Strict with his own children, he insisted they spend hours each Sunday reading the Bible, memorizing verses and keeping quiet. Daddy told us that he hated those Sundays.

On rare occasions, when all of us lived in India, our family took the train to visit Grandfather Gould and Cousin Carrie. I followed Daddy into the sun-lit, smoke-spiralled room where his men-friends gathered for a game of caroms. Grandfather never seemed hurried, always took his time, face lowered, glasses flashing over the suggestion of a smile. I liked watching his hands. At eye level for me, they moved onto the table instinctively and with assurance. After transferring a smoldering cigar, he braced the bent index finger of his right hand against the puck. The room quieted. When the time came, his finger sprang forward, flicking the ivory disk the length of the polished surface. Grandfather invariably hit his target. I was impressed by his cool confidence. He knew he was good at something. Would I ever be?

Villagers often sent runners to ask for his help when cattle or children were dragged off by tigers. Respected as a great *shikari* or big game hunter, he relished the adventure, and would ride through head-high grass on the back of an elephant with his gun at the ready, or sit still through the night in a tree-blind, waiting for the faintest shift of a leaf at the big cat's approach in the pre-dawn chill. I was horrified, imagining the soft-eared goat tied as bait to the trunk below him, bleating and unable to escape.

Once, Grandfather shot such an enormous tiger, he sent the pelt to Abecrombie and Fitch in New York City. The store paid him enough money to buy a car, the first to be seen in northern India. He was also honored by a British gunsmith who gave him a beautifully-fashioned wooden gun stock, especially fitted to Grandfather's arm. The family was proud of his marksmanship. Today I am ashamed of the deaths of all those tigers, leopards, bear and gazelle killed for sport and status—not just by Grandfather, but by generations of privileged Britishers, Americans, East Indians and Europeans. I mourn the loss of these wild and beautiful creatures who could yet save us from ourselves if we cared enough to protect them.

I had forgotten Grandfather's house until Bill reminded me of its walls full of trophies—the dulled eyes, the startlingly-pointed horns and antlers, the musty guard hairs—and how Grandmother Carrie served tea in delicately-flowered china cups.

When I pestered Mother to tell me about Grandfather's first wife, Helen Reed Newton, she seemed only to know that Helen had been a doctor in India and had died of spinal cancer. Aunt Betty remembered more: Helen had trained as a doctor in the States at a time when women weren't allowed into the profession. To counter the prevailing discrimination, a medical school for women had finally been established in Pennsylvania. Helen earned her degree there, going on to specialize in diseases of the eye. However many doors were closed to her in the States, she was welcomed in India, and soon became head of a large women's hospital in the town of Ludhiana. Indian women seldom received treatment for medical problems because their husbands, fathers and brothers wouldn't allow them to be seen by a male doctor. Once Helen arrived, women with children on their hips, many half-blind and in pain, lined up, dawn to dusk, to have cataracts removed, boils lanced, conjunctivitis treated.

More of Helen's time was spent caring for others than in caring for her own children. She is said to have trusted that God would keep them from harm. Perhaps he did. More likely, society gave little support to parenting and much to having a profession and healing others. India, with its colonial tradition of servants, and its own history of not valuing the life of an individual, fostered such choices.

Her children survived the dangers of heat stroke, poisonous snakes, rabid dogs, dysentery, drowning and whatever broken bones, thorns and cuts three brothers and a sister accumulate as they take on the world. Just as surely, however, more invisible scars shaped their destinies. How did they cope with loneliness and fear, competition and bullying? Even though all three boys grew up to marry and have children, they each suffered a divorce, leaving behind damaged lives.

Dad was eleven when he and his brothers and sister were left in America during a family furlough. Although the Board of Foreign Missions would no longer pay their fare, how could the parents bear to return to India without their children? My guess is that they were more invested in their work and in adult company than in parenting.

The children stayed at Wooster College in Ohio, which served as a holding pen known as Inky, for Presbyterian missionary kids. Like others before them, they went to school and took care of each other as best they could, swallowing their losses. Did they ever see their mother again? If so, it would have been seven years later, during another furlough.

Helen died in India at the age of fifty-six after years of acute suffering from spinal cancer. Dad would have been twenty-one, a sophomore in college, half a world away. Whenever I asked him about her, he had little to say except that she had been a wonderful mother. He never mentioned how he felt about losing her. She was buried in the town of Dehra Dun in the Himalayan foothills in 1927. I wish I had known that sooner. On my return trip to India I was in Dehra Dun, and it would have meant a great deal to me to visit her grave.

After his wife's death, Grandfather Gould, meeting his own needs, married Helen's cousin, Carrie Janvier Newton. Billy and I called her Cousin Carrie. She was the only grandmother we knew.

Carrie and Betty took care of Grandfather until he died. My lasting memories of her were formed during our summers in Alabama where, after retiring from the mission, she and Grandfather lived out their lives in a cottage near K's family.

Carrie went to the considerable trouble of cooking *Hindustani khanas* for the entire clan every Sunday—memory-laden curries, fragrant rices, *dhals* and *chapatis*. Thick waisted and plainly dressed, her salt and pepper hair wound loosely in a bun, she had only enough money for necessities, making use, as Betty did, of store-bought flour which came in colorful cloth sacks that could be used to make an apron or summer skirt.

Despite her years as a missionary, Carrie took a decidedly upbeat delight in religion, once inviting Betsy and me to walk with her to the Holy Roller church service nearby. The room was full of swaying, dressed-up Black people, murmuring and calling out *Praise the Lord!* and *Amen!* I was excited by the intensity of it all, by the preacher's dramatic delivery and the congregation's singsong responses, by their radiant faces. This religion felt more like a celebration than a lecture.

But Carrie also wanted to convert me. While I was at Shipley, she bought me a subscription to *The Upper Room*, a small magazine for daily devotions. Each page offered a parable for the day, and a quote from the Bible, followed by brief instructions on how to live a Christian life. After many years of Sunday School, church sermons and chapel talks, I found the advice familiar, took it to heart, and applied myself diligently to the task of self-improvement. Eventually, however, I let the subscription lapse, feeling both guilty and relieved as I loosened Carrie's attempt to hold me to the religious life.

For my next five or six birthdays, Carrie also sent me a silver-plated teaspoon. Each bowl was delicately shaped and the handles scalloped and beaded. I wasn't quite sure what to do with these slightly ornate objects, and knew she could ill-afford them. After keeping each one wrapped in tissue paper for several years, I offered them to Mother who suggested I keep them for my hope chest. What was that? Marriage? Good grief, I wanted only to be free. Mother kept the spoons for a few years and eventually gave them to a friend. My not wanting them left me feeling guilty, and set up a series of conflicts in me as I weighed generosity against attempts to proselytize. I felt Carrie's was the right road to travel, but I wasn't on it. On the other hand, I kept Aunt Betty's presents: a beautifully illustrated book on ballet and a large photograph of her that I had asked for. They reminded me of our love for each other without strings attached, a bond I cherished.

I did admire Carrie for something I read about years later in Betty's family history: Carrie once saved her Muslim cook by hiding him under blankets in a wagon and driving him from Hindu-dominated India into Pakistan where he could be safe. Betty also noted that

> *Carrie's little terrier saved her and Aylmer's life one night. It set up a barking beside their bed. Grandfather slowly opened one eye to see a large cobra on the foot of the bed, apparently attracted by the warmth. The terrier kept teasing the snake and gradually enticed it off the bed as it struck at the terrier upon which Grandfather shot it. It was the custom to have a terrier and an Airedale raised together for protection in the yard. The terrier would wake up the Airedale and the larger dog would do what was necessary in the circumstances. As in the Kipling stories all the children had mongoose pets [that] were an added protection.*

THE CHURCH'S HOLD ON me waxed and waned. I was once briefly determined to become a nun, taking pride, along with my ten-year-old friends at Woodstock, in not wearing makeup or drawing attention to myself. I vowed to save lives and serve the poor. But when a new missionary family arrived in the hills, enrolling their two strikingly beautiful girls in school, they caused quite a stir. The sisters, perhaps fifteen and sixteen, had elegantly cut blond hair, ivory skin, and wore bright lipstick. They seemed lovely and un-abashed by their good looks. With what pleasure I stared at them! I wondered if I could copy them, but took the moral high ground instead, insisting on remaining unadorned and pure, whatever that meant.

13

WHEN THE SUMMER IN Alabama ended, Mother and I drove to Pennsylvania for an interview at the Shipley School across from Bryn Mawr College. Shipley was run by two headmistresses, the Misses Margaret Bailey Speer and Augusta Wagner. Both had been missionaries in China, and were interned for two years in a Japanese prisoner of war camp, nearly dying of starvation. Together, they had organized the camp into areas for food preparation, sleeping, waste disposal, and a children's play area, in this way saving many lives. Even so, over half of the prisoners died before the war was over.

A tall, broad-shouldered, quiet-voiced individual, Miss Speer drew up a chair beside her desk, and engaged me in friendly conversation. My feet didn't quite touch the oriental carpet, but my shoes were carefully polished, my socks clean, and I wore a pale pink and blue cotton dress bought especially for the occasion. Matching ribbons covered the rubber bands cinching my blond braids, and I was alert and well-mannered, even self-assured. I was granted a full six-year scholarship covering board, room, tuition and books. For the first two years, I walked from my dorm to the nearby lower school, and spent the next four on campus, attending the upper school.

Miss Speer and my teachers were kind to me, and it didn't take long before I made friends with other girls. But that first day, when I saw them in their silk stockings and fashionable hairdos, their make-up and graceful ways, I felt childish, lonely, homely and awkward: I knew myself a foreigner. I was the only eleven-year-old boarder. Parents of all the younger students kept their children at home.

Sometimes even my vocabulary set me apart with words like *pinafore* and *counterpane* instead of apron and bedspread. I had never heard of French— required along with Latin—and struggled to memorize a poem my peers quickly mastered. Decades later, I can still recite a line or two: *Le cigale est enchanté* —the grasshopper is enchanted—the ant, of course is industrious. I was definitely on the side of the grasshopper, however much church and school had imbued me with the virtues of the ant. I was different: both privileged and bewildered, eager and vulnerable.

That first year, as I walked from one campus to the other, I loved shuffling through the pungent piles of autumn leaves, and in the spring, hearing the warblers return. But I kept dropping my books in the shrubbery, then blocking out the knowledge, and being truly baffled when I arrived in class, and the teacher asked me what had become of them.

Letting the books slip into the bushes or under the leaves must have been my way of freeing myself from having to go to school. I wish now I could hold that child in my arms, bring her home for keeps, show her the mountains not far from our house in the Pacific Northwest, and our house overflowing with books that have saved us both. I wish I could let her meet our children and theirs and the others we have cherished in the way she also wanted to be loved.

Much of Shipley's classwork left me feeling defeated. What were The States? How could I possibly learn their names or understand the map that everyone took for granted? What did the periodic table mean? I couldn't grasp the concept. What were nickels and dimes, quarters and dollar bills? How was I to learn French, which most of the girls already knew from governesses or from traveling abroad? And where were my beloved mountains, and the sound of harness bells, the whistling thrush?

Latin, geometry, history, biology, English literature, algebra, French, art history. Eventually I caught on. My grades weren't spectacular, but at graduation from Shipley I won more awards than anyone—not in academics but for Promotion Of Interest In Music, and Promotion Of Interest In Literature. . . In Poetry . . .

In Art History, as well as For Honesty, Integrity and Leadership. I was given a book, the letters and journals of Beethoven, my hero, inscribed by the headmistresses.

During my Shipley years, the school had no applied art department. Just as well. I would have camped among paints and paper. Still, I loved my English teacher, and wrote my first poems for the school journal. I also studied piano and often practiced several hours a day, pouring all that I felt into the music. The notes in their soft and widening range, their mixed rhythms and adventurous melodies reflected feelings I owned but couldn't name. I sang, too, in the school chorus: *Pat-a-pan*—or *Where E're I Walk*—absorbed by the shared discipline and soaring sounds.

Besides acquiring knowledge in the courses I studied at Shipley, I began to learn some things about myself: that people liked me and I liked them, but that having friends wasn't enough to keep me from feeling alone; that the copper beech's wine-dark leaves looked silver in the glancing sun; that the upper part of the gauzy curtains in my room stayed on the iron rung that held them, but on a blustery day, the lower part escaped through the open window. It suddenly became clear to me that these contradictions were interesting and everywhere possible, even within myself. I tried talking about that in an early poem.

I learned, too, that I had never belonged—and only much later, that maybe no one ever did. During a school production of *Playboy of the Western World*, when a visiting Broadway director came to help us, I discovered odd things about myself through her—for instance, that I noticed the relationship of objects in space. A lean, thin-haired, somewhat gruff woman with hooded eyes and a husky voice, she walked briskly on her cloppety, wide-heeled shoes, or draped herself over a folding chair on the gym floor with her loose-leaf notebook open on her lap, suggesting moves to the players. I became her partner, instinctively arranging a shawl on a table or placing a pair of shoes just so on stage. I had no desire to act, but the play itself called out to me, and she seemed to know that, to understand how deeply I took it to heart.

The director herself once strode onto the stage, pulling a soft hat out of her pocket, shuffling under it as she turned herself into an old man or, again, pushing the hat back to become an eager boy, both characters so convincing, we students were astonished.

Clearly, neither props nor costumes made the difference; stepping into another person's life did.

In these and other ways, I learned I could inhabit a poem or story, a painting or piece of music. Unable to make sense of the homesickness I couldn't name, I found solace in the brilliance of a scarf or the song of a warbler. At home in the blustery trees and the unasking grasses, in the hard bright berries, I was drawn to the language of the visible and the mystery behind it.

Then there was our French teacher. Arrogant, bitter-mouthed, she nodded at us as we scuffed into class between bells: *Bonjour, Mademoiselle Perron!* I never knew her to smile.

Nor did she seem to have any lips, just a smear of lipstick, a dark red gash where a mouth should be, plucked eyebrows, pancake makeup, hair swept up in a French roll. The stringy tendons around her neck moved in and out as she stood at the board. Her short, perfectly-fitted dresses were always of black, grey or beige wool, but at the neckline each carried a dazzling piece of silk. *Americans!* she would say, *You have no sense of style, of how to wear a scarf!* Hers flared at the shoulder, the chantung fabric stiffly luminous: celery-green; black and gold striped; burnt orange crushed against gunmetal; magenta; turquoise; sometimes a confetti of black and white polka dots. Each scarf made a statement in a handful of silk—the flag of her anger; the banner of her loneliness and courage; her defiance.

Back at the dorms, we made fun of her, working our neck tendons in and out, straightening our backs, fierce-eyed, haughty.

Before I graduated, she came into the sunny utility room where I worked feverishly at the school sewing machine, attempting to make a white organdy skirt and blouse for graduation. After her greeting—as always, a wordless nod—she asked what I was sewing, and then offered her advice:

> *You must not get your hopes up when you leave this school. The world is a hard place. While the rest of the students will spend summers sightseeing in Europe, and winters skiing, protected by families of wealth and privilege, admitted to the best of the Ivy League colleges, given coming out parties*

*and cotillions, soon married to men of rank and power, you
will spend your life behind a counter selling, or at a desk typing. No one will look after you. Work hard; pay attention.*

I LISTENED AND THANKED her. But clearly her words were not
meant for me. I was too giddy with the excitement of soon being free, my grand adventure with the world about to begin. Years
later, I realized she was trying to reach out and help me. Her life,
very likely, had not been one she'd chosen or found joy in. A spinster, correcting endless papers, carrying groceries back to a lonely
one-room flat in a country that offered her work: she must have
missed home.

I often wonder what became of her, wish I could have been
kinder and understood her history. She only worked for a few
years at Shipley. What then? Did she ever let her hair down, swim
in the ocean, make love, share years in the warmth of another's
affection? *Je suis, tu est, il est, elle est.* How little we know of each
other!

MISS YOUNG STOOD WITH her back to the window, light glancing
off her reading glasses, light silhouetting her small pear-shaped
figure, her hands quickly at home in the pages of books.

What was tangled or opaque in Yeats or Shakespeare, she
opened with the stops and starts of her voice, language playing like
a flute straight into our young hearts.

And yet she stayed ordinary and old-maidish, her powdery
cheeks pale, her two suits often mismatched, the brown wool jacket thrown carelessly over the blue skirt, or the other way around.
Strict and undivided in her attention to us and to the text, her face
wore a perpetual and barely perceptible smile.

She'd read aloud or call on one of us to read, ask what we had
discovered, have us look up new words, pay attention to phrasing,
breath stops, enunciation, the subtleties of meaning and language.
She once taught us to read in unison as if we were a chorus and
she the conductor, the varied pitch of our voices, the up and down
cadences, another kind of song.

Our papers came back, neatly-inked with comments that addressed spelling, organization and clarity of thought, sprinkled with fresh ideas to think about. Two of us started writing poetry. Miss Young referred to our pieces as verse. Poetry was of a higher order. Her precise notes lead us forward without our knowing how. When she read Yeats outloud to us, she gave us mimeographed copies of several poems to keep. The rhymes and rhythms, the striking imagery, resonated through my body with such intensity I felt seen, known, given voice. Introduced around the same time to Thomas Hardy's novels, I raced around telling everyone about him, thinking I had discovered a great new writer. Then it was Shakespeare's imagery that rained down on me like magic. Miss Young had us memorize long passages, which we eventually recited on stage. My life opened to the voices hidden in books. They spoke beyond the clamor of the daily to what lay buried in my heart. She gave me entry and permission to a lifelong partnership with literature.

Pale hands together, she might sit quietly at her desk and listen. Or stop us in the middle of a reading to have a look out the window. On the bare branches of a wintering shrub, we suddenly saw bright, hopping birds. She named them for us: warblers—Audubon's, Wilson's, Blackburnian—their sweet shapes and tidbits of color gathered like petals flown in from the sky.

By the time I was out of college, where I'd successfully petitioned to write a book of poems for my senior thesis, Helen Young was dead. I wish I'd been able to put my poems in her hands, to tell her how she changed my life by loving literature and sharing it with me, sharing herself.

WITH A FEW CLASSMATES and a chaperone, I rode the Paoli local to Philadelphia to watch Eugene Ormandy conduct the orchestra. I'd never heard an orchestra before. Who had made the massive building, the chandeliers? Why did all these people gather to sit and listen? The dark silks and wools, the hushed laughter and conversation, the white flags of programs shuffling their wings like doves, all absorbed me.

In the tuning of instruments and the convergence of "A's," I heard myself and the others drawn together. Ormandy walked in briskly, bowed, and then turned his back on us, both arms raised, baton at the ready. Before that first down-stroke, he held us in suspense, as if waiting to cross the boundary from one world to another. And when his arm fell, it freed those first, declarative notes, acknowledging both a sense of community and singularity in a language that thrilled me.

In 1953, by this time a high school senior, I found myself in the same concert hall, wildly applauding two men on an empty stage, one slight, the other tall and lean: Norgay Tensig and Edmund Hilary. They had just returned—the first people to reach the summit of Mount Everest. Diminutive in his Sherpa's shirt and trousers, Tensig looked achingly familiar and reminiscent of my left-behind homeland. The standing ovation went on and on in that packed auditorium as the two men bowed and smiled and bowed. Tears ran down my face. The clapping, like rain on a tin roof, thundered around me in unstoppable waves.

Shipley's headmistresses occupied offices on either side of the carpeted hallway that stretched between the common room at one end with its grand piano, stuffed chairs and book-lined shelves, to the dining room at the other end with its formal center table and smaller surrounding ones. If girls stopped by Miss Speer's open door, she looked up from her desk, reading glasses balanced precariously on her nose, a small smile welcoming us. We knew her to be dependably fair with students, faculty, and staff. In brown, low-heeled shoes, earth-toned, slightly rumpled wool suits, hers was a steady and calming presence.

Miss Wagner was short, short-tempered and stout. She wore dark suits and frilly blouses. In spite of her beautiful silky white hair, she struck us as combative, even when she smiled, which wasn't often. Her face flushed easily with anger, her jowls jiggling. We students rarely interacted with her unless we were seated at the center table where she and Miss Speer presided over meals. Occasionally, Miss Wagner gave a talk in chapel, or we passed her in the carpeted halls. Tending the school's finances was her full-time job, one for which she was apparently perfectly suited. She was also known to be an excellent cook.

Each senior was required to meet with her for an evaluation and overview of their work. When I knocked at her door, smoothing the pleats of my dark green jumper, a school uniform worn with a white shirt, black bloomers and black cotton stockings, sweat slicked my palms. *Come in!* she called. I turned the brass door knob and stepped into her office as she swung her chair away from the desk and motioned me to have a seat, teachers' comments and grades covering my six years as a student at Shipley spread before her. She got right to the point. I was well-liked but not college material. I should get married and have children; I'd be good at that. Her words struck me like a slap in the face, turning everything black. I could barely breathe. I had received A's in some classes, notably English and Art Appreciation, B's and C's in others, a D in Latin.

She reminded me that Shipley was a college preparatory school with a reputation for academic excellence, and that, statistically, about 99% of the graduating seniors went on to college, many to the best of the Ivy League schools. A substantial number received graduate degrees as well. Did I understand the rigors of studying? Did I have any idea what discipline it took to earn a Ph.D. in economics as she had? To have her thesis published? To sit at her desk day after day for a year to complete the work? I heard everything she said, and nothing. My future in pieces, her words confirmed a life-long sense of how I had failed.

Thanking her, I fled.

14

DURING THE TIME I was at Shipley, Bill (no longer Billy), boarded at an all-boys' preparatory school in Massachusetts called Mount Hermon. Its sister school, Northfield, from which Mother had graduated, stood on the opposite bank of the Connecticut river. Bill later told me how he valued those years at Mount Hermon, its excellent teachers and the students who became his friends, its beautifully tree-lined campus and fine chapel.

Unlike Shipley, Mount Hermon's curriculum centered around a work-study program. Every student not only attended classes but had a job on campus or on the school farm. Bill peeled potatoes and washed dishes his first year, and from then on, worked in the science lab, which he enjoyed, cleaning equipment or setting it up for the next day's classes.

Chosen for the swim, tennis and soccer teams, Bill also served as sports editor of the school newspaper. He earned high grades and went on to win a scholarship to Oberlin College in Ohio.

At Oberlin, while working in the kitchen at one of the girls' dorms, again peeling potatoes to earn money, Bill met Ruth. He dropped out of school at the end of his sophomore year to marry her—she had just graduated—bought an old greyhound bus, and drove across country, stopping in Seattle to visit uncle Lindsay and introduce Ruth to the family. That would have been the summer of 1953, the year I graduated from high school at Shipley.

Boeing offered Bill a job, but he decided, instead, to volunteer for the army. During his six weeks of basic training at Fort Ord in

California, Ruth continued to work in Seattle, joining him when he was sent to Fort Bragg in North Carolina where he became a paratrooper for the 82nd Airborne.

One of Bill's letters describes that first jump. Having to step through an open door into a rush of cold air, the earth so far below him, he thought he'd pass out. But once his parachute opened and he started looking around, he felt the euphoria of floating through space.

Dad had taken risks also, but without any training or proper gear. When Bill was around ten, the two of them had attempted to scale a massive rock face to reach an eagle's nest. No ropes or equipment. Mother scolded and begged them not to go. We were camped in a remote area of the Himalayas, medical care a good five-day hike away. In spite of falling rock, and the eagle's attack as they neared its nest, the distant, tiny figures returned unscathed and full of the thrill of adventure.

When Bill took on risk as an adult, white-water rafting, hunting, working the woods, he was again without the training or safety measures he might have needed.

After his tour of duty, he spent four years at the University of Colorado in Boulder, graduating in 1959 with a degree in electrical engineering. Ruth worked full time at the National Bureau of Standards, and Bill joined the staff there during the summer months.

Once he had his B.S., the Martin Company hired him as an instrumentation supervisor on a Titan missile test stand. Ruth, who also worked for Martin, fell in love with a colleague, and asked Bill for a divorce. He moved to Denver where, a few months later, he met and married his second wife, Joan. Their son, Mark, was born in Denver while Bill worked for Sundstrand. He later accepted employment with Hughes Aircraft in California where his twin girls, Lisa and Lynn, were born. Bill went on to work for the University of Denver, moving his family back to Colorado, and then, in 1968, to Carbondale where he taught for four years at Southern Illinois University.

When Bill came up for tenure in 1972, life seemed too predictable—a wife, three kids, two cars, a house, steady work—the American dream, but not his—and he decided to make a change. He had never felt comfortable teaching, and perhaps the sixties gave him permission to quit. He and Joan sold their house and most of their belongings, bought an old laundry delivery van, and loaded it with essentials, along with a big white canoe and a pop-up tent camper.

With enough money to live on for a year, they headed south to hunt for land but found it too expensive, and ended up, twelve months later, near the Canadian border in Eureka, Montana. Through a lucky meeting with old-time residents who hadn't yet put their place on the market, they bought two hundred acres for a hundred dollars each. The land was richly-timbered and fed by a small creek. It was home to a wide variety of birds and wild game, and afforded fine views of Lake Koocanusa and the Eureka valley.

One evening as the family hunched around a camp fire finishing dinner, snow on the ground, the house not yet built, one of the twins looked up puzzled: *Now tell me again, Why did we leave home?* On another occasion her sister piped up, *Where our friends are?* Before winter closed in, the family—having worked hard cutting and poling trees, firing up the one-man sawmill to make dimension lumber—built the house and an outhouse, and finally, with the help of townsfolk and neighbors, raised the roof. Home at last! They went on to work the land as a certified tree farm.

We visited them several times a year, the house fragrant with Joan's freshly-baked Dilly bread and delicious stew, the children lively and growing fast. Sitting on aspen rounds at the wooden-spool dining table spread with a colorful cloth, we talked and laughed, glad to be part of each others' lives.

During our four or five days together, the land drew us adults out for walks while the cousins played raucous card games or practiced riding the shaggy horses bareback. In winter, Carl and Mark snowshoed and tried camping out, but got too cold, and burned the bacon. They had more fun day-skiing with their cousins at Big Mountain. We helped cook and clean, learned to stoke the furnace with fire wood, and throw ash into the pits of the three-seater outhouse with its view of the trees and its icy plywood seats. The living room, where we talked politics, jobs and family, was stocked with good books and music. But the past was with us too, and darker moments surfaced.

Once when Mark was about fourteen, he was lying on the rug reading instead of bringing in the fire wood his dad had requested. Bill grabbed him, spanking him hard, his face enraged, Mark howling and in tears, all of us riveted and wanting to intervene. I suffered for Mark and was ashamed of Bill but realized he was in the grip of our self-destructive past, handing on unhealed wounds to his own son, widening the gap between them.

In the meantime, Joan had been investing more and more of herself in the children, leaving Bill feeling isolated and unloved. In spite of all of their accomplishments, and the pleasure they took in their surroundings, by 1983 the two were drinking heavily. Bill became active in local politics, met another woman, divorced, and moved to Kalispell.

The pattern of hard work, not enough money, successes bruised by self-destructive habits, continued to be handed down with heart-breaking regularity throughout the family.

Bill and I both worked when we were young, but as an adult he had to rely on himself to earn his own and his family's keep, while I, as a full-time mom and wife, did not. I always felt he had the harder path, and I admired him for taking it, but wondered if he resented mine.

As a child, Bill had adored Dad, and naturally identified with him. Long after he had became a father himself, and had learned that Dad was a pedophile, Bill suffered Mother's remark that he would never amount to anything because he was too much like his father. Her lack of faith in him kicked out the final underpinnings of whatever self esteem he had been able to muster.

Bill and I had never been close, but I identified with what he was going through. Mother had undermined me in a similar way. When I was home once during a college break, she told me that she'd thrown out all my letters and poems because if I hadn't succeeded in my early twenties, I never would.

Unfortunately, both of us kids, somewhere deep inside ourselves, felt Mother's assessments were true. Self-doubt became a deeply-ingrained habit hard to unlearn.

During a job review at Hughes Aircraft, Bill's supervisor commended him for his work, but asked him why he was afraid of success. Bill found the question both startling and accurate. So did I. Not only did it apply to Bill, but to Dad and to me as well. A painful truth.

On a recent visit, Bill shared one last memory: he was five, on his way to the States for the family's first furlough. As he and

Dad walked down the gang plank, Bill remembered he didn't have his beloved teddy bear. He wanted to run back and get it, but no matter how he pleaded, Dad wouldn't let him. Does that hurt ever go away?

Both Bill and I had always found solace in the natural world—in the texture of a tree trunk, the smell of rain, its cantoring sounds, the cleverness of a crow, the quietness of a flower. Nature not only surprised and interested us but was never judgmental. We were free to be ourselves, to adventure and discover.

Recently in Montana, visiting Bill and his third wife, Bobbie, I watched him quiet his losses by stroking their beloved cat, Elvira, as she lay on his chest. I thought of the puppies in Allahabad, and how they had comforted me as a child.

But if nature offers solace, it also remains disinterested. And however many people we had lived with, we had seldom found true companionship.

DURING THEIR SECOND FURLOUGH, Mother earned her Masters in Family Life from Columbia University, and Dad completed all but the last of his PhD thesis in Comparative Religions. Typically unconcerned, he triggered her frustration, as he often did, by failing to complete the work, losing both the status symbol she valued and the additional earning power he would have had when applying for jobs in the States. He had no wish to compete. While studying at Columbia, they lived in a Mission-owned apartment on Riverside Drive. Bill and I spent fall, winter and spring at boarding school, Christmas and spring break with our parents in New York, and summers with relatives or friends.

Because she was so seldom available to us, I felt bitterly neglected by Mother. When I voiced these feelings to her as an adult, she seemed surprised: *I didn't smoke or drink*, she said, *and I saw that you went to good schools.* True. As a parent, Mother was curiously honest, energetic, dissatisfied and selfish.

She was also gifted in many ways. Her eye for color was apparent in everything she touched—color and line, an innate sense of proportion. She cut and arranged flowers beautifully and designed her own garden as well as the interior furnishings for each of the houses we lived in. Later in life, while living on her own, she became a respected potter and weaver, selling her stoneware and richly colored wool blankets, jackets and table runners.

No work that had to do with her own creation seemed too demanding. Completing a blanket was a laborious process but she never withheld herself from it. First she made a pencil sketch of the pattern. After choosing colors and deciding on the width of stripes or plaids, she wound the yarn around a ruler to model a sample and see if she liked it. Then she'd string the loom, often with the help of her tireless master-weaver friend, Marg, who urged her to work for an hour or two every day until, a month later, the piece was finished.

Once the blanket came off the loom, Mother knotted the fringe ends to keep them from unravelling, and knelt over the tub to hand wash her work. Several rinses later, she carried the heavy wool in a dishpan to the washing machine to spin the water out before carefully spreading it on the grass in the back yard to dry. By now it was almost weightless and she brushed it gently, as she'd been taught, with prickly teasel to fluff it up. Finally, after sewing on a label bearing her name, the piece was ready for the gallery.

I wanted to be cared for like that. To be looked at the way she looked at fine wool or a lily, to be drawn in, the way she spread grain for the golden-crowned sparrows. I wanted her to brush my hair straight as longing and lustered as silk.

By the time, along with other six-year-olds, I sat on a wooden stool with my back to the *aya*, her strong, overworked hands pulling the bristles through sleep-tangled hair, drawing the skin of my temples taut as she braided, I had vowed to grow up quickly and take care of myself.

WHEN HE WAS PAST fifty, Bill admitted he didn't ever remember Mother hugging him. I'm sure she hugged both of us, if only on special occasions, but what registered were the daily criticisms, her irritation at our being underfoot, our inability, no matter how we tried, to measure up. In those days, to marry and have children was expected of women, but for her, the work was without reward. She wanted men's power and privilege in the world, and resented not having it. After a childhood full of painful losses, she fought for an adult life of her own. Children were fine as long as someone else took care of them, and when they were grown up, she expected them to help her.

15

ALL AT ONCE THIRTEEN, I now called America home. Dad had secured a well-paying job teaching English at a private boys' school
in Blairstown, New Jersey. When Bill and I visited during the holidays, we could see that he and Mother were excited to live in their
own house by the green, tree-lined campus. They went about making the rooms comfortable and welcomed faculty members over
for tea.

The white, two-storied clapboard house came with a small
back yard, shrubs and a few trees. A living room, study and kitch-
en occupied the ground floor, and above them, the bedrooms and
bath. Bill had his own room at the top of the stairs, and turning a
corner, was mine. Our parents slept on the other side of the landing. Just outside their door on an old work bench, Mother grew
African violets. Each in a clay pot with its saucer of water, the
plants sat in rows under fluorescent lights that stayed on all the
time, ghostly and white. The flowers flourished, their leaves thick
and hairy, their velvety throats dotted with bits of yellow. But to
me they felt pampered and ominous under that strangely artificial
glow, cared for like illicit beings never allowed to sleep.

I remember being home on vacation once when Daddy tip-
toed into my bedroom before first light. Curled up, with my back
to the door, hardly breathing, I hoped he would let me sleep, but he
never did. I tried pushing him away, and could feel myself disap-
pearing, as if the girl in the bed wasn't me, and I was somewhere
out of his reach.

Now that I was a teenager—even though his penis had never

entered me, it had spilled semen on my thighs—he talked about babies, how we'd have to be careful, how Mummy didn't want any more. On several occasions he said he wished he could carry a child within his own body—not only to relieve Mummy of the pain of delivery, but for the thrill of it.

That summer Mummy found me a pretty dresser. After Daddy sanded the wood, she painted it a pale mint green. Fitted with an oval mirror, it curved around two small drawers and a matching stool. I had never been given any of my own furniture before. I liked its shape and color. But sometimes the mirror blinded me with light or caught strange shadows, and I was easily frightened.

In the same way, I wasn't sure what to expect when one frosty morning, Daddy woke me while it was still dark, but instead of climbing into bed, told me to dress quietly and meet him outside by the car. We were off to look for wood ducks. I remember only the glassy water, the cold of the heavy, black binoculars, and then, as if I could touch it, an arched neck and wary eye staring into mine. Feathers shimmered with a dazzle of blues and greens as a second bird glided into view beside the first. Suddenly, in a swift clapping of wings, the wood ducks lifted, circled, and were gone. I had peered through binoculars before, because ever since we could hold them, Daddy had shared with us children his excitement of the world. But until then, I hadn't felt so close, so startled by the revealed life of a wild creature. The birds' perfectly arranged feathers filled me with awe. Beauty mixed with danger.

A day or two later, a boy drove up to our house with a cardboard box full of baby wood ducks and asked Daddy to raise them. Daddy called the Natural History Museum for help. I was assigned the job of digging up the earthworms which he then diced for food. How they clung to the earth when I pulled! Their strength startled me. And even though they were slippery and icky, I didn't want them to die or be taken from their homes. Still, I pulled them out, wanting the ducklings to live.

The birds soon wore sweet, furry coats and greeted us with a chorus of cheeps. I could hold them in my hands, one or two at a time, and bring them up to my face. Daddy reminded me that we couldn't keep them; once old enough, they needed to be set free. Eventually, he banded all of them and drove them to a tree-sheltered lake, releasing them into the wild.

After the holidays, I went back to boarding school in Pennsylvania, homesick but glad not to be on guard. I dreamt of running uphill as some shadowy figure in an overcoat chased me, running fast and faster to gain the summit and the lift I needed. If I reached the top before being caught, I could jump off and fly, escaping the man's grasp. Every so often throughout the years, I dreamt the same dream, always barely making it, but making it, and feeling the freedom of flight, the magic of floating out of reach over a canopy of trees.

The summer I was sixteen, I worked as a baby sitter for a family in Pennsylvania. They had three small boys, the youngest still in diapers. The dad left each day for work or was away on business trips, and the mom stayed home while I helped with the children and house work. I was supposed to stay for the whole summer, but on a weekend when the dad was clearing brush in the yard and I helped him rake and feed the fire, I came down with an almost fatal case of poison ivy. I didn't know about the plants until the itching began. We tried soaps and salves but nothing worked. One of my legs turned purplish black and was swollen to twice its size. I felt sick all over. Finally Dad came to take me to a specialist in New York who administered cobalt treatments that dried up all the rotting flesh.

Although the Board of Foreign Missions paid each family's fare between India and the U.S. when the children were little, by the time they reached their teens, only the adults were covered. If our parents had returned to India for a third term, they wouldn't have been able to afford our passage. Dad was determined not to leave us behind. He remembered being eleven in the States after his mother's death when his father returned to the subcontinent without him and the other children. Dad and his brothers and sister felt abandoned and lonely, bringing each other up haphazardly on the Wooster College campus. He didn't want that to happen to us. So, in 1949, he resigned from the Mission and we settled in the U. S. for good. Both Bill and I were relieved; we desperately wanted our family to stay together.

DURING ONE OF OUR summers in Alabama, a letter arrived for Betty and K from K's brother, Lindsay. We gathered around to hear his news and look at the photo of his new bride, Sally, standing on the pontoon of his beloved Seabee. Sally looked beautiful and glamorous and Lindsay radiantly happy.

When Lindsay invited Billy and me to spend a summer with his family in Seattle, we were thrilled. All we knew about our uncle was that Dad was fond of him, that he was a doctor, that he had a daughter about my age, was the only one of our uncles who was rich, and owned an airplane. It would be decades before I pieced together more of his history. Two years older than Dad, Lindsay was born in 1904 in Kasur, India (now Pakistan), and boarded at Woodstock along with his brothers and sister. He completed high school and college in Wooster, Ohio, earned his medical degree from Case Western Reserve University, and interned at Chicago's Percy Clinic where he specialized in abdominal surgery.

Having completed his training, Lindsay decided to head west, driving across country to Seattle in a rickety model A. An old photo shows the main road crossing one of the mountain passes still unpaved: muddy, rocky and full of potholes. He was homesick for mountains, and looked forward to exploring Washington's wilderness trails. Before long, Tacoma General Hospital invited him for an interview. He had only one suit, and had to hitch-hike. Once they hired him, he finally received a steady pay check.

In 1934 he married Stella Fritts, and two years later their daughter, Lindy Ann, was born. In 1939 Stella left Lindsay for another man, pinning a brief goodbye note on her three-year-old daughter's pillow. Because Stella had sued for divorce, the courts granted Lindsay custody of Lindy Ann. He proved a good father.

1942. Lindsay joined the navy and served in the South Pacific during World War II as a PBY pilot and flight surgeon on the troop/cargo ship and seaplane tender, U.S.S.Chandeleur. For risking his own life to save the lives of others, he received a bronze star from Rear Admiral Perry, and a commendation ribbon from Admiral Nimitz.

Once his tour of duty was over, Lindsay settled in the Seattle area, establishing his practice as a surgeon and general practitioner in the University District. His office, on the eighth floor of the General Insurance Company building, afforded stunning views of the Cascades and Olympics, the air in those days still pristine. When our parents, at Lindsay's urging, moved to Seattle, he took care of the family's medical needs.

To experience that magic summer, Billy and I rode the bus out from New Jersey. It was hot and crowded, and I was itching with poison ivy. Five days and nights later we arrived rumpled and dazed to find Lindsay, Sally and a little girl in a frilly white dress, white gloves, white socks, and shiny Mary Janes, looking like something out of a fairy tale, waiting on the gritty Seattle platform to greet us. The little girl was Lindy Ann. She and I soon became friends, but I could see that she was anxious about our taking over her household. It wasn't until weeks later that I met Sally's daughter, Tammy, whom I liked at once even though she was only five then, her bright spirit and quick mind already in evidence.

Lindsay seldom talked about his childhood in India or his military experiences, and instead, praised America and his beloved Northwest landscape—*God's Country*. He never tired of hiking in the Cascades, keeping extra boots, jackets and ice axes in a closet for visitors who shared his enthusiasm. Besides hiking, he enjoyed flying the family to Dabob Bay or Gold Lake to fish, dig for clams, or just to picnic and have fun. If I questioned him about the war, he looked at me to see if I was serious, and then said only that what was hardest was to comfort young pilots traumatized by night landings. Their eyes told them to land, but their instruments told them they were off-course and not to. To trust their eyes plunged them into the ocean and certain death; not to, betrayed their own senses.

As soon as he was able to put money aside, Lindsay started saving for land on which to retire, and after years of searching, found property on the southeast coast of San Juan Island, flying up whenever he could to camp on its shore. Later, he built a tiny cabin there out of driftwood, designing one wall to swing up, propped on poles, opening, on bright summer days, to frame the glittering bay with its picturesque shoreline of drift logs, rocks and evergreens.

Once, when the girls were gone and Lindsay was at work, Sally took me shopping. She liked expensive clothes and wore them well. I was startled, in an upscale boutique, to watch the owner choose a fitted suit and red felt hat for her, his wandering hands not only tucking in her blouse but lingering there, his voice soothingly appreciative as she preened in front of the mirror.

But she also took me to a department store where we chose

patterns and fabric she paid for, so that we could sew identical summer dresses. Sleeveless, with bandana-collars above a row of buttons and pleated skirts, they'd be fun to wear. The glazed cotton fabric came in two colors. I liked the corn-flower-blue, but so did Sally who had first-choice. Like hers, the Kelly green bore a subtle imprint of flowing lines. Sally helped me understand the instructions as we pinned and cut, basted and sewed, working together step by step. I liked her cheerful disposition and unhurried manner. Once a pattern piece had been used, she folded it neatly back into its envelope, her groomed fingernails rosy under a clear polish. I compared my own plain, girl's hands to hers, and wished them as elegant.

Sally also let me help in the kitchen. I liked working with her fruit-embossed china and shiny table ware. In her house, too, I first saw boxes of Kleenex and blocks of dark chocolate: lovely, soft, white tissues; bitter-sweet chunks that soothed the palette. I stole several of each when Sally wasn't home, feeling sinful and indulgent.

Our summer felt like a golden reprieve from all the tensions at home. We often ate at an outdoor table on which Lindsay had laminated a flight map of the Puget Sound area he loved to explore in his Seabee. He showed us where we had dug for clams, or where he planned to take us next, introducing the place with a story of past adventures. We could catch a glimpse of Lake Washington through branches of the madrona tree, and after we helped with the dishes, he'd catch Sally around the waist, swing her down as she batted her eyelashes and call her his gorgeous hussy. Later, we'd play badminton in the front yard, shouting with excitement.

Lindsay took Billy and me on several long hikes, one of which was to climb Little Tahoma on the shoulder of Mt. Rainier. Rainier loomed overhead in its dazzle against the blue, its icy green crevasses and rumbling avalanches. Little Tahoma (Little Rainier) rose to 11,000 feet, giving us the illusion, once we were high on its slopes, that we were looking down on the big mountain. With dark glasses protecting our eyes from the blinding snow, we first crossed the vast snowfields of Frying Pan Glacier. Each step took us a little higher. Occasionally we stopped to peer over the edge into the light-struck maw of a beautiful cobalt and jade crevasse a few feet wide and terrifyingly deep. As we sweated uphill on the look-out for avalanches, or stopped to admire the sweeping views, and to slow our beating hearts, Lindsay showed us how to rope up and how to jam our ice axes into the snow should one of us slip. The seductive scenery and our own young exuberance—always in tension with the fear of falling—gave us a sense of safety. We felt both heroic and blessed by the mountain. But we never reached the summit. In spite of our begging, Lindsay had us turn around just a few dozen yards from the top because of a change in the weather.

A difficult choice, and the right one, a lesson I came to re-spect, one that neither of his brothers would likely have made. The descent was tricky. I tried not to look down, but to concentrate on each step, as my crampons bit securely into the ice. Once back on Frying Pan Glacier, we took them off and Lindsay showed us how to glissade, leaning back on our ice axes as if they were rudders, while sliding on our boots.

In this way we traveled swiftly down the slopes we had la-bored up. It was great fun and felt like flying. Nearing the end of the snowfield, however, I slipped, losing control of the ice axe which flailed around its leash on my wrist. By digging my hands and boots into the snow, I finally came to a shaky stop—and just in time—above a catch basin of jagged rocks. Badly frightened, but otherwise unhurt, I eased around the rocks and slid from the snow onto solid ground. We celebrated with handfuls of raisins and nuts and welcome gulps of water. Back on the trail with renewed en-ergy, Lindsay sent a series of yodels to base camp where Sally and Lindy Ann greeted us with big grins and bear hugs as the stories began. Maybe that was what Lindsay gave us—our own stories, a way to join the larger collection, its mythic significance.

On another trip, this time to Whitehorse where my ankles ached from the long side-stepping traverses, we returned to the car bone-tired only to find all four tires punctured by vandals. Why would people do that? Who were they? No answers, but with Lindsay we always felt safe.

Sally and Lindy Ann were with us when we hiked to Summer-land, an idyllic area, little-known at the time, its mountain mead-ows strewn with wildflowers and pristine streams, sun warming us each day, and the cold nights flooded with stars. Lindsay got up early and fried bacon and pancakes for breakfast, in high spirits, as we emerged from our sleeping bags, blinking at the new day's dazzle, the brimming world. He was our hero and we loved him. By the time George and I took one of our sons to Summerland, decades of hikers had worn down the meadows; only our memories held.

Lindsay also took us salmon fishing at Neah Bay. Riding the swells that surged in from the Pacific, we trolled at various speeds in an open boat, along with two or three dozen other small craft, hoping for a bite. When the run finally came, every rod bent double at about the same time, the water exploding with fish. I watched a nearby Indian in his dugout. Skillfully maneuvering the great swells and eddies around rocks where the fish gathered, he suddenly caught a silver on each line and had to cut one loose. Proud as I was to be hero of the day by catching a twenty-five-pounder, I never wanted to fish again. How that hook must hurt in the mouth! Through my hands I'd experienced salmon-power, and knew they shared the mystery of a vast and fluid world beyond our fleeting lives.

To Bill and me, Lindsay was always kind, full of a zest for living, and unencumbered by vows of poverty or church doctrine. Wilderness was his church, discipline and hard work his mantra. He shared his love of the world with us, and was generous. But he was also very much the head of the family and could be both judgmental and a harsh task master, holding himself and everyone else to high standards, intolerant of what he perceived as weakness. I felt I had to do my very best around him. When I brought a boyfriend home, Lindsay wanted to know if he had good teeth and bones and wanted to test him on a hike, giving him a heavy pack and seeing if he complained. He had no use for people who couldn't *pull themselves up by their own boot straps*, or who were drunk or lazy or fat, who littered or didn't appreciate *God's Country*.

If a person measured up, however, Lindsay shared whatever he had. Night or day he'd fly his plane into remote areas of Alaska or Canada when an emergency arose where someone had been knifed or suffered appendicitis and was unable to get help locally. On one of these occasions, while he sutured up an open wound on one man, another held a gun on him, in case his work wasn't successful.

Lindsay also loved a good time with friends, a shared story, an adventure recollected. Favoring Debussy, he played the piano well, and, like his brother, K, took fine photographs—especially of the sea and mountains. He had several enlarged and framed as gifts for physician friends. Wood-working was another hobby. Lindsay made a number of sturdy work benches, giving one to Dad, thinking it might inspire a new hobby, but Dad only used it as a catch-all for flower pots and old newspapers.

For over half of Lindsay's professional life, he worked to establish a much-needed hospital on the outskirts of Seattle. Convincing businesses, individuals, and the community at large, he set about raising funds and tracking down land, until finally the collective dream became a reality, and Northwest Hospital opened to the public. Decades before the environmental movement, Lindsay worked closely with the architect and builders to make sure trees were saved and buildings designed around them. When the hospital eventually expanded, adding a new, large auditorium, it was named after him.

Lindsay delivered our second son, Todd, at Northwest, and two years later, when I needed back surgery, attended the orthopedist in charge. For forty years, he went to work every week-day, retiring in 1972.

I like to think of him measuring and cutting wood at home in the San Juans, wearing frayed coveralls or paint-stained suntans, stopping long enough to raid the kitchen for a slice of French bread and butter—luxuries he never had as a child. He'd sprinkle salt on the bread before taking a bite, murmuring his pleasure, and return to the shop to finish building a shelf or a bird house. Once, I came out to find him facing his black Lab who sat trustingly as Lindsay pulled porcupine quills from his muzzle. His touch was gentle and steady. He never veered from a difficult assignment.

When Sally died of cancer in her sixties, he was not only heartbroken, but felt he should have recognized her symptoms earlier and saved her. Lindsay himself died four years later of lung cancer. Cancer claimed his daughter too. Lindy Ann and her husband, Ken, had had two boys, and, by the time the boys were in their teens, their parents were divorced, shadowed by verbal abuse and an extramarital affair. Lindy had already withdrawn into the Christian Science church which became her refuge.

Of the three brothers—Kenneth, Lindsay and Stan—Lindsay, seemed the steadiest and most dependable, the happiest with his life. But each carried a legacy of pain that was handed down, one generation to the next.

16

ONCE SUMMER WAS OVER, Bill and I returned to school, tanned and full of stories to tell and write about, with snapshots that caught some of the magic we'd experienced. Our uncles and aunts were beloved role models. They and our cousins were the family we had always wished for. At the same time, big changes were under way: our hormones were on the move.

During one of the school holidays, a classmate invited me home with her. She lived on a small farm in Doylestown, Pennsylvania, and ran with a fast crowd. She wanted to be with her boyfriend, and her mother said she could go on a double date only if she found a partner for me. She did—a boy named Keith whom I liked in spite of his acned face and few words. Even though I felt awkward and nervous, his direct, unaffected manner helped me relax. He had earned the money to buy his own carefully-washed, beat-up car, for which I admired him, and confided his dream of going on to art school. Eventually, he put his arms around me in an easy way that made me happy.

We talked about our lives and hopes, he with his quiet voice and disarming smile. Over the weekend, we saw each other several times. Once, he stopped by while I was washing dishes. I had borrowed my friend's light blue angora sweater, and, uncharacteristically, thrust out my newly-developed breasts. He smiled and said, "I see you; you don't have to poke my eyes out." Ashamed, I turned away, but he gave me a hug and said not to worry. He had a present for me. It turned out to be a wonderful, seated figure he'd carved out of wood, the first art work I'd ever owned. I kept it for decades as a reminder of our friendship, and always hoped he was able to become the artist he clearly already was.

At Shipley, too, I met gifted students. One of them was a girl named Woody, an upperclassman, whose life revolved around the piano. Her dark, long hair framed an ashen face. She was heavy, and seemed heavy-hearted, forlorn-looking, but at the keyboard everything about her was beautiful. She leaned into the notes, losing herself in the intensity and rapture of the moment, playing the most difficult pieces with ease. Woody had a boyfriend. Both of them planned to attend a conservatory and eventually marry. Because they were seniors, I suppose, and on their way to a concert in Philadelphia, I was allowed to go with them, unchaperoned. I don't remember her boyfriend's name, but he linked one arm into Woody's and one into mine, on that cold, bright winter day, each of us wrapped in our heavy coats, happy to be together. I'm sure I flirted with him, laughing more at his stories, listening more intently than I should have, knowing full well he was Woody's and she adored him. I wasn't trying to steal him away, I was simply enjoying my new-found powers, but I sensed that it hurt Woody's feelings, and later, I was ashamed. By the time I reached college, I would stand in her shoes, feeling my own losses.

It must have been the summer of my sophomore year at Shipley that my parents found temporary work in the Catskills as camp counsellors. I helped by leading the littlest kids in camp songs, art work and story-telling. Many of them had been to camp before, and knew all the words to songs I was still learning. They paused between syllables in the one about Noah's Ark where the animals climb aboard by *ones* and *two-zies*, anticipating the joy of calling out in one voice, *el-e-phants and kang-a-roozy-roozies, chil-dren of-the Lo-ord.* Before the summer was over, they'd incorporated my name into the script.

Both the little ones and the older children all seemed to know each other, as did their parents. Their hero, and someone very much in charge, was the boys' counsellor, Eddie. Among other skills, he taught tennis, dazzling the girls with his deep tan, blond crew cut, muscular build, and Colgate smile. Self-assured, well-mannered, his tee-shirt, shorts, socks and gym shoes always blindingly white, he sauntered about, dispensing smiles to those in his favor. Eddie had a sister whose chestnut hair, stylishly-cut in a page-boy, swung teasingly above her shoulders. Her comments were laced with irony, and her knowing smile and serious eyes suggested secrets as she patrolled the camp, keeping track of her brother and those he drew into their circle. Brother and sister often conferred. She told me their dad had just returned from Paris, bringing her a fifty-dollar bottle of perfume and a charm bracelet. I could see that she and Eddy ruled the Kingdom of Camp, and their parents the Kingdom of Commerce. Summer to them was a place you could always fly to. Like the others, Eddie seemed at ease in the sunshine and playfulness of privilege.

I had never been to camp before. It simply meant work to my parents and me and was a way to observe how other people lived. Before driving up to the Catskills, we had fretted over finances, logistics and library books in order to gather enough songs, games, stories and projects to keep children busy every day for several months. For Eddie and his sister I was a source of novelty and amusement. Eventually he asked me out. It was my first date. I felt grown up and accepted, and when I asked my parents for permission, they said it was O.K. I washed my hair, rolled it up in lengths of torn cotton to give it some curl, put on my prettiest dress, and waited. Eddie bounced up to the door in his tennis shoes, pressed slacks, a sweater casually knotted around his shoulders, and met my parents with a smile and a handshake, assuring them he'd take good care of me and have me back by ten.

I've forgotten most of the evening. Did he take me out to dinner? By the time he had parked the car on a little hill with its family of trees, it was dark. Once the headlights were off, and the ticking engine cooled, the quiet of evening flowed in. Eddie's voice was soothing and friendly. He leaned into his corner so as to face me as we talked, then reached an arm around my shoulder and drew me to him, stroking my hair. I felt his wide hands that so easily wrapped around a tennis racket, gentle against my face, the muscles in his arms that threw a ball high before slamming it over the net, encircling me tenderly. I was happy.

He told me how beautiful I was, how much he liked me, how good it felt to be close. Soon he was kissing my throat, my eyes, my lips, and I was kissing him back in a surge of desire. He reached in, cupping my breasts. Then a hand locked on the back of my head

and slammed me down as suddenly as a leopard pounces on a gazelle, his penis shoved into my mouth. I recoiled, gagging, struggling, desperate to breathe, to escape, the world turning black, as if
time had stopped. After the hand let up, the lights went on and the
engine started. I was crying and spitting and buttoning my dress.
In some dim way, I wanted to please him, but was repulsed. He
drove me back before ten, as he'd promised, seemed happy and
chatty, kissing me lightly good night before walking away.

The next morning I could hardly step outside, assuming everyone would know, would notice my embarrassment, but no one
seemed to. Several days later, when the children saw me enter the
playroom, they burst out singing, *Char-lotte and Edd-ie are go-ing
stead-y, stead-y, chil-dren of-the Lo-ord.*

That was my first and only date with Eddie, but he grinned
at the kids when they teased him, and made sure I was chosen as
that summer's Toga Princess since he was the Prince. I was scant-
ily wrapped in a sheet and crowned with flowers, applauded as
we walked down the aisle to be seated at the head table. After a
glass of wine, things felt wobbly and surreal. While the others went
on dancing and partying, I was escorted by one of Eddie's older
friends to the friend's apartment where he fed me black coffee and
buttered toast to sober me up before driving me back to my parents' rooms. When the summer was over, I returned to Shipley,
glad to be safe and in school again.

Other encounters followed. During my junior or senior year,
I received a long, typewritten letter from an unknown American boy who had grown up in India, also of missionary parents.
His family had apparently learned that I was boarding at Shipley
and suggested he write me, that we might enjoy meeting. Leon
explained he was a sophomore at Princeton, and wondered if I'd
like to be his guest during the weekend of the big Yale-Princeton
game. My dorm mates were thrilled and made a big fuss about the
invitation. I received permission from the school authorities, was
loaned a suitable wardrobe, and was chaperoned to the train, ticket
in hand.

There he stood at the Princeton station, neatly groomed and
courteously introducing himself. We were both nervous. He drove
me to the campus and showed me where I'd be staying—probably a
supervised guest house Shipley had approved of—but I remember

none of that. The next day's game was exciting, the stands packed, the air crisp. We shared a blanket on one of the bleachers jammed with people, and our voices roared along with theirs. Afterwards, there were parties. Leon took me from room to room, introducing me to students. I had the distinct feeling he was showing me off. Since he cared as little as I did for football or liquor, we soon left the parties to walk around campus while talking about India, school work and the future.

What I remember most vividly about the weekend was dinner. Leon ushered me into a vast hall filled with tables where hundreds of seated young men waited for their food. The minute they saw me they picked up their silverware and started banging the tables and cheering. The thunderous attention—a tradition, apparently, when a girl arrived—both thrilled and unnerved me. I shied, ready to bolt, but Leon took my arm and led me to a table, where conversation soon resumed and the food, mercifully, arrived. Once back in school, I had an eager audience, and for many months, received three- and four-page, single-spaced, typed letters from Leon, letters I answered, but sadly, without feeling any of the ardor he expressed for me.

I don't know how Walter appeared on the horizon. He might have simply asked to take me out for an afternoon walk around the neighborhood. These sign-in and sign-out "dates" were allowed seniors if the visitor had the appropriate credentials and had received permission. I worked a few hours each week, greeting visitors at the front door and answering phone calls. After recording name, phone number, message, time and date on squares of lined paper, I then delivered them to the recipient on a small, round, sterling silver plate that was heavy, well-worn and carefully polished by one of the maids.

At any rate, Walter and I met and walked through the beautifully tree-lined residential community around Shipley while he told me about his life, and I recounted mine. An exchange student from Germany, he seemed less a boy than a man, conversant in many subjects, eager and somehow intimate. He was tall and thin, with impeccable European manners, talked about his studies and how he was homesick, soon held my hand and, when we were tired, spread his coat on a grassy out-of-the-way knoll and nuzzled my cheek, told me how lovely I was, called me his little *Liebchen*, planted a kiss, and then another, and asked if I'd run away to Germany with him.

Easily drawn into the warmth of anyone's attentions, I nevertheless sensed the dangerous terrain we'd embarked on, and managed to say no. That was the last I saw of Walter, though he, too, sent letters for a while, this time on onion skin paper that crackled over the long blue lines of his sloping penmanship.

IN THOSE DAYS, ESPECIALLY as missionaries' daughters, girls were taught modesty at church, in school, and by the example of other women. We knew very little about how our bodies worked. Bill and I grew up on scraps and hunches. Even though our family members saw each other nude in the act of bathing or dressing, as a child, I instinctively avoided looking directly at genitals, knew not to ask questions, and felt vaguely ashamed and uneasy about *all that down there.* Dad seemed at home in his body and liked exercising and staying fit. Mother shied from exposure, embarrassed by her big, drooping breasts which she said were the result of having us children.

Ignorance, and the fear of being caught doing something "wrong," were tempered by the occasional aside, such as Dad saying, *Anything you do in sex is O.K. so long as both people enjoy it*—whatever *it* is.

Religion and sex. One was talked about, held up as sacred, a standard to live by; the other silenced, an unspoken language surrounding the body: profane, tabooed, hidden, shameful. Yet, oddly enough, the scriptures referred to the body as a tabernacle to be revered, God's dwelling place. And Hindus, in the culture I grew up in, openly celebrated eroticism and the pleasures of the body in public sculpture, painting and dance. Both male and female figures appeared beautiful and energetic, full of joy in their intimacies. I was trying to sort these contradictions while making sense of my own developing figure, which went on evolving without instruction from me.

As a pre-teen in the States, I came across a Japanese fan, its black, lacquered wood, opening to an ivory ground delicately painted with nude men and women in various acts of coupling. Shocked by their positions, I was also unnerved by the realization that someone had watched, had painted them for others to see.

And how was it that the fan had lain hidden in a musty trunk full of Aunt Jessie's moth-eaten fur pieces? I had met her. She was the Victorian pillar-of-the-church spinster my mother had lived with and worked for as a teenager.

With a brother two years older and able to pin my shoulders when we rough-housed, able to bicycle and read before I'd learned how, my perception of boys, from the start, was that they had more power than girls. It didn't occur to me that I could develop my own authority. Mother was helpful in voicing her anger and frustration at being a woman in a man's world, but she didn't demonstrate how to turn that anger into constructive living.

At Shipley, girls were encouraged to think for themselves. It was assumed they were intellectually as capable as boys. Knowledge sprang from a democratic playing field, open to everyone. But even at Shipley, in the forties and fifties, *nice people* didn't talk about sex. Although we were given lots of help developing our mental, spiritual and physical (as in, exercised) selves— sexuality was not acknowledged. I had seen words like *vagina, breasts, penis* in books, but—except in doctors' offices—they simply weren't voiced. Even in college, I hardly ever heard them spoken out loud.

At first, as boys made tentative moves in my direction, I felt awkward and uneasy. But if a boy liked me, I was also pleased, even if I didn't like him. Being included felt good. Later, young men who found me attractive helped me to feel grown up and pretty, and my own hormones responded by flooding my body with pleasurable sensations. Dad's abuse had left me feeling ashamed, isolated and different. To have people my own age like me was a relief. I worried that I would only appeal to older men. They made passes at me, and left me feeling preyed upon and helpless, the way I felt during one of aunt Gertie's Thanksgiving dinners.

Our family was about to leave the crowded house on Long Island, and I'd opened the closet door to retrieve my coat, when a slight, wiry man slipped in after me, closing the door, pushing us up against the winter woolens, grabbing me for a kiss. I was thirteen, revolted by his bad breath, scratchy chin and clutching hands, and fought to escape, but was badly shaken—again, too ashamed to think of telling anyone.

Fortunately, boys differed from men. Their awkward uncertainty and tentative moves seemed less threatening, and helped quiet my fears. However, some of them, too, as they grew older, would become possessive and predatory.

As with most girls of my generation, I had been taught to be obedient, good, brave and honest, thoughtful, kind, self-effacing and of service to others. Such an up-bringing, while socially expedient, proved destructive. To say *No* felt selfish. I had no sense of my own rights, my own boundaries. I granted men and boys whatever power they assumed.

As a result, the cost of incest became a slow death—an invisible smothering of the spirit. Sometimes, yes, my body stirred with a strange flair of pleasure as Daddy's hands stroked me. But more often it shut down, the way an anemone closes when it is touched by a foreign object.

Withholding myself created a sense of guilt for *hurting* the parent, not giving him what he wanted. I risked banishment from his love—which, like life itself, was essential for my survival.

A child has no language, no understanding of the concept of sexuality and adult desire. But even a toddler instinctively feels uncomfortable and threatened by abuse. Although the idea of incest was never shaped into words or consciously understood, it was felt.

Having believed what I was taught, and what I experienced day by day—that my father loved me—I gradually came to learn that it was safer to dislike myself than to dislike him. I didn't, as an adult, go around consciously hating myself, but years later, during counseling, I learned that depression was anger turned against the self, and I had certainly experienced depression. Plagued by feelings of inadequacy and unworthiness resulting from those early years, I tried to develop my own strengths and to affirm the belief in myself that others offered along the way, but I never got very far. Abuse is hard to understand unless it has been experienced. It eats away at life, leaving a person untethered and exposed as they drift in and out of danger.

There were other, closer calls with boys. My body surged passionately toward young men I hardly knew, and once, during a love scene in a rare movie shown at Shipley, a fiery wetness appeared between my legs. Even though I resented chaperones and tried to escape them, their presence gave me the boundaries I didn't have on my own.

After graduation, I felt almost independent. But not entirely. Living with the headmistresses provided a steadying influence even though we seldom saw each other. I respected them. However, because they belonged to my parents' generation and were spinsters, they weren't the easiest people to talk to, especially about sex. I was still in need of the parenting I wasn't receiving.

Our family doctor, Dr. Gates (center)

Picnicking on the white sands of the Jumna river: Mother, Billy
behind her, Charlotte, British RAF soldier, Eric

Billy with pigeons he shot, circa 1943

Faculty and staff at Ewing Christian College, Allahabad. Stan Gould third from upper left; Nehru visiting, fourth from middle right, 1940s

Gandhi and two men in Allahabad

Quiet India rally, circa. 1946

Dhudh wallah, milkman, in the Himalayas

Kishan with Billy
and our family
hiking in the
Himalayas

The Nehru family at home in Allahabad

Banyan tree in front of Ewing Christina College. Note people standing in the foreground.

Charlotte and Mother's passport pictures, 1947. We leave on furlough for the United States

Billy and Dad's passport pictures, 1947

Family photos with pets,
circa 1942

Charlotte at Zig Zag

Cobras entranced by flutes

Pilgrims bathing and worshipping in the Ganges

17

FORTUNATELY—DESPITE MISS WAGNER's ultimatum confirming my own sense of never measuring up—my determination to go to college never wavered. I was finally free of boarding schools, chaperones, churches and parents. Free to decide which school I wanted to attend, whether to live on or off campus, and with whom, free to choose my own major. I felt giddy with excitement.

The college I had chosen was Reed, in Portland, Oregon. I needed a scholarship, but Reed didn't give me one. Instead, their letter recommended I enroll at an accredited four-year institution to see if I could do the work; my grades at Shipley weren't up to their standards. I could re-apply.

Once Bill and I had graduated from high school, we knew we had to work to pay our own way. Our parents were barely able to make house payments and support themselves. Understanding their situation, Miss Speer invited me to stay with her and Miss Wagner, board and room free. I jumped at the chance, looking forward to "a real job" and feeling proud that I'd be able to contribute. Their spacious, Victorian house stood a few blocks from campus, in the quiet, tree-lined neighborhood of Bryn Mawr. My room was perched on the third floor under the sloping roof of the attic. I loved looking down through the great hardwoods just outside my window where warblers gathered in the spring. With a bed, a desk and just enough space for a small trunk, I felt like a girl in a novel, a poet, a free spirit.

Soon I had a job in the nearby town of Ardmore. I traveled

back and forth by train on the Paoli Local, sack lunch in hand. Most of the commuters were clean-shaven men on their way to Philadelphia, men in dark suits and starched white shirts, their hats and briefcases stowed neatly on the overhead racks. Rarely glancing up, all of them seemed to be reading *The Wall Street Journal* or *The New York Times* folded into long, narrow widths so as not to intrude on their neighbors. The paper-shuffle, when a page was turned and re-folded, was the only notable sound besides the rhythmic heartbeat of wheels riding the track. I loved looking out the windows and into the eyes of people at each station as we slowed, imagining their lives.

At Peck and Pecks, a small, up-scale women's haberdashery, I sold cashmere sweaters, tweed suits, fine wool coats and pearl jewelry. Folding the soft pastel sweaters into neat piles beneath the glass show case, my hands took pleasure in the rabbit-like nap. I made sure the suits and coats stayed in their size categories, and matched them up with sweaters for customers— wondering, as I did so, which outfit I'd like to wear, lifting single strands of pearls, heavy and lustrous, from velvet display boards for matrons to consider.

Except for two of us, the clerks were older women with lined faces and families to feed. They wore heavy make-up and high heels. As soon as we climbed upstairs for a lunch break, we kicked off our shoes and propped up swollen feet as we settled into the battered couch and stuffed chairs. The windowless room was Mary's domain. She was the alteration department, and moved between her sewing machine, the ironing board and a mannequin. With pins in her mouth and threads clinging to her skirt, her hands performed magic. I loved her reckless laugh, her dark, liquid eyes full of mischief, her fiery wit which kept our spirits from flagging. Even though Mary was a seamstress, surrounded by colorful garments, she always wore black, the hem of her flared skirt wildly uneven. Irish Italian, generously built, her thick, naturally-curly hair crowded her shoulders.

If Mary was kind, the manager, Miss Watson, seemed every bit as fierce. With her hair pulled into a tight bun, and her tall, thin figure encased in narrow skirts and high heels, she criss-crossed the store briskly to sign for deliveries, cut open boxes and haul armfuls of heavy coats to the display rails, price tags fluttering. She kept a sharp eye on her salesgirls, spoke brusquely, arrived early to open the store, and left late after balancing the books. We were all a little afraid of her. It took me several months to realize her kindness was there, but hidden. I had an eight-hour shift and carefully banked my paychecks. Once I won ten dollars—or was it a hundred?—How could I forget?—it had seemed a fine bonus back then—for placing first in a company-wide writing contest about selling.

EARLY SUMMER. THE TREES full of bird song. I began to spend my free time with a young man named Pete who lived only a few houses away. His mother, Miranda, was Miss Speer's secretary at Shipley, a person I had grown to love during my six years there as a student. Now, Miranda often invited me to her house for dinner, which is where I met her husband, Dizzy, an affable, unflappable broker, and their two sons, Pete and Jay. Pete was as kind and quietly accepting as his mother, but with a merriment in his eyes all his own. He must have just graduated from college and had his heart set on being a jet pilot in the navy. I don't remember any formal dates with him. We simply liked being together, sharing thoughts and feelings. At family dinners I was treated like a loved daughter. Miranda made wonderful pot roasts that we enjoyed after a brief prayer and a tiny glass of sherry. The table was set with white linen and sterling, but that formality never got in the way, only seemed to celebrate the warmth we felt for each other. Pete's brother, Jay, then a gangly, red-haired, attentive teenager, was eager to have a girl in the house, and their father, clearly glad to be home after a day's work, also welcomed me.

Once, I was invited to stay overnight, maybe because Miss Speer and Miss Wagner were away. As it happened, the guest room had an adjoining door to Pete's bedroom. After lights out, he whispered to me to come in for a visit. Up until that time we had enjoyed each other more as favorite cousins. I had on pajamas, so did Pete, and he pulled the covers back so that I could lie beside him, covering us up again, his long body stretched out beside mine. We lay there talking in whispers, enjoying each other's warmth, exchanging companionable stories. I felt protected and content instead of passionate with Pete, and he seemed happy to be with me in the same way. But soon, there was a brisk knock on the door, and Miranda's alarmed voice asked if we were together, said that wouldn't do, she had expected better of us, and that I was to return to my own room at once. The next morning we had some explaining to do.

Before the summer was out, Pete started talking about marriage, but never quite committed himself. I was not quite eighteen, but already sensed the resemblance to Dad's lack of decisiveness. As it happened, Pete had earlier introduced me to a friend named Bill whom I started taking walks with, bird-watching, visiting as we enjoyed an ice cream cone, and within months Bill had proposed.

The only formal date I remember with Bill was when he took me out to dinner. He said the restaurant would be a surprise. It was. I was enchanted. I'm sure the food was delicious, but what I remember was the restaurant's signature music, all of it Beethoven. It seemed to give voice to everything I'd ever felt, the beauty and the heartbreak, the irrepressible spirit of life itself.

I had seldom eaten at a restaurant, and here I was, feeling very grown up, wearing the pale green and gold silk scarf Aunt Nan had given me, a dress I had probably made, and a lovely blond winter coat I'd bought with my own money at a considerable discount from Peck and Pecks.

Exuberant but alone, I had no idea how to choose between Pete and Bill. Bill had enrolled in law school, liked music, taking walks, and bird-watching. His father played cello in the Philadelphia orchestra. Ten years my senior, at twenty-nine, he still lived with his parents. An older sister, also unmarried, had only recently moved out of the house. These clues should have meant something.

At one moment I was certain Pete would make the best husband; at another, Bill. What did it mean to be in love? Was I? I liked both of them, but maybe love came later. Getting married felt exciting. Still, I wanted to go to college. Each of the three of us seemed drawn to the other, not so much by passionate desire, as by the pleasure of having a special friend. Bill was, finally, the more verbally persuasive, and as summer drew to a close, I said yes to him, but when I went to tell Pete, I felt crest-fallen. Had I made the wrong choice? Miss Wagner had registered surprise that I'd managed to attract two such nice young men. She continued to cut me down.

Now that I was engaged, Bill took me to meet his parents. His father, who greeted me in passing, was ushering several friends into a sitting room to practice music. I wanted to stay with them and their richly gleaming cellos, basses and violins, admiring the musicians' ability to draw from their bows such haunting sounds. But it was Bill's mother I was left with, a woman of few words and much power, stocky, formally dressed and coiffed, with make-up unable to mask her disapproving eyes. I could tell she wasn't happy with me, and the tea she poured tasted bruised by that barely-hidden verdict. At some point she brought out a catalog of table service, and asked me to choose the pattern Bill and I would use. I'd never given thought to such matters, but had clear opinions about design, and didn't like the elaborately ornate styles crowding most of the pages. When I found what I saw as a plain but elegantly balanced shape, I chose that one. She grudgingly approved but was not in the least interested in putting me at ease or having me like her. Where was Miranda and her warm-hearted family?

Back at Peck and Pecks, everyone congratulated me, and Mary helped pick out a pattern for the wedding dress I would make. I wanted lace on the bodice and she said she could order Chantilly lace from France for a fraction of the retail price, that it would be lovely. It was.

During my final months at Peck and Pecks, I took on extra work at a soda fountain in Bryn Mawr. Sodas, milkshakes, banana splits—I hadn't a clue how to make them but soon learned. Worn down from working two jobs with the hope of making more money, I contracted mononucleosis and was hospitalized with a high fever. Before long I also developed hepatitis. My bills cost me everything I had saved that year. The doctor ordered six months of rest, and Miss Speer suggested I move to Seattle where my parents now lived. Lindsay had urged them to come to the Pacific Northwest where they could find work, and he could help them. Miss Watson wrote to cheer me up, enclosing a card from my co-workers, along with a bus ticket. I was overwhelmed by everyone's kindness.

From Seattle I wrote Bill frequently. We occasionally talked on the phone as well, and set our wedding date for late summer. I had bought him a camera as an engagement present, and he had bought me my first pair of binoculars, knowing how much I loved to study birds.

Mother had told a friend at the church that I was engaged, and her friend offered to have a party for me, inviting a dozen other women. As we left home on the day of the shower, I suggested we pick up the mail, and was happy to find a letter from Bill. Reading it as we traveled, I soon discovered he was changing his major from law to medicine and asking me to wait for him for another four years. I knew then that he wanted out. Should we turn around and cancel the shower, or proceed so as not to disappoint our hostess? We chose the latter.

I arrived in a state of shock as I shook hands with Mrs. Hewitt and each of her friends who greeted me warmly. When I saw the card table piled with beautifully-wrapped presents, I burst into tears, and once my guard was down, I couldn't stop. Much as I was hoping not to, I explained that the wedding had been called off and I was sorry to have caused so much trouble. I had never met any of the guests, but was touched by their kindness, their words of comfort and encouragement. They were all women who had raised children and were able to empathize with me. I asked that they keep the presents for another occasion, but they insisted I carry them home: soft new hand towels, colorful place mats and table cloths, glasses and bowls.

Once home, I read the letter again and again, talked the situation over with my parents who agreed that Bill was trying to cancel the engagement. When I reached him by phone, he apologized, but remained noncommittal, saying only that he would return the camera. No, I said, I gave you the camera because you wanted one, and because I cared for you, just as you gave me the binoculars. We can't undo that past, but clearly our engagement was over.

I felt hurt and rejected, but, for once, my parents offered emotional support. Looking back, I see I had gotten myself involved with two men as easy-going as my father, and as unable to commit themselves. Unfortunately, I had more such lessons ahead of me.

18

By the end of my six month recovery period from mononucleosis, I was strong enough to attend school, and had become an official resident of Washington state, eligible to attend the University, able to afford its low tuition. Between classes and my part-time job helping with secretarial work in the economics department, I continued to write poems, and was eager for feed-back. Not knowing anyone in particular, I found my way under the big-leaf maples to the old pre-fab offices on campus that housed the English department. I knocked on several doors, some locked, some wide open with empty rooms. Eventually a voice answered, and I introduced myself.

Wreathed in cigarette smoke, his desk top-heavy with papers and cantilevered books, the man I happened on was Nelson Bentley. He looked up, ruddy-cheeked, through eyes crinkled as if from mirth. The pocket of his comfortably-rumpled plaid shirt bulged with a dime store notebook and stubby pencils. He might have just stepped in from cutting wood, sleeves rolled up, sturdy arms resting calmly on the crowded desk. As I reached for a chair, I explained myself, and handed him a sheaf of poems.

Even though I was not one of his students and had no appointment, Bentley read page after page, noting each comma and cliche, the run-on dots and strings of adjectives. He could easily have criticized them or suggested multiple changes, but, instead, made a few comments, praised the effort, and encouraged me to come back often. I did, week after week. At eighteen, the notion that people had other commitments had not yet dawned. Nelson always welcomed me. I later learned he helped countless students over the years. His generous spirit and personal kindness made a huge difference in my life and in the lives of so many others. Besides introducing me to contemporary poetry and the Little Magazines, he showed me how to clarify and condense my writing, invited me to read in the University's Castiglia series, urged me to send poems out, and cheered when something was published. When he died some thirty years later, the room where his life was being celebrated was crammed with former students, family and friends. After all the eulogies, tears and laughter, someone started clapping. One by one each of us joined in, until the sound swelled to a thunderous wave of applause for Nelson, his steadfast encouragement, his love of language, of family, his droll sense of humor, and belief in his students. I still have a quote of his on my work table: *Seldom a day without rejoicing.*

As one of two student secretaries in the economics department, my job was to type in triplicate through thin sheets of carbon, or wrap waxed impressions around the mimeograph machine's inky drum. By summer, I needed work off-campus, and found it in a busy restaurant in Seattle's University District. Four horseshoe-shaped counters attracted people with an hour off for lunch who expected fast service—a bowl of soup, a sandwich, the day's special. I was quick to wipe down counters, set up napkins and silverware, ice water, greet customers and take down orders. But as more and more people arrived, I began to lose track of who sat where and what they had ordered.

The seasoned workers, middle-aged women balancing six heavy plates at a time on their arms, sailed back and forth, throwing us new-comers guarded looks. They had long since figured out a numbering system for each of the places on their counters, and could handle the heat, even though, by the end of the shift, they, too, snapped at each other, eyes clouded with fatigue. I could see that my lack of competence only added pressure to everyone's days. Within a week I left.

My next job, instead of being in the University District's hub, was on the outskirts, in a narrow restaurant with eight booths. The owner was a cheerful, energetic man of about thirty who liked bantering with the regulars, kept an eye on everything, and helped the cook as needed. He called me Blondie.

I rode the bus to work, a trip of forty-five minutes each way from my parents' house in the Northwest district. The bus grew more and more crowded as we neared the city, and once when I stood with others to get off, someone squeezed my bottom. Mortified, I spun around, but all eyes faced forward. I learned to stand next to women.

Behind the restaurant's kitchen, a utility room crammed with shelves held canned goods, sacks of flour and sugar, cleaning equipment, and a section for our white uniforms. A row of pegs had been installed on which to hang our clothes. One day, as I stood in my slip prying open the starched uniform to pull over my head, I looked up to see the laughing eyes of my boss hiding behind boxes in the opposite corner. Embarrassed and flustered, I hurried into my uniform and out the door. Later, when I carried an order to a customer, I found a note in the mashed potatoes telling me I had a great figure.

Another time, as I put my coat on to go home, the boss stepped past one of his buddies to ask if I'd look at his etchings. I hadn't heard the expression, but knew, as his friend rolled his eyes to the ceiling, that he was up to no good, and kept on going. I laughed off such exchanges, acting grown-up, but wished my parents could have been on hand to warn me of the dangers, or teach me how to handle them. They never visited the places where I worked, and if I talked to them about my fears, their statements were too generalized to help.

Finally, when I went to collect my bimonthly pay check, the boss promised he'd have it the next week, but pushed it forward another week, and by the time I told Dad about it, and we tried tracking it down, the restaurant had closed and the owner skipped town.

It wasn't until my senior year at Reed that I worked as a waitress under reasonable conditions. Portland's upscale eatery, Pulaski's Hill Villa, hired me on weekends, and since people came to spend a leisurely evening over good food, each of us had fewer tables to serve, and were responsible for our own money drawer. The tips were generous, the setting pleasant, and the work load manageable. We still carried heavy trays—this time up and down carpeted stairs I once slipped on—but back at my room, having counted my night's earnings, I felt well paid, and slept soundly until the alarm went off the next morning.

At the University, I had made A's and B's, and was therefore able to try Reed again. Nelson encouraged me to do so. Invited to lunch in Seattle to be interviewed by a professor from Reed's admissions committee, I was scared but determined. He at once put me at ease, and I found him charming, felt myself a butterfly just out of its cocoon. This time, I was awarded a scholarship—a small one, but one that stretched my summer camp counselor and after-school waitressing earnings just far enough, along with my parents' all-they-could-afford contributions, to pay the bills. Both Bill and I fretted that our parents were so poor we needed to help them. As a result, our own needs often went unmet.

The summer before I started Reed, I worked as a camp counselor for the American Friends Service Committee, a Quaker organization. High school students, recruited from across the country, volunteered to help. We had been asked to build a firehouse and paint tribal homes on the Lummi Indian Reservation outside of Bellingham, Washington. A slight, wizened, wrinkle-faced Native American master carpenter guided our work. I soon had a crush on the boys' counselor, Larry, a gentle, steady young man who liked spending his free hours with me as we sorted out the eternal questions of life and death, war and pacifism, love and loss. By summer's end, he had decided to return home to the east coast to finish his education. We kept in touch but only for awhile.

On the reservation, whenever there was a salmon bake or dance, our entire camp was invited to join in the festivities. One of the Lummi teenagers, Daryl, taught us to swing to the then new hit, "Rock Around the Clock." I was instantly attracted to Daryl, his dark eyes almost always full of laughter, his thick hair combed back over his collar as he spun me around on the dance floor, and later tried to get his hands down my blouse. He was young and his kisses were urgent and sweet. I was a counselor, and, besides, there was Larry—What was I doing?

Now, decades later, it's clear that I was afraid to rely on any one person I cared about. Because men seemed attracted to my body, and that appeared to be their way to share tenderness and closeness, I offered it to them. I wanted to be loved, but instead, was being played with. I needed to sort out the difference.

19

ALL THROUGH GRADE SCHOOL and high school, my teachers had been women. In college they were men, now bearing the title professor. Even if standards of scholarship were the same as they had been at Shipley, men's view of the world, their voices and perspectives, differed. I found myself not only attracted by men's ideas, but by the subtle tug of electric current running between us. They were older, more experienced academically and socially, and because they held positions of power as faculty, any special attention they gave us students was seductive. I found myself easily taken in.

As for the male students, I no longer had to meet them in evening dress and make-up on the dining-room-turned-dance-floor of an all-girls' school. I could talk to them in commons over a sandwich, or on the way to the library; slouch over bitter cups of coffee at the coffee shop; or hold hands with strangers at a line dance on weekends. I talked to these boy-men about Plato's *Republic and the City State*, about *Paradise Lost* and *Light in August*, and there was still time to find out where they called home and what flavor of ice cream they liked best—men who looked like everyday boys in their soft shirts and jeans, their pocked faces and thoughtful eyes. They proved as jittery as I was—young colts, both shy and curious, bold and ready to bolt, but with enough assurance to charm me. I fell in love easily and several times, and they did too. But all of us studied.

Even though I had had a year at the University of Washington, I started over as a freshman at Reed, living on campus in the

new dorm with two upperclasswomen. Each of us had huge reading lists, papers due constantly, small classes filled with cigarette
smoke. Our heads bent over multiple texts— Chaucer, Heroditus,
Kant, Kafka—or tipped back at lectures. Burnished by language,
ideas cast vivid images onto the caves of our minds—Plato's cave
notwithstanding. Slowly we sorted evidence that led eventually to
a sense of how things were and how little we knew. Beginnings,
returns, revisions, heartache, excitement, change. I was exhilarated
by the community of scholars surrounding me, the heady thrill of
ideas and learning we shared.

THERE WERE OTHER KINDS of challenges. Early on at Reed, one of
my roommates invited me to an off-campus party. Old neighborhood houses with sagging porches, dilapidated couches, scarred
oak tables and claw-footed bathtubs were rented out to students
who crowded in, five or ten strong, to keep down expenses. Content as I was with the new dorm, I would eventually live off-campus.

The party was upstairs in a room packed with students and
the occasional, indistinguishable, faculty member. When the door
opened, a surge of cigarette smoke, music and conversation greeted me, along with *Come in's*. What little furniture there was had
been pushed against the walls, including a desk covered with sliced
cheeses, bread and jugs of Gallo. I was one of several nervous fresh-
men acting as if I were at ease. Pale-faced, stubbly young men in
black turtlenecks talked to women without make-up whose loose
hair sizzled in the fall light, everyone smoking or eating, some in
earnest conversation, others looking hopeful. I recognized a few
people who came over to say hello and introduced me to others.
We talked about our classes, where we lived, had I read *The Odyssey* yet, what did I think of my Humanities lectures? I had some
cheese and bread, which I'd heard kept you from getting drunk,
then some wine so as to quiet my hands, which seemed ready to fly
away. Within minutes, I felt strangely warm, wobbly and amusing.

My roommate was talking rapidly with a dark-haired, spec-
tacled young man in the corner as she tapped out another Marl-
borough from its crisp, red-and-white box, and he bent towards
her, cupping a match whose flame cast a glow on their faces. Even-

tually someone asked me to dance, the floor crammed with shuffling feet and dreamy-looking figures. Keith was soft-spoken but merry, wore thick glasses, and leaned towards me attentively. He held me close as we swayed to the music, telling me something about his major—sociology—and asking about mine. He was an upper classmen, said I was lovely and sweet, such fun to be with— everything I longed to hear, especially from someone my own age.

Before long, he suggested we move into the other room to escape the smoke and noise of the party, taking my hand and drawing me through the crowd to a side door that opened onto a tiny bedroom heaped with coats. While kissing, we fell into a nest of coats. In the dim light, he asked if I was a virgin—yes—and told me I was wonderful, that I'd love Reed, as he groped my clothing aside and entered me. Then he said he'd leave the room first, and I could fix myself up before coming out, that no one would know. The experience was intense, if swift and unexpected. I was glad to find out what intercourse was like, but it hadn't occurred to me that I might get pregnant. Fortunately, I didn't. Later, I heard that as Keith left the party with some of his friends, he bragged that he'd taken another virgin. I was mortified and ashamed. How could I call myself virtuous, a Christian, or be so naive? I needed to grow up fast.

By the following year I had a boyfriend who at least tried to protect me from an unintended pregnancy by taking me to a doctor's office where I lied, saying we were about to be married and I needed to be fitted with a diaphragm. The woman doctor's eyes bored into mine as I tried to steady my gaze. She knew I was scared, that this was illegal, but that the consequences of inaction could be even worse.

Again, I had taken charge of getting myself into college, of holding down jobs and saving money, but I seemed incapable of managing my sex life—feeling powerless, as if choice belonged in other people's hands.

DURING THE FIFTIES, REED was often praised in one breath and damned in the next—as a college with exceptionally high academic standards, but one which promoted Free Speech, Free Thought, Free Love, and even Communism. The faculty had been devastated, as had those on many campuses, by the McCarthy hearings. However, even though Reed was socially liberal and humanitarian, it was an institution in search of truth, not anarchy.

After World War II, when most institutions shunned Jews, Reed offered them refuge. Unfortunately, the same could not be said for African Americans, who seldom chose Reed, no matter how actively the college recruited them.

Arguably, Reed may have been too permissive in the fifties, placing a great deal of responsibility on students still in their late teens and early twenties. Alliances between faculty and students too easily crossed social and sexual boundaries. Students were expected to regulate their own lives and take responsibility for their actions, to uphold the honor system and to respect the welfare of others, but few support systems were in place. We swam or sank.

Humanities, at the core of Reed's curriculum, was required of all students. Wherever possible, texts for classes were based on original material. We studied Plato's own words, for instance, instead of a scholar's interpretation of them. Although lectures were held with fifty or sixty in attendance, classes were kept small: ten to fifteen students. Faculty served as facilitators in a conference-style discussion, students contributing ideas and exploring material together. Reed gave no grades unless specially requested, except upon graduation and to meet the requirements of graduate school and other institutions.

While faculty remained exceptionally bright and gifted, their primary focus was always to teach rather than to publish.

EVEN BEFORE I MET Lloyd Reynolds in his ink-stained apron and thick glasses, I was under his spell. As I walked across campus between my biology lab and a lecture on *The Odyssey*, I came across a banner of white butcher paper announcing a poetry reading, the lettering in stark, black ink, clean-edged, spirited and stunningly beautiful. Who drew that, I wondered, and how?

Eventually, I was lucky enough to take a calligraphy class with Reynolds. He filled our ears with the history of lettering, and patiently taught us how to hold the wide-nibbed pens. But what captivated me was his own hand moving across a slant board to demonstrate the long sweep of a Chancery cursive "f" or the generous bowl of a Roman capital "O." Sheer magic! He made it look easy—those lovely transitions between thick and thin lines, the strong ascenders, the light, sure touch. Such mastery could only be achieved after years of disciplined practice and passionate attentiveness.

Decades later, while my children played around me in the basement of our house, I often stood at the light-table that my husband had made for me, and practiced my lettering—like folk dancing, or apples shared in winter with the deer—an unexpected gift during those rigorous student years.

DURING MY THIRD YEAR at Reed I faced Junior Qualifying exams. They terrified me, but I passed. I was then free to petition for the privilege of writing a book of poems—instead of the usual critical paper—for my senior thesis. At first I was turned down, but I persisted and, after showing my work to several people in the English department, my wish was granted. I loved the challenge and, much to my surprise, at graduation won our class award for excellence in creativity.

In high school, my poems had been more or less about love, death and nature. They tended to be sentimental and vague, the images over-drawn. By the time I reached college, I was using a richer, more interesting vocabulary, and beginning to experiment with rhyme, meter and form.

The chance to work with an advisor who was also a distinguished poet was a heady experience. Quiet, alert, non-directive, Kenneth Hanson read everything I showed him, going over it with me at the desk in his light-struck office behind the library where we met for an hour every two weeks. I had no idea whether he thought what I wrote was any good or not. Without praise or blame, he handed back each page, pointing out a word that seemed especially apt, or one that wasn't needed, asking questions, and saying things like *Yes*, or *Well*, or *I see*.

Occasionally Ken made interesting suggestions for me to consider. For instance, one weekend, having bought a pair of five-dollar wooden skis at Goodwill and driven to Mt. Hood with friends to learn a new sport, I had broken my leg. He said, *Write a poem called To My Leg In a Cast using a four-beat line, no more than*

fourteen lines—something like that. Or he'd suggest I try a sesti-
na, using a river as the central metaphor. I'd hand-write all of the
rough drafts, then type the latest version for him on Dad's manual
Corona, a gift he gave me when I went to college, one I treasured.
The work was endlessly time-consuming and exhilarating—carbon paper, erasures, smudged offerings, but the final drafts, to my
unschooled eyes, looked impressive.

Several times Ken asked if he could send a poem or two of
mine to poetry editors he knew, and a few months later one would
appear in print. I was grateful, of course, but assumed that this
was the way things worked, that soon I would send out poems in
every direction, and most would be published, eventually ending
up in books. I wanted my poems to resonate in other people's lives,
move them, as poems by Stafford or Sappho had moved me. To be
published seemed to verify their existence. Little did I know what
was ahead.

Was it in college or afterwards that I came across Keats' concept of negative capability? His words sprang open a door that
felt instantly liberating. Being in uncertainties, mysteries, doubts
was where I lived. That this dwelling place could be an asset, especially for a poet, startled me. It encouraged me to accept my own
contradictions, to hold opposites in the same level gaze, embrace
diversity, welcome surprise and withhold judgement, paving the
way for metaphor. Metaphor, in turn, illuminated life and breathed
life into art.

I felt safe being with Ken, if awed by his intellect. He was
clearly focused on my work, not my body. I respected his writing
and teaching, his exceptional knowledge of modern poetry as well
as the classics, his impatience with sham and pretense. Although
he could be biting in his criticism of the establishment, he was
unfailingly kind to students, and patient with our not-knowing.

Ken didn't own a car and walked to campus from home, taking a bus or cab downtown, or riding with a friend. Sometimes
I drove him on errands or stopped at his house for a visit. Those
were edgey moments. I strained to find something to say that
wasn't hopelessly mundane, and shied toward the colorful modern
paintings on his walls, the beautiful scrolls and vases from China
and Japan, the orderly books. Careful not to over-stay, I was always
glad to have caught a glimpse of his rarified world.

At casual student-faculty parties, Ken sometimes asked me to dance, one hand holding mine, the other counting the beats in a syncopated way as if he were listening to a free verse poem.

If a visiting poet gave a reading at the college, Ken often introduced me afterwards, or took me along to the dinner given in their honor. Once, when Auden came to town, he invited me to join him and Carolyn Kizer at a nearby restaurant. I had met Carolyn before, her deep, rich voice, assertive manner, patrician bearing, her mind probing and articulate. This time, blond hair wound up on her head, a glittering silver pendant swinging provocatively against her black dress, she served as both muse and companion to Auden. He looked exactly like the picture on his book jackets—that deeply tanned and fissured face inscrutable and untamed, the eyes almost lost in the massive, motionless head, a head crammed with poetry, criticism, the history of literature.

We were seated in a high-backed, quiet booth, and after brief introductions, Kizer and Auden plunged into a sophisticated exchange of literary shop talk about publishers from London to New York, anecdotes and apocryphal stories about their peers, reminiscences of restaurants in Prague, paintings in Florence, concerts in Madrid. They swept through the whole of western civilization, Beatrice to Bishop, Kafka to Moore. I couldn't follow any of it, and sat dumb as a sheep, except for a few quiet exchanges with Ken, but I was unnerved and wept in the car as I drove him home. Ken said not to worry; he hadn't understood much of what they talked about either. Kind, if not true.

When I heard that Marianne Moore would attend our Arts Festival and give a reading on campus, I wrote a review of her poems for the college paper. We didn't have an auditorium then but used the gym, the only space big enough on campus to hold a large crowd. Every chair was filled. A diminutive woman with a quick wit that kept us laughing during her opening remarks, Miss Moore recited her poems, our absolute attention paying them full tribute.

During her stay, someone gave her a copy of my article, and she asked to meet me. I felt awed in her presence, but her quiet, attentive voice helped ease my fears. She encouraged me to visit her when I came to New York, and to bring some of my poems. I was briefly tempted, but felt I would be imposing on her unfairly, and knew I was no match for her well-stocked mind. Still, her kind words buoyed my spirits.

At other readings, and through Ken's friendship, I came to know Carolyn, William Stafford and Richard Hugo, as well as the sculptors, Lee Kelly and Manuel Izquierdo, and the painter Milton Wilson. Another faculty member who befriended me, Kaspar Locher, invited art and literature students to his home where I met Carl and Hilda Morris, the Russos, and other members of the Northwest School whose work made a lasting impression on me, their large, abstract canvases reflecting the muted landscapes and figures of the Pacific Northwest.

20

IN HIGH SCHOOL, LIKE so many girls, I had suffered from menstrual cramps, often painful ones, my periods irregular and dragged out. My roommate had told me about Midol, which I had carried around in its pale blue tin case hinged at the back, the thin tray holding a dozen or so tablets. The pills never helped, but offered hope, and served as a badge of sisterhood, as did having a heavy flow or using Tampax, which struck us as fairly risqué. Menstruation was more alluded to than talked about, and I had little understanding of how the body worked, only that it hurt a lot and wore me out.

By the time I was admitted to college and needed a physical, I went to see Uncle Lindsay, and asked him if there was anything else I could take for cramps. He prescribed APC's, a combination of aspirin, phenacitin and caffeine. They helped more than Midol, but only by taking the edge off the pain. Nothing relieved that week to ten days of misery.

Masked by feelings of exuberance at growing up and being freed into the world, of going to school and making friends, of dating and being popular enough to feel included, periods of bleakness and isolation had surfaced more often in my teenage years, and I didn't know how to talk about them or who to confide in. Once, while I was still at Shipley and home on vacation, my parents said I seemed depressed. I was, but when they asked what the matter was, I didn't know, and said so.

One particular downward spiral in college was triggered by a

boy's rejection. An upper classman, his job was to help us fresh-
men feel welcome and to answer our questions, show us around.
Everyone liked him; most of the girls had a crush on him. He
wasn't tall, he wasn't handsome, he wasn't talkative, but his eyes
twinkled with intelligence, his quiet voice was soothing, and he
seemed steady and dependable. Besides his rumpled everyday-
ness, an air of philosophical inquiry endeared Victor to us. The
sixties hadn't quite arrived, but he foreshadowed them, wearing
sandals and a folded Mexican blanket over one shoulder, rolling
his own cigarettes, their smoke causing his eyes to squint.

I found myself especially attracted to him one weekend. After
intense days of studying and working on papers, I would be drawn
like a moth, Saturday evenings, to the Student Union building, lit
up and throbbing with music. Taking the steps two at a time, I
kicked off my shoes by the open door and moved onto the wooden
floor that vibrated with life. Along with others, Victor welcomed
us newcomers and taught us Israeli line dances. His patience impressed me. Once we knew the steps, we no longer had to stumble
about but could join hands anywhere in the circle and dance our
hearts out. I loved the music's measured pace and haunting melodies, and the freedom of not having to have a date. Anyone in the
line became my partner-of-the-moment. In one of the dances, a
boy's hands at my waist, I was half-lifted as I leapt forward and
became momentarily air-borne. If that person happened to be Victor, I felt especially lucky. He was a good dancer, strong and light
on his feet.

I didn't have official dates with Victor, but we often visited
over books and coffee or at folk dancing or during casual weekend parties where everyone was welcome. He seemed fond of me,
but before long, had chosen another girl to court, and soon after,
marry. She confided, once, that he forbade her to cry in his presence, and forty years later, when I caught up with her again, she
told me she and Victor had had four children, moving the family
from one university teaching position to another until the day he
said he needed to fulfill himself spiritually and experiment in free
love. He left her, with little warning and no money, to bring up the
children by herself.

At the time, I felt his rejection as another joy dashed and another failure on my part to measure up. One day, I pocketed the

APC bottle and walked off campus to a nearby park. It was late afternoon, the weather sunny and mild, and I found a sheltering tree in an out-of-the-way spot cushioned by grass. Scooping handfuls of water from the nearby pond, I swallowed all the pills, then curled up under the tree and went to sleep. I thought the water might kill me if the pills didn't. If I died, that was O.K.; if I didn't, at least I wouldn't hurt so much. I never thought of it as suicide. I simply wanted relief from the pain—not only the pain of cramps but of my life.

It was on that day that I vividly came to the conclusion that no one truly loved me, that if I died, my parents would worry about what the neighbors said and miss me for awhile but would essentially feel more puzzled than hurt. My friends would be startled and saddened but soon too busy with their own lives to think of mine.

I slept deeply, covered under the sky's dark blanket, and woke around two or three a.m. to wander back to the women's dorm. It surprised me to see lights on in the entryway and down the first floor's shiny, long hall. As I walked past one of the rooms, my name was called and there was June, a kindly upper classwoman, our dorm adviser. She asked if I was O. K., and said she was glad to see me, she'd been concerned and left the dorm unlocked for my return. I hadn't thought of that, or that I'd be missed. I was tousled and drowsy and said I'd fallen asleep outside, but something about my story troubled her. I must have mentioned Victor or cramps or that I'd taken some APC's, because although she urged me to get a good night's sleep, the next morning she stopped by to say she needed to report my absence to the dean. She added that Victor wanted to see me.

He and I sat across from each other at a small wooden table. He seemed so genuine and kind that my story tumbled out as I sobbed uncontrollably. The poor guy looked on in shock. He said he had no idea I felt so unloved or had such strong feelings for him.

After my outburst I felt a huge sense of relief, apologized, and we made up with a parting hug. Before he left, Victor reminded me that the dean was expecting a visit. I returned to the dorm, washed my face, brushed my hair, walked across campus and found the door with its opaque glass bearing her name. The secretary's welcoming smile put me at ease, and I was soon standing in a large office, facing the desk at which Ann Shepherd was at work.

Her reputation was one of fairness, a no-nonsense, right-to-the-point conversational manner, and a wise heart. I noted her auburn hair flecked with silvery gray, wound loosely on top of her head. As she looked up, light from the windows caught in her glasses; she smiled, extended a firm handshake, and had me sit down. Her face, clean of make-up, looked rosy and weathered. She said she was glad I had come to see her. Did I understand that the college needed me to meet certain obligations if I were to stay in school? I was to see a doctor and bring back a written release stating that Reed was not responsible if I took my own life. I was to tell my parents what had happened. Finally, I was to see a counselor on campus until he was satisfied I could cope.

While her tone of voice was kind, she noted that suicide was a cowardly act, not one she imagined I'd aspire to. She commended me for agreeing to carry out the college's requests and said she would help in any way she could. She advised me not to talk with anyone except my parents, the doctor and the counselor about this event because it would only make other students anxious and vulnerable.

Suicide. That was a new word, a new concept in my universe. A year before, I had bought a 1957 Chevy with a girl friend, Ilka, each of us paying half of the fifty dollar price tag. The car had running boards, four doors, bald tires and a working engine. We were thrilled! Within the next couple of hours I packed a small bag, drove the six hours to Seattle and told my parents briefly what had happened, the three of us sitting in their modest living room.

Dad said, *What did you do that for?* Mother's response was a clucking sound and then silence. I told them I had to see Lindsay to get a written release, and the next day met him at his office in the U. District. He said, *Well, the APCs probably didn't cause any harm, just relaxed you. Now, go back to school and forget about all this. You have a healthy body, a good mind. You're an attractive person. Concentrate on your studies and you'll be fine.* He signed the letter of release, and I drove back to Portland.

Besides my studies and part-time work in Commons, I now saw a counsellor once a week for several months. Tweed jacket, teeth clamped on a pipe, desk dimly lit and busy with papers, he immediately told me he'd been a *mish* kid in China and knew exactly how I felt. I had no idea what a *mish* kid was, and I didn't think he had a clue.

But over time he gained enough of my trust as he read my poems, listened to my stories and acted as both guide and ally, that I told him about the incest. Not with that word, which I didn't know yet, not with abuse, but in phrases I came to haltingly, dry-mouthed or in tears.

Even though I was twenty by then, schools hadn't yet introduced sex education into the classroom, and parents I knew never spoke openly about it, especially not to young people. I didn't know that incest had happened to anyone but me. Forbidden to tell, I hadn't confided in a soul, and actually felt loyal keeping the secret. Loyal and deeply ashamed. I could see no way out. I had become good at acting as if life was fine and everything was O.K.

The counselor's response was heart-stopping: *It was not your fault.*

Those words felt like the first click of a key unlocking the door to a dungeon. I would find others in books decades later: *The Courage To Heal. The Drama of the Gifted Child. Because I Remember Terror, Father, I Remember You.*

He went on to give me another astonishing bit of information: *This happens in many families all over the world.*

I HAVE WONDERED OVER the years why I didn't say *No!* when I was twelve or when I was seven. Would that have saved me? In fact, I did say no on several occasions, even as a very young child. I said it, but it never worked. I said it not only with words but with my body pushing Dad away. He always responded by telling me he loved me and that I was his little sweetheart, his goldilocks, and he'd never hurt me. I believed him, needed his love, loved him too. But why did he leave me feeling trapped and used and no good? For months he might not put his hands on me, and then they'd be there again.

Although he never physically hurt me, little by little he clouded my mind with fear and forgetfulness, with shame, doubt and self-erasure, and with a life-long sense of my own worthlessness. At the same time, he comforted me, encouraged me, and made me feel lovable. I wish I'd gotten angry and confronted him, but I didn't know how to, except—as a counsellor later explained—by being depressed. *Depression was rage against the self.*

By using me for his own pleasure, Dad robbed me of a sense of who I was, stole my ability to trust and to claim my own needs, my own boundaries. Decades later I found out there were more than twenty children, not only girls, but boys, he had victimized. The school in New Jersey let him go because of the first such public allegation. Mother must have known. Must have known long before that, when her own sister, Gertie, took care of us children during our first furlough. Mother herself told me when I was an adult that Gertie had warned her Stan couldn't keep his hands off anyone. Then why didn't she protect me, and why, in my twenties, didn't she believe me? I hadn't learned to disentangle love from loss, or predator from prey. It was as if there were two fathers, one I needed and cherished, one that sickened me.

Growing up became a life-long battle for survival in a world of contradictions, starting with a mother who said *I love you* but pushed me away, and a father who delighted in my company but moved past protectiveness to predation, calling that love. Nothing, after that, seemed clear or simple.

I grew aware that the trauma of the individual psyche plays itself out in the moral fabric of countries as well. America, founded on freedom and respect for others, stole land from the Indians, massacred them, enslaved Blacks, separating families, torturing, burning and killing. Japan achieved a fine appreciation for beauty—from the drape of a kimono, the calligraphy of a brush stroke, to the artful placement of rocks in a garden, or flowers in a vase. With such a deep-seated love of aesthetics, how could the Japanese, then, so mercilessly murder civilians and torture prisoners of war when they invaded China in the 1930's? In India, Gandhi's passive resistance gave way to hand-to-hand combat and an ethnic blood bath.

Beauty and terror, comfort and catastrophe, love and betrayal seem forever bound to each other in the human experience.

So I cut myself in half. One half saw my father as good, kind, funny, dependable; the other as someone who woke me early to murmur, caress and imprison me with a thousand hungry hands I couldn't escape. One half of me wanted to be like my mother, a woman, an artist; the other half felt endangered, swallowed up by her, never good enough. I lived my life always on the brink—wildly exhilarated by the world, by other people, by books and music, and the hope of escaping to a place of inner contentment. On the other hand, I was unable to come to terms with depression, tears easily triggered, a wobbly self that never felt wholly sturdy, a self I couldn't depend on.

During the eleven years in boarding school—or at least the six in the United States—I felt safe, but homesick. Except home was in my imagination, the place itself always shifting. I was no longer surrounded by the tropical flowers, the sun and rain of Allahabad, its people in saris and homespun, the fragrance of cardamom, the crush and drama of life there. Nor was I in the mountains where the air was pure and the forest remained home to birds and monkeys, leopards and barking deer. Sociable and well-liked at school in the U.S., encouraged instead of criticized, I still felt lonely and different. At home, even though I often experienced a sense of belonging, I also felt captive and on guard. Many people helped me— teachers, other caring adults—and I succeeded on a number of levels, but as I entered adulthood I saw myself as almost-but-never, persistent but mediocre, a failure, a loser. I understood where that image of myself came from, but why had I continued to claim it, and what could I do to break free?

IT WASN'T UNTIL I was in my fifties, our eldest son in college, that I felt able to afford long-term counseling. I knew I needed help but felt ashamed not to be able to cure myself. I wanted to work with a woman who might understand what I'd gone through, someone who'd raised a family, someone in our own community so that I wouldn't have to drive to Seattle, a day's round trip too painful for my back. I learned of just such a person, a therapist who specialized in child abuse cases. I saw Margaret on and off for seven years.

Sometime during our work together, she mentioned a group of women incest survivors who met on their own to talk about their lives. I decided to join them. Their stories not only validated my own, but broke my heart, the abuses shocking: women burnt with cigarettes and hot irons, cut with knives before being raped.

Women beaten with belts and boards, their lives terrorized. Most were quiet-voiced, some pretty, some plain, some educated, some not, all working long hours as well as raising children. I sobbed as I listened. When I told Margaret how I couldn't stop crying during their stories, she said, *It's easier to cry about someone else's pain than to cry about your own.* She helped me by listening, by her deeply compassionate nature, and by her ability to demonstrate in herself the strength that I needed to acquire.

21

I HAD OTHER JOBS in college besides serving food in Commons. One year I spent every other weekend with an elderly couple who needed looking after: the Bensons. She was a retired physicist, bedridden, her attentive brown eyes still lively, her salt and pepper hair thick and wavy, the fingers of her right hand curled from arthritis, nails often dirty and in need of trimming. Except when she ate or slept, she smoked, staring out through the open doors to the living room, or inward to memories, the ash from her cigarette leaning precariously before being caught by the glass tray on her bed. Throughout the day she belched loudly without seeming the least self-conscious, and ordered lunch or a mohair throw with the abruptness of the privileged. On the other hand, she was kind to me and asked about my studies, her hand compulsively circling a place on the covers as if to acknowledge some steadying design.

Mr. Benson, white stubble on his head and chin, managed to shuffle to the dining room table for meals where he dribbled egg onto his shirt, hands fluttering like young birds at feeding time. At night, or in the afternoon when he and his wife slept, their separate rooms vibrated under a chorus of snores. It wasn't pretty. I understood that they were ancient and besieged, and empathized, but I shuddered at the thought of getting old. They needed help, I needed money, so we cared for each other as best we could.

Alternate weekends, another student spelled me off, and on one of her watches, Mr. Benson died of a heart attack. The house was quieter and his absence felt, but his wife seemed only a bit more introspective, and my job was easier. A few weeks later, her son paid a visit. A professor of English Literature at Columbia University, he livened up the house, entertaining us with stories about students and faculty, recent political controversies, Broadway productions. He also argued with his mother about family holdings, and pocketed pieces of silver. At the dinner table, his eyes glinting beneath a mass of curly salt-and-pepper hair, he quoted a line from *Macbeth* or *Hamlet, Twelfth Night* or *The Tempest*, scolding me when I couldn't name the play, or the act and scene, they came from. *How can you be an English major if you don't know your Shakespeare!* I felt stupid.

That evening as I turned out the lights and unfolded my blankets on the living room couch where I slept, I went over the day's events, vowing to better inform myself. Dozing off, I woke to a faint brushing sound on the carpet, and then felt hands stroking my hair, my face, whispered words saying how wonderful I was, lips on my neck, thick curls against my cheek. In spite of my shock, I was drawn to the comforting embrace, but alarmed that his mother might wake up. When I pleaded with her son to go back to his own bed, he did.

The next morning I brushed and tied up my hair with more than usual care, returning his smile over breakfast. He was attentive and full of cheerful banter. Afterwards, he cornered me quietly to ask if I'd run away with him for two weeks as his guest in the Bahamas. I was tempted for a second and flattered, but couldn't imagine leaving school. "Then come to New York," he countered, "and spend a weekend with me during the summer holidays." I'd think about that.

On the following day, without warning, I was introduced, like one of the servants, to his wife, all the warmth her husband had sent my way suddenly detoured and sparkling toward her. She had just flown in from the east coast, young, intelligent and attractive. What a fool I was! And how hurt! The two of them changed into shorts and bounced down the front steps, laughing, as they left for tennis.

Not until I was in my fifties and seeing Margaret, a counselor, did I grasp the fact that I needed to define myself instead of relying on others to do so, that I had the right to protect myself as well.

〜

BACK ON CAMPUS, I met a boy at folk dancing I grew to care about. His vitality attracted me, dark eyes lit with laughter, slim body easy-going in jeans and rolled-at-the-cuff shirts, thick, dark hair swept back. He was dancing with another girl that evening, but our eyes locked for just long enough to register intense interest. Before the night was over, we had managed to introduce ourselves and join hands in a line dance. Within a week we were seeing each other often—for lunch in the commons, for a hot drink in the coffee shop. We studied together in the library, strolled the campus, talking out our lives, went on to spend the rest of the term together as friends, then as lovers. Mark was Jewish, not religious but used to traditional Yiddish phrases I enjoyed and quickly picked up. By his sophomore and my junior year, we had moved off campus to share a rickety houseboat and, later, a tiny cottage not far from the college. We even adopted a stray dog, creating enough of a semblance of family to help us feel anchored during our last years of school.

Mark was a history major. We weren't in any of the same classes— except for drawing—which gave us space and time for other friendships. We felt brave and adventuresome. The sixties were right around the corner.

One summer, pooling our resources to pay for fuel and food, we drove back east with several friends, taking turns at the wheel, sleeping in the car or outside under blankets, rolling up stray clothing for pillows. Mark wanted me to meet his parents, and assured me I could find work in the city to earn money for college. I did—a part-time waitressing job at a Mayflower Coffee Shop several subway stops down the line. We stayed with Mark's folks in their street-level Manhattan apartment. His mother, a strong, ruddy-cheeked, hard-working home-maker, greeted us warmly and cooked great Italian meals, scrubbed and polished the hallway, then covered it with newspapers to keep out the dirt. Mark was clearly the apple of her eye.

His father presided as head of the table, saying the blessing and acting gruffer than he actually was. Mark and I listened to family stories, shared some of our own, helped clean up, and spent hours walking the streets, riding the subways, visiting Coney Island, the Port Authority Building, and kosher shops in the neighborhood selling lox and bagels and briny pickles glistening in barrels. Most of the merchants knew Mark, teasing him about his girl, and eyeing me mischievously. I felt happy and secure as I loped along in summer sandals, eager to take on his world. But meeting his attorney-brother and fiancee, both of whom seemed poised and self-confident, intelligent and handsome, I could just as easily feel insecure.

We joined the extended family for a vacation on the Jersey shore, and later ran three-legged races at his other brother's employee picnic, winning first prize in the egg-balancing contest. Mark seemed more of a boy than a man next to his protective older brothers. But I liked him best, his sense of humor and irony, his fighting spirit. He was street-smart and I was naive, shocked to learn that the cops at the Port Authority Building—and by inference, elsewhere in the city—routinely took bribes, cops I'd always looked up to as trustworthy protectors.

Mark's mother had friends in the garment district, and during the first week of our visit, she surprised me one day with a pretty blue dress. I wasn't used to gifts without an occasion and loved her generosity. She had a no-nonsense way of laughing or scolding lustily and was a great story-teller. We had taken to each other at once, but eventually, in her straight-forward manner, she told me I was a nice girl but a *goy*, and should marry someone of my own faith.

Marriage. Mark and I had talked about it occasionally. But neither of us could make up our minds about the prospect, or commit to a lifetime together. He was too young; I wasn't ready.

When fall arrived, we returned to Reed. During the next two summers, Mark worked for a cruise ship company out of New York while I stayed in the Pacific Northwest. Because his oldest brother was a member of the dock workers' union, he was able to facilitate Mark's getting one of those coveted jobs. It paid handsomely and gave him a glimpse of other countries. The stories he told, once he returned to Reed, were rife with partying, intrigue and sexual liaisons with passengers. I was uncomfortable imagining them, even though I understood his excitement at being sought after and admired. Mark made light of it, as if it were all part of growing up and discovering what the world was about.

Decades later I met him again, curious to see him as an adult, each of us wondering whether we'd made the right decision. It was strange to find that he now dyed his hair black and looked somewhat portly. Nevertheless, he was able to express his thoughts and feelings in an easy and unaffected way. He told me he had married, had a daughter, divorced, become an alcoholic, eventually received treatment and recovered. He spoke of his countless affairs, a self-styled Don Juan who still dallied in women, claiming his goal was to sleep with at least one from every country in the world. He also prided himself on having had a long affair with a married woman while living with her and her psychiatrist husband, a *menage a trois*. It sounded sick to me. I imagined the lives he had played with, the corroding losses. Had we stayed together, I would have been one of the discards.

What had happened to the young, exuberant, life-affirming student I had once loved? He claimed he liked being a free spirit and was happy now, but I wondered.

22

BY THE END OF the fifties, after Mark and I had graduated from college, we said goodbye to each other amicably, and a year later I met someone I wanted to marry. Once George and I planned our wedding date, I phoned Dad to see if he could meet us for lunch. *Oh, no,* he said, *I have a son to care for now*—his new wife's teenager. *And what about me,* I thought, *aren't I your daughter, and won't George be your son-in-law? And what about your own son?* I hung up the phone feeling hurt and angry. As I continued to think about it, however, I realized Dad and George would have had nothing to say to each other, especially since I had told George about the abuse. From that time on, whenever I needed to contact Dad by mail, I addressed him as Father instead of Dad or Daddy, my encoded moral stand that, of course, no one understood. I already disliked his new wife, Shirley.

Dad had lost his job at the University Congregational church in Seattle, and was now the pastor of a small community parish in the northeast district. He had moved into Shirley's house and invited me there to meet her. A member of his congregation, she still addressed him as Reverend, and looked up at him adoringly. He wanted me to love her and call her Mother. I was insulted. I already had a mother. Besides, Shirley seemed sugary and insincere, not someone I was drawn to. Her house was cluttered with knick knacks and everyday stuff: plants, puffy pillows on puffy couches, old newspapers. No touches of beauty, no artwork or bright colors, no books or quiet spaces. Even her clothes seemed indifferent in shape and style.

After our visit, still trying to sort feelings of disappointment, anger and confusion, I climbed into my old Chevy, glad to be leaving. As I backed down the curving driveway, I hit something that thunked. I couldn't see anything but thought I had hit a rock, a piece of pottery, or a sign when my wheel cut the corner. I should have stopped but I didn't. Dad called me that evening to say I'd damaged Shirley's property on purpose just to be mean. How could he think that of me! I wrote a note of apology to Shirley but that didn't erase my resentment at Dad's accusation. Once again, I was hurt that the parent who all these years had trusted and believed in me could be my accuser. Besides, he seemed not to appreciate that the visit had been stressful for me. I was reminded of his divorcing Mother and how he had wanted both wives to be friends and live together with him—no sense that that was humiliating and hurtful. I had to help him move out.

Realizing Mother wouldn't come to the wedding if Dad or Shirley were present, I didn't invite them. It was an easy choice. My brother agreed to walk me down the aisle. A few weeks before the ceremony, Dad came over to Mother's garage to pick up some tools he'd left behind, and I helped him carry them out to the car. We small-talked to stay on neutral ground. I still felt loyal to both parents and responsible for keeping them from hurting each other. Dad seemed untroubled, even happy, but Mother cried every day. Besides feeling ashamed that they were getting a divorce—at a time when divorce was frowned upon, especially for members of the clergy—she anguished over not having any money and never having worked outside the home. I tried to comfort her.

That day, as Dad put his tools in the trunk and opened the car door, talking casually, his voice trailed to a lower register: *There's a rumor going around that I sexually abused you.* Barely controlled anger rumbled in his voice as if he were the victim instead of me. I was stunned. He had never acknowledged his abuse, never named it in over twenty years, never referred to or hinted at its presence. Why would he do so now? I felt struck, caught off-guard, as if, again, he were silencing me, maneuvering me into the belief that he had always *just loved me*, that I had portrayed him as someone bad, that whatever had happened was my fault.

Could it be that he felt truly bewildered? That what he had done to me was too painful to acknowledge and no longer available to him? Was some deeply-buried trauma in his own child-hood threatening to find its way into his consciousness and over-whelm him?

Before I could gather my wits and say *Yes! Why did you do that? What sort of person would molest his own daughter? Have you any idea what grief and turmoil you've caused?* he closed the door and drove off. Of course, I should have gone after him. I was filled with feelings of shame, betrayal, defeat and vulnerability, and had no idea what to do or how to behave.

What had I done besides asking him to stop? I had reported him to Mother, as the Reed counselor advised me to. At the news, her face had turned ashen even though all she had said was, *Oh, no, he wouldn't do that. He was probably just being friendly.* But something in her eyes had acknowledged the truth, and she must have talked to Dad because he never bothered me again. Within months of that confrontation he was returning the attentions Shirley showered on him, and soon told mother he wanted a divorce.

ONCE GEORGE AND I were married, I was totally immersed in the joy of our being together. By the time we moved to Shelton, besides housework, I concentrated on writing. A year later, when Simpson transferred George to its northern California plant, I was again en-gaged in home-making and getting to know the community, and at the end of those two years we were ready to start a family and I became a full-time mom.

By then, Shirley was dead, reportedly from an overdose of drugs. Dad had moved to Montana, where he lived for a while with Bill's family, and then rented a place in town, working as a substitute teacher. How many children had he gotten his hands on there, I wondered? Years earlier, when Bill and Joan visited us, I had warned them about leaving Dad alone with their three young-sters, since he had molested me. At the time, they stared at me, and after an awkward silence, changed the subject as if to erase what had just been said. It didn't help that George, working in the kitchen, kept to himself instead of standing up for me. I was hurt and humiliated, and felt dismissed by all of them. These were the first people, besides George and a counselor, I'd spoken to about the incest. Did my warning save their children? I don't know. No one in Bill's family ever wanted to talk about it. Perhaps it was too painful, perhaps their own lives were all they could manage as they focussed on parenting, jobs and their own problems with alcoholism. But I wish they had acknowledged and comforted me. We could have helped each other.

My last visit with Dad came when George and I drove with the children to Montana to visit Bill and his family. I thought it would be a good idea for the boys—then, maybe, four and eight— to at least meet their grandfather. As it happened, we met him in a parking lot carrying groceries to his car. I wanted our family to experience the warmth and playfulness, the kindness he'd shared with us in India. But we had all changed. He shook hands, said a few words to the grandchildren he barely acknowledged, and told us he had things to do, needed to get going. He left us there in the parking lot, and we drove through town and up into the forested hills where Bill and Joan and their three youngsters greeted us, the fragrance of freshly baked cookies drawing us into the house.

Dad married a third time, a woman named Elvira who lived in Arizona. Within a few years, they, too, divorced, and he returned to Kalispell in Montana. In early December of 1975 our phone rang. It was Bill on the line. He seldom called, but his voice was bright and conversational so I chatted about whatever I was up to that day. Then he said, I have some bad news: Dad is dead. First the shock, then the questions. He had drowned ice fishing on Moran lake. He had asked a fishing buddy to go with him but the friend declined, saying the weather was too mild and the ice not safe. Dad went anyway, probably because he loved the natural world and felt it would protect him. Who knows? A couple of days later he was supposed to substitute teach at the high school and didn't show up. Then his truck was found. Then his body. A strong swimmer, he floated face-down in about thirteen feet of water and ice, approximately sixty feet from shore. He'd been there for three days. I imagine he struggled, trying to move back when the ice began to crack, and to flatten himself and get out once he fell in. My heart went out to Bill who was called on to identify the bloated body found by strangers. Bill had lost the only parent he felt had ever truly loved him.

After that phone call, we left our young boys with George's parents, filled the station wagon with poinsettias for the service, and drove to Montana. I was relieved that Dad was gone, but grateful that he had left me an abiding appreciation for wilderness, and that he had taken care of me during the times he was able to be a good father. I wished his own life had not been so damaged, and hoped mine and my family's would move forward, freed from that numbing history, knowing it would always tug at us. My needs as a young daughter to be cared for by a loving father tangled painfully with my rage as a grown woman facing incest. I wanted out. I wanted to make a new life for myself. And gradually did—but even after years of counseling and friendships that helped sustain me, whenever I was under too much stress, I reverted back to that wobbly, fractured self, the past faulting me for who I was; reaching out to swallow me up.

ONCE WHEN I WAS ten or eleven, I asked Dad how he stood all the years of criticism from Mother. He said, *She was the cross I had to bear.* Even then, the words sounded too easy, too preacherly, making him the martyr and her the scapegoat. Bill and I had always been on Dad's side in their arguments, and we still were, but now there were questions: *Why didn't he battle it out with her? Why had they married in the first place? Wasn't it for love? Why had they fallen out of love? Was it our fault? What was wrong with us that made us hard to love?*

By the time we were fourteen and sixteen, Bill and I were able to put the unsayable into words: *Why didn't Mother and Dad get a divorce, since they never seemed happy together?* Six years later they did. Mother said they waited that long "for our sakes," but it was Dad who asked for the divorce. Mother felt ashamed to face the community, and wondered how she'd survive. She finally signed up for classes at the University of Washington. The woman who headed the department of Family Life took her under her wing, helping her to look for work and eventually offering her a part-time job so that she'd have a paycheck. Two years later, after many tears, application forms, interviews, Mother landed a well-paying position as Dean of Women at Linfield College in Oregon. For the first time in her life she had enough money to live on comfortably and no one but herself to care for. She made a down-payment on a house a mile or so from campus and lived there contentedly for the rest of her life, dying on her ninetieth birthday. She continued to be productive but was critical of others to the end.

23

2002. TIME IS RUNNING out. I am in my brother's house, visiting him in Montana. I ask him for his stories, but he says he can't remember anything. So I dredge up some of my own. Yes, he remembers the game we played in the deep, moon-lit sand on the banks of the Jumna river. And, yes, he remembers being given his first gun, and how he hunted pigeons on the same riverbank. I was there, too, watching from a distance as he and Kishan, one of our servants, lay hidden against a sand dune, waiting until a large flock flew over. The rush of their wings whistled like arrows. He pulled the trigger again and again as the flock lifted and swerved, first one, then another dark shape falling from their midst, somersaulting, thudding to earth. Sometimes, one wing trailing, a bird turned in the sand or dragged itself away, eyes blinking rapidly before they glazed over. Billy and Kishan strung them by their feet and stood in the yard later, Billy's nine-year-old grin facing the camera, his gun upright beside him.

Do you remember our pet crocodile? he asks.

No, just the alligator Uncle K kept in Alabama

What alligator?

The one in the pond that liked its belly scratched; and the hawk K kept in a cage, teaching us to feed it chunks of raw meat; the raccoon in the screened back porch; the chickens whose warm eggs I carried carefully into the house for Aunt Betty, glad to be safe from the fierce-eyed birds; Bessy, the cow, whose milk steamed and frothed as cousin Edward jetted it into a bucket. How comfortably he leaned against her black and white side.

BILL REMINDED ME THERE were two cows, one a holstein, one a jersey. When he and Edward milked together, they had fun squirting milk into the cat's mouth. Carrying a full pail up to the house, sometimes Edward tried swinging the bucket fast enough to keep the milk from falling out. Such daring!

Tell me about our pet crocodile, I said.

From the Jumna.

Bill tells me Kishan took him pigeon hunting; that they bicycled up-river, shot a small crocodile, thought it was dead and tied it onto the bicycle rack. Halfway home, the croc started thrashing. They dragged it the rest of the way on the end of a rope. I was shocked.

What happened then?

I don't remember.

What I remember is the white rabbit Bill bent over in the front yard. He slit the skin of its belly with his hunting knife, chin to tail, then peeled it back like a glove, pulling the drape of the fur neatly away in a handful: my first lesson in anatomy—and in the distance between us.

WHAT NEXT, I WONDERED? I had earned my college diploma, but how was I to earn a living? Teaching, nursing and secretarial work were the options offered women of my generation. Because college teaching would steep me in literature, it held the most appeal. But I felt far too uninformed and insecure to stand in front of a class and assume responsibility for the minds and lives of students. On the other hand, I had no appetite for secretarial work, and little for nursing. So I turned myself over to Portland's downtown employment agency, took a battery of typing and written tests, and was encouraged to apply for the job of Group Worker that had just opened in Multnomah County's Juvenile Detention Center. I had never heard of such a place and wondered what it was all about.

Days later, I found myself seated at a long table opposite five men and one woman who questioned me about the choices I would make in various critical situations with children, and, finally, which professional journals I subscribed to (none). Several were recommended. Within a week, I wore a lanyard around my waist linked to an authority of keys that gossiped as I walked.

Each morning, I left the sunlit world of the parking lot to unlock doors that bolted behind me while I made my way down a labyrinth of waxed and gleaming hallways to the girls' wing. It, too, became a hallway, on either side of which seven- to seventeen-year-olds slept in individual rooms with barred windows. At the far end of the hall stood a glass-sided office, housing a long, built-in desk, a telephone and a log book in which we entered daily reports. We had been instructed to barricade ourselves inside this office if a riot ensued or someone chased us with a butcher knife, and to call for help. The office looked out on a spacious common room and kitchen. Each morning we unlocked the girls' doors, letting them out for the day's supervised activities. Danger and heartbreak stalked that shiningly clean space, as well as occasional glimpses of hope.

The youngest children were usually held for only a few days while the courts settled their parents' divorce cases, assigned custody, or found foster homes. But the older ones often served long sentences and returned more than once, caught stealing or at prostitution, for violence at home or in school. I remember one massively-built Black girl, put in solitary, who refused to talk with anyone, hurled her tray of food against the wall, tore her pillow apart and stuffed it down the toilet. The hatred and defiance in her eyes were palpable. She would go down fighting. I wanted to help her, much as she frightened me, but, besides my being white, I was part of the society that had brutalized her. Why should she trust me?

Daily, I wrote extensive reports on as many of the girls as I could. I was on their side, not their parents'. The adults were the ones who should have been locked up, I thought. Better still, they needed help: to undo the cycle of alcoholism, neglect, poverty and abuse with which they battered these children. Clearly, the system itself was flawed, society's priorities contributing to the chaos. I realized that if I chose to continue working here, I would want to train as a social worker, an attorney, a judge, a psychiatrist and a congresswoman with enough clout to alter national priorities to help educate, employ and support families in need.

Somewhere toward the end of my first year, my co-workers asked me to draw up a list of changes we had all agreed on, which would improve the plight of these children and better enable us to care for them. I typed up the suggestions, thirty some in all, signed the letter on behalf of the staff, and submitted it to the director. It seemed like a manageable list and a good faith gesture on our part, but it caused an immediate storm. I was marched down the halls by a heavy-shoed, militarily-stern supervisor into the grand office of his majesty the emperor as if I had just blown up the castle. The superintendant was a tall, imposing man I had only glimpsed on occasion and had assessed to be a reasonable person. Now, he told me, if I continued to *stir up trouble*, he would see that I never found a good job again. My behavior was not to be tolerated. I was to watch my step.

This sort of intimidation was frightening, but I had never experienced it before. I felt as if I were in a war movie or a social satire, and wondered how that had happened. What had I expected? Praise for our initiative? A meeting with the director to discuss suggestions and arrive at consensus before taking action? Despite this kind of treatment, I stayed at work, and kept writing suggestions in the log on behalf of the girls. But, at the same time, I enrolled in a graduate class at Portland State to begin earning credits for a degree in teaching, a job I felt would allow me to be of more use. Not long afterwards, I met George.

24

OUR PARENTS HAD BECOME friends during committee work at Seattle's University Congregational Church when Dad was one of the pastors. Now that he and Mother were divorced, Elizabeth invited her to join their family for a few days at White Pass while George and his cousin, Bill, skiied. Since I was coming home for the Christmas holidays, I was included.

Initially, I felt myself part of a package put together to keep George entertained and at home after his tour of duty in the navy. Although I had met his mother and father several times, I hadn't known they had a son. I was determined not to serve as his weekend date, but looked forward to skiing.

Mother and I drove from Seattle, George and his folks from Hood Canal. We had agreed to meet at the Shell station in Enumclaw, not far from the White Pass ski area, and from there follow the family's red and white Jeep to the tiny logging hamlet of Packwood with its cafeteria and rough-hewn cabins.

When we pulled into the Shell station, our windshield wipers pushing a fine rain, George was filling the Jeep's gas tank. I could hear his mother say, *Son, it's raining. You'd better put on your coat,* and was struck by how incongruous her remark seemed, considering the report I'd heard of his responsibilities on an aircraft carrier, and how the tall, trim young man went about his task with a natural ease. We introduced ourselves, exchanged a few pleasantries, and were soon back on the road, winding through dense evergreen forests, the rich canopy sparkling with water drops during sun-breaks, or curtained off by low-hanging clouds. I thought of Mount Rainier, the great white massive, not far from us to the south, holding up the sky.

The following day the weather cleared, and we three young people went skiing. I was surprised, while pulling on wool socks in the Jeep, that George knelt beside me to assist in lacing up my boots. He was so unassumingly helpful. Both he and Bill were good skiers, while I was a beginner, floundering about, pitching forward onto my face, or spinning spread-eagle into others on the hill. The cousins stuck by me and helped as I gained confidence, and although I was unable to ski with the grace and speed they enjoyed, the bright, snowy world thrilled me, as did our mutual camaraderie.

In the evening, sore-shinned and suddenly light-footed after stowing boots and skis, we joined our parents for a simple dinner before walking them back to their cabins for the night, and re-grouping around a pitcher of beer to quiz George again on his ex-periences in the navy. I was already attracted by his quiet patience and his pleasure in the mountains. Now he described his under-water inspection of an aircraft carrier's huge propeller, the blades improperly locked and beginning to turn, imperceptibly winding up his air hose. Or how, during night training swims in the black Atlantic, he and his buddy made it to shore and back to the ship ahead of their classmates by devising hand-to-hand signals that kept them from being separated. How he almost ran out of breath swimming through a submerged tunnel while free-diving in Italy's Blue Grotto when he was on leave.

I was an English major, Bill a physicist; what did we know about George's world except to hold our breaths?

One evening, a full moon drew us out, and, taking the Jeep, we decided to explore the old logging road in front of our cabins. Snow, studded with frost, sparkled in the moonlight. Even the air blinked back at us, ice crystals refracting the light like tiny fire-flies. When we moved up out of the forest into a clear-cut area, the mountain suddenly rose, white and shimmering, barnacled with star light like a breaching whale. We sat looking out the windows while the Jeep's engine cooled, then stepped into that immense si-lence, the vapor from our breathing silvered and visible.

I think that was the turning point. George and his parents drove me to the train station the next day so that I'd make it back to Portland in time for work and classes. But when he and I said goodbye, it felt more like hello. I wrote him a letter inviting him to visit if he were ever in town, and the next weekend he drove down the length of Hood Canal to meet me. We saw each other steadily for six months. I'd hear his black Volvo's harmonic shifts climbing the hill toward my tiny rental house, and soon he'd be at the door with a smile and a clutch of daffodils behind his back. For an exuberant moment we leaned into each other, then gave the daffodils a drink. While I finished cooking dinner, George sat on the step that separated the kitchen from the living room, and practiced sailors' knots with his patient hands. We ate looking out across the city as lights floated up in the gathering dark.

During that spring, in lieu of rent, I was in the midst of scraping layers of paint off the sides of my little house before applying a new coat, using a blow torch to loosen the weathered surface. When George saw what I was up to, he offered to help. We rented a second torch and worked together until the job was done. I remember, too, experimenting with empty bottles and a glass cutter, scoring the neck, tightening a wire around it before heating it with a torch, then tapping the bottle smartly to break off the top. Once the cut edge was sanded smooth, we had a new drinking glass. I especially liked the sea-green ones.

George was easy to be with, and whatever work we shared, reflected our joy in being together, a prelude to nights of love-making filled with passion and tenderness. All the terror of my years with Dad and other men fell away. I'd found someone I could trust.

Before long we were drawing house plans, imagining, on graph paper, a life together. By the time our talk turned to marriage, I told George he needed to know something about me that was painful and that might change his mind. He wrapped his arms around me and told me he loved me and always would. Neither one of us had any inkling of how abuse would haunt us. We planned an August wedding, and were married that fall of 1961, eager to start our lives together.

BROUGHT UP A PACIFIST, I had chosen to spend my life with a man who had just completed his tour of duty in the navy. Even though we shared the same moral values, my thinking about the military differed widely from George's. Through him, I grew to respect the need to defend a country we both loved, and to honor the men and women who protected us with their lives. Through me, he learned to appreciate the peace-makers and the moral courage they exerted in the face of violence. Even though war still felt like the ultimate failure, and my admiration lay with the peace-makers, I recognized that the democratic freedoms I cherished, and our own family's day-to-day lives, could only survive with protection from both.

George had trained as a diver, specializing in ordnance disposal, dismantling nuclear and conventional weapons. He also served as underway officer of the deck on the aircraft carrier, *Lake Champlain*. Having graduated from the University of Washington's College of Forestry, he went to work for Simpson Timber Company in Shelton after we were married, spending his time in their technical services department on dimension lumber, plywood and doors.

Together, we found a cottage for rent outside of town, its resident mouse looking up at us from a kitchen drawer. The house stood on a bluff at the edge of a field beside Hammersley Inlet. From our front window we could watch rafts of bufflehead and scaup, an occasional eagle, a passing boat, and were thrilled to be together in such an unspoiled setting.

For a few months, the living room was occupied by a narrow skiff George built, one fine wooden rib at a time. On weekdays, while he worked at the plant, I stayed home sewing curtains and couch covers, cooking, cleaning and, most importantly, forging ahead writing poems. Wood shavings mingled with metaphors and the fragrance of pot roasts and cookies. Instructed by a fox that pounced on mice under the apple trees, I felt singularly alive.

When the skiff was ready, we paddled up-stream, exploring the still-wild banks and waterways that drew us to them. Once, drifting under a full moon, a sudden pattering against the hull mystified us until a flurry of bright, flat shapes leapt in, flopping about on the floorboards. We had disturbed a school of perch. As we rescued one batch, another flew in.

On one of our daytime outings, the boat snagged on the water-swept branches of a toppled red alder, capsizing. We righted it and hauled ourselves back in, unhurt, just as I caught sight of the jumbo jar of tuna-noodle dinner I'd made the day before tumbling away in the current, sealed off even from the fish.

What stayed with me was how water, like wind, played through the fallen alder leaves, brushing against their dark green covers and white undersides, turning them this way and that, like a flock of sandpipers wheeling in and out of sight against a leaden sky, each engaged with the other, and how the leaves gave new voice to the water's thrumming, how the tree would die there, drowning, giving back its nutrients to the land, but staying always in my mind, as green and alive as we felt then.

25

WORKING ON poems in Shelton, away from academia, I focused on the world outside my window, assuming that the excitement nature aroused in me would saturate my writing and turn it into poetry, that my job was to observe and faithfully record. But gradually I began to realize that no matter how intently I paid attention to the fox, no matter how faithfully I described its leap and pounce or its light-catching whiskers—that, in itself, wasn't enough. Something more was needed—a letting go, a welcoming of mystery. It was as if all the observations and details were necessary ingredients, but had to ripen and meld with whatever I was able to offer out of my own life. Some sort of alchemy between the outer world and the human heart begged to be given voice. Only then was language able to transform the landscape it relied on into art.

And language itself mattered. As I began reading in a more focused way, it occurred to me that if the poet said too much, the work was spoiled. Also, if two dissimilar things were brought together, the reader would find correspondences. Differences intensified each subject's special qualities without the need for comment.

I came to these realizations, and others, in a vague and groping way over time as I struggled to write. Clearly I couldn't *will* a poem onto the page, or expect that just because I'd worked hard, it would come alive. Poems seemed, instead, to seek me out when they felt welcome. Being engaged and open to the world had something to do with it. Life continually offered itself up, as the fox did, full of rich diversity and beauty. But something more was expected from me as well. I felt both the kinship and the distance between us.

The subconscious had a way of making its own connections. Years later, when swans flew close over our house, the thrill of seeing them and the loss of losing them reminded me of the mixed feelings I'd had about our sons growing up and leaving home. Why would swans suggest sons? Together, both subjects were able to carry on a conversation in the poem, bridge a gap, give rise to feelings and impulses that would not have occurred with just one of them, and which I would have missed.

Gradually I was learning that connections didn't have to be spelled out—in fact, couldn't be spelled out—and that these odd links and tensions within the poem gave it strength. I wasn't able to *will* leaps, juxtapositions, metaphors any more than I could will a poem; they tended to arise intuitively and with a sense of urgency that energized the work.

Again, chance came into play on an early morning after our move to the Olympic Peninsula. Still half-asleep, I stood at the window wearing the kimono a friend had given me, enjoying its warmth and drape, my thoughts drifting back to her and our times together before she died. Just then, a fox trotted by, jolting me into the present. My friend and the fox, in this way, became linked, their odd partnership suggesting a dialogue. I started scribbling down the lines. The fox provided me with a metaphor for the complex feelings I had about my friend, and the friendship provided me with a way to talk about endangered wildlife.

With the rest of the household still asleep, I had chanced on a moment of solitude and good fortune that allowed the poem to emerge. It then took me several years and dozens of revisions to find the language that both captured those initial feelings and presented them in such a way that a reader might also make them his own. Sometimes a poem insists on being written down, and that first rush of words holds. More typically, revision and more revision reveals the poem's strengths and deepens its capacity to carry life.

And so I wrote, and discovered that words linked to other words in the right order and stirred by emotion could arrive at complex and buried truths; that bits and pieces of experience could come alive on the page. Every time I despaired of being a writer, I tried again, and however often a poem fell short, the next one lured me on.

I read hungrily, and marveled at the exciting body of work available to the public, the variety of voices, and the endless possibilities language offered. In college, my friend Connie had presented me with Theodore Roethke's *Collected Poems*, knowing how moved I had been by the reading Roethke gave on campus. In the lilting lines of "My Papa's Waltz," Roethke caught the complex relationship between himself and his father: the joy of closeness as he stood on his father's shoes and clung to his sides to be danced around the room, the menace of closeness to that stern parent, perfectly rendered by the belt buckle scraping his cheek. How could such a small poem encompass so much? I wanted to write like that! The poem expressed my own mixed feelings about my Dad, the shameful ones and the joyous ones. I admired Roethke's long poems, too, his appreciation of women, his intimate rendition of the natural world, his genius for the music hidden in language.

26

WEEKDAYS, I DROVE GEORGE to work, and picked him up afterwards in our new 1961 Volkswagon bug, its candy-apple-red paint
catching the light. At four-thirty, he'd be waiting for me in the yard,
a solitary figure, tall, slim and heart-stoppingly unencumbered,
carrying nothing but himself. Perhaps in his jacket pocket he'd
have the folded paper bag I'd filled that morning with sandwiches
and an apple, re-cycling the sack for tomorrow's lunch.

Ten minutes late! How could I have kept this new husband
waiting again! Within a day or two, he commented that one could
be early or late but not on time. What a novel idea! I was still having trouble learning to schedule activities and watch the clock. I
felt respectful of others, but needed to show it by honoring their
commitments as well as my own.

Some afternoons I arrived wearing dark glasses to hide tears
threatening to spill over when I saw George. Hadn't I looked forward to being at home, observing the world, getting it down on
paper, keeping house? And wasn't I married to a fine young man,
both of us in love and delighting in each other's company? Yes. But,
only months before, I'd been accustomed to a full-time job and
daily contact with co-workers and friends, including other writers
and artists. Then, as newlyweds, George and I had been insepara-
ble, driving through Germany, Switzerland, France, Denmark and
Greece, the trip a wedding present from his parents.

In Greece I had come down with a fever of 105 and nearly
died of typhoid. By the time we reached Bari, in southern Italy,

I was admitted to a tiny hospital run by nuns. They wore lovely swept-wing headdresses of the sort I'd seen in paintings. George stayed in my room to watch over me. The townspeople, walking past my bed to use our bathroom, greeted us with shy smiles and *Buon giorno*.

Now I worked at home while he had a *real* job and a pay check, and whatever he accomplished seemed more important than what I did. I was lonely. However much I loved him and loved being with him, he was gone all day. I missed, too, being able to talk to artist friends about painting, writing, music, books, the hubbub of our inner lives.

When George was home, we worked contentedly side by side, read, listened to jazz or classical music on the radio, rode bicycles late afternoons in the country, our Woolrich shirts of gray tweed blending with the muted colors of the northwest landscape. Nearly invisible in the fields, deer raised their heads as we passed.

To save money, and because we liked being self-sufficient, we occasionally did our own dry cleaning, dipping dress slacks or a skirt in a round tin tub outside half-filled with solvent, hanging the clothes up to freshen. When friends visited, they laughed at us. I had never had clothes dry cleaned; besides, I relished our independence. Looking back, I recognized our patterns of frugality and how they mimicked my father's and George's mother's Spartan natures, however generous each was in other ways.

Often during the winter, I made a casserole and George packed the car with the tent and cookware, securing skis upright on a rack in the rear. After I picked him up from work, we drove to La Wis Wis forest camp, set up the tent, heated dinner, and then snuggled into the bulky sleeping bag I'd laboriously sewn and quilted. From high up in the quiet evergreens, we'd listen to the melodic whistling of a bird we never saw, even in daylight, dubbing it *the twee bird*. Years later, having identified it as the varied thrush, we enjoyed its annual visit to our yard, its robin-red-breast decorated with a dark brown vee, its singular, high notes reminding us of our special time in the woods.

By morning, even our drinking water inside the tent was frozen solid. We pulled on army surplus wool pants and jackets, cooked hot oatmeal with a handful of raisins, and spent the day skiing at nearby White Pass. What fun! To glide instead of stumble! To follow the raven's path and the snowshoe hare's! To merge with the sparkle and bite of winter, and share each other's lives! I couldn't have been happier.

The weekend that a camping buddy of George's came along, one of us inadvertently knocked over the casserole, spilling dinner. After groans of disappointment and laughter, I scooped up what I could, heated it on our tiny, round primus stove, and we ate hungrily, mindful of stray fir needles and bits of gravel. That night it rained. The tent wasn't big enough, and when our friend rolled against the wall his sleeping bag got soaked. He never complained but must have been glad to find dry clothes in the morning. We often wished we could have made amends for that miserable night.

At the end of a year in Shelton, Simpson transferred George to their northern California plant in Eureka where we again set up housekeeping, and explored the mudflats and rocky shore for birds and mammals. On our first drive down the coast, I thrilled at the sight of snowy egrets flying up out of the grassy sloughs, trailing their lacquered legs. The canals meandered close to the highway and served as feeding stations for countless birds and animals. Sometimes a solitary egret, intent on fishing, held motionless as we passed: a painted scroll in an emperor's study.

Always, the world stayed miraculous: a chipmunk high-tailing across the road, an osprey nesting on a platform above a lake, hardwoods holding the sky in their arms, the rise and fall of ordinary hills. It was many years later, though, that the egret and the crane—two birds which oddly moved me—registered as those I'd seen as a child, fishing on the shores of the Jumna. They spanned both worlds, the crane's haunting cries, the egret's snowy cut-outs in the sky, each lifting wide wings to connect me to my life.

When we moved to Eureka, I addressed the isolation I had felt in Shelton by involving myself with small groups whose values I respected, especially the League of Women Voters. George and I joined Arcata College's community chorus. We made friends and participated in civic activities.

In addition, by the end of that first year, I was engrossed in my first pregnancy. It began with a few weeks of nausea and queasiness, with no more periods, and with thousands of changes the body magically invoked without my knowledge. Among them, a sense of competence and wholeness. To carry a child, to make of our love someone new and alive, to nurture and connect, filled me with joy as well as purpose. I would be the best mother ever!

The queasiness gradually eased, and I was grateful not to have been sick enough to throw up the way some women did. I sewed colorful cotton smocks for my changing figure, read Dr. Spock to make sure I had anticipated our baby's needs, and stayed active in the League. Evenings and weekends, George and I explored the coastline, took walks and bicycle rides, visited friends, and worked at home.

George made a crib from two-by-fours he'd found on the beach, new lumber, presumably washed up from a tug and barge at sea. The bed was sturdy and spacious. He laced its sides ingeniously with fine twine. I painted it white and fitted the new mattress with a pad and soft sheets, then sewed a zippered cover for the piece of cut foam I fitted to the top of a dresser for diaper changing.

At the end of the first trimester, I experienced a spotting of blood, was hospitalized for two days of observation, and given a new drug, Depo Provera, to stop the uterus from aborting. Fortunately, that intervention seemed to work, and I was soon off the medication. Ultimately, Depo Provera came to be considered dangerous to a fetus. Brought up, as my generation was, to respect authority, I never thought to question doctors or hospitals, assuming they were the experts and had my best interests at heart. I couldn't imagine losing this baby, remained fiercely protective, and was determined to keep him healthy, alive, and growing steadily inside of me. From the start, I had been careful to keep my weight down, eat healthily, exercise and avoid alcohol and coffee.

On a sunny day in November, my contractions started getting close together, and George drove me to the local hospital, St. Joseph's. It was a joyful time for both of us. I was twenty-eight, George twenty-nine, in good health and spirits, married two years and ready for a family. I could hardly wait to hold our baby, welcome him or her into the world, gaze into those eyes. Everything was ready: crib, changing table, cloth diapers, diaper pail and disinfectant, tiny cotton T-shirts and sleepers, soft blankets and fitted sheets. It never occurred to me that anything could go wrong.

While an aid took my vital statistics, I slipped off my ring and wristwatch for George to keep. The aid soon returned with a basin of warm water, which she placed on my bedside table. After pulling the curtains closed, shutting George out, she prepared to *prep me*. I had no idea what that term meant but followed instructions as she went about scrubbing my private parts with a soapy wash cloth, then shaving off my pubic hair, startling my skin to involuntary shivers. Rinsed, dried and back under the covers, I felt plucked and exposed.

Once the curtains were open, George and I were again free to visit. Contractions continued, and hands on the overhead clock moved slowly. Periodically, a nurse stopped by to check my progress. Before long I was fully dilated, contractions hard and fast and the pain ratcheting up.

In those days, no parenting classes or prenatal exercises existed in our small town. I knew to breathe deeply and to try to relax, but soon the pain was so intense I begged George to call the doctor. By nature reserved, he was reluctant to interfere. Finally the nurse explained that the baby was caught on my pelvic bones, its head too big to pass through. Our doctor was out of town. His partner—currently with another patient—would supervise my delivery. When he arrived, he decided the birth should be induced and prescribed intravenous medication. At once, the contractions ran into each other without mediating intervals. Seared by pain, deep, visceral groans coming out of my body, I hung onto the rails behind my head, wondering if both the baby and I were going to die. George was concerned, but to him, also, a hospital was a place where trained people were at work, and to interfere by asking for additional help would have seemed inappropriate, even meddlesome.

Finally, in the delivery room, an anesthesiologist administered a shot of Nembutal and I quickly lost consciousness. An unusually large episiotomy followed, and Carl was delivered by forceps, face-up, instead of in the typical face-down position. In recovery, I woke to a dream so vivid I still feel its imprint—I was that baby, as well as its mother, willing it through miles and miles of a dark, rocky, windingly narrow passage. We traveled together, and I became both the current pushing him forward and the one being pushed, until, finally, we both emerged and woke to the light.

After hours in recovery, I was grateful to be back in my room holding our son, a sweet, small bundle of life. For Carl's middle name, I'd chosen Eliot, after a poem I had loved in college, T.S. Eliot's *Journey of the Magii*. Carl nursed hungrily and then went back to sleep, bundled off to the nursery until it was time for another feeding. I felt an inexplicable joy in holding this tiny, new being. We bonded instantly.

What I did not know, was that the day before Carl's birth, President Kennedy had been shot. I heard the news later from friends who stopped by to visit, their eyes red from crying. As I watched the funeral procession on T.V., I joined a nation in mourning, the lone, riderless horse symbolizing our bewilderment and grief, my own family's joy tempered by history.

Within three or four days, I stepped back into the dazzling sunshine, George helping me to the car and then handing me our baby. I cradled him in my arms—no infant seats in those days—excited finally to be heading home. Carl was an easy child to care for, feeding hungrily and sleeping soundly, bright-eyed when he woke, crying lustily if he needed something, and quickly soothed.

When I took him in for his six-week check-up, the doctor told me he had a hernia and needed an operation. My heart stopped. What was a hernia? Why did Carl need surgery? He was only a tiny baby! *This is a common occurrence*, the doctor's quiet voice assured me. *Babies heal quickly. The abdominal wall isn't always completely formed when they're born. He'll be fine in no time.* Whenever I entered the hospital and heard any of the children cry, my milk started to flow, soaking the front of my blouse. I couldn't bear seeing Carl in that big metal child's bed, but he was safe, well cared-for, and the inch-long incision in his groin healed as if by magic within a week. I was immensely grateful to have him back home.

As for my own body, for the first weeks after delivery, I was so uncomfortable I couldn't sit on the toilet, stood, instead, over a plastic waste basket in the tub. When I went to see the doctor, his comments were dismissive—both of my physical condition and of the tears that started falling as I spoke: *Women have been giving birth for thousands of years. Pain is all in your head. Get a hold of yourself or get counseling.* I felt shamed, and responsible for not measuring up. George was away at work, and I began to long for a mother who could help and comfort me. My own mother would not have known what to do with a baby, and would have wanted attention herself. Within minutes of her arrival, she would have stirred up criticism and hurt feelings.

I didn't know then about postpartum depression, but became keenly aware, for the first time, of what it was like to love and care for a baby, to realize that I had once been just as innocent and dependent on my own parents. I couldn't fathom how they had neglected and molested me. How could anyone do that to a child? Tears started falling more and more often, especially when I nursed Carl, felt his hunger, knew I was needed, and that loving him, protecting him was what I could do best. I had come to realize my parents were products of their own upbringing and had given what they could. But the child I had once been still felt at risk.

I phoned an older woman friend, someone who had already raised her own children, a social worker I respected, and shared my feelings. She urged me to get help, said she'd watch Carl for an hour a week while I saw a counselor, recommended a psychiatrist she knew. He was wonderfully supportive, and helped me regain my sense of well-being within a couple of months. Not until Carl was grown and in college did I embark on the kind of long-term counseling I would have benefitted from earlier. As a young woman, I felt ashamed to need help, and to pay for it would have put a huge strain on our family budget. What was wrong with me that I couldn't *pull myself up by my own bootstraps*? My parents' generation saw emotional problems as character weaknesses, and so did I, even though I knew better.

BY THE TIME CARL was a few months old, he would wake in his crib chortling and singing, tossing notes in the air like surprising discoveries, as if to entertain the world. While nursing, his cheeks pumped steadily, small fingers grazing my wrist, my throat, reaching up to touch my eyes or stroke the satin binding of a blanket. We rested comfortably in the wide-armed oak rocker. As time passed, sighs and sucking sounds gave way—started up again—gave way, until he fell deeply asleep, the two of us rocking quietly as I gazed into his face or out over the field in the arms of the evergreens.

Laying Carl on his back to scooch a folded diaper under him, snugging it with one hand while running a safety pin through my hair or into a bar of soap with the other to ease the shaft through layers of fabric, fingers automatically guarding young skin, I pinned and tucked and buttoned.

As any mother does, I touched my own nose, and said *Nose!*, Carl soon brought his hand up to the middle of his face, and— *Yes!* I'd laugh—and we'd grin at each other. We played peek-a-boo while I stretched the neck of his soft T-shirt, pulling it over his head, covering his fist with my hand to guide it through his sleeve. Finally he could stand up, pat the mirror, pat my face or plant his mouth on mine in a drooly kiss, clutching my hair to steady himself, his voice its own instrument and companion.

Set down, off he'd go, crawling about the floor, the flat of his hands slapping out their rhythms the way Shunkar's wife slapped the *chapatis* back and forth between her palms. He liked to pull out pots and pans to play with, or pad over to the living room couch and tug himself up to reach the sleeping cat. Soon he was teetering around upright, cruising the room. A huggable, inquisitive child, he grew to love exploring, and registered every nuance of his world intently.

27

WE HAD LIVED IN Eureka for two years, enjoying the months of sunshine, the rocky beaches full of wildlife, our friends and small family. By 1964 George was ready for a career change and a place to raise our children and put down roots. When his uncle needed help building a small real estate office, and offered temporary work, we bundled up the baby, two cats and the household gear, and moved to Washington State's Olympic Peninsula where the salt water and mountains felt like home. Our rental house shared Anderson road with a few old timers, and was surrounded by alfalfa fields alive with marsh hawks, coyotes and meadowlarks. Once the real estate office was up and running, George contracted for work as a commercial diver, inspecting dams and bridges, as well as turbines at the Hanford Nuclear Plant. Between dive jobs he worked locally as a land surveyor.

That first year in Washington, when Lindsay gave me a routine physical and pelvic exam, he asked what had happened—*You look like you've been butchered.* I told him about my experience with labor and delivery in California, wondering if a Caesarian would have been safer for both the baby and me. He shook his head in disbelief, and said he was glad I was now within reach of Seattle's professionally-staffed hospitals.

When the rental we had lived in for over a year was sold, we moved down the road to a little cottage, and from there, drew floor plans and hired a neighboring contractor to build us our own house. It took shape on just under an acre of land surrounded by evergreens at the edge of a wooded ravine about a mile from the Dungeness Spit. In 1965, we moved in, and have lived here ever since.

Over the last four decades, trees have been cut down and re-planted, fields of alfalfa we once played in, have vanished, and the old barn has been replaced by houses. Weathered fence posts no longer hold meadowlarks. I miss their vibrant, carolling songs. The foxes are gone. So are the owls. But long, wavering lines of Canada geese still call us out of doors as they fly over, and children's voices mingle with the sound of lawn mowers and cars.

After four years of trying, our second son, Todd, was con-ceived. Lindsay delivered him in the spring of 1968 at Northwest Hospital, the one he had worked so hard to establish. I hadn't wanted to risk another bungled delivery, so a three-hour journey, including a ferry ride, from home to Seattle seemed well worth the effort. I trusted Lindsay to take good care of my baby and me.

On May 24th, at three in the morning, my water broke, and not knowing that to wait could endanger the baby's life, I woke George, and we readied ourselves for the trip, but delayed leaving so as not to wake his parents or Lindsay. Two hours later, I put a clean, dry hand-towel between my legs, bundled up a sleeping Carl, and drove with George across the floating bridge to his par-ents' house at Lofall. Once there, I phoned Lindsay, who said to get right to the hospital. We hugged Carl, still in his pajamas, content to stay with his grandparents, knowing his dad would be back by dinner time.

During my hospital stay, I was comfortable and well cared-for, and didn't mind the head nurse scolding me for not coming straight in when my water broke. Yes, I should have known better, but I didn't.

An hour or so before delivery, I became deeply chilled. The nurse was quick to cover me with what looked like an insubstantial white, cotton blanket, but it had been in a warming oven and felt like a blessing.

George was able to watch the delivery, as was my cousin, Tam-my. Lindsay was in good spirits, and the four of us celebrated the occasion with smiles and tears. I'd had a spinal, so could feel noth-ing from my waist down, but was alert and able to watch through an overhead mirror the unexpected sight of my own dark blood threading past the sharp and oddly painless knife, and then the baby's head emerges as I wept with wonder.

Once aspirated, weighed and measured, Todd's body was laid across mine for a few moments of deep contentment. Before long, I was in my room with the bed cranked up, cradling him, stroking his tiny, waving hands, George beside us again, and our world complete.

I couldn't wait to have Carl meet his baby brother. After being an only child for four-and-a-half years, it wouldn't be easy for him to share his parents. I spent extra time with him to ease his fears, told him often how much we loved him, and always would. However, no matter how much I affirmed him, no matter that his brother looked up to him and wanted to be his best friend, rivalry eventually intruded into their relationship. Even as adults, if one reached out, the other distanced himself. My hope continues that they'll come to respect and value each other.

Todd grew quickly, his long, narrow torso predicting a tall adult, his platinum hair and bright eyes tapping into Nordic ancestry. Like Carl, he ate hungrily, slept deeply, and woke ready to explore the world. From a young age, his steady nature and friendliness engaged him with others. He loved anything that moved— tricycle, swing, bicycle, ski, car, airplane, motorcycle. By the time he was five or six he was dragging pieces of plywood, propped up by firewood, to make ramps for his bicycle. As he grew older and mastered the art of riding, the ramps grew higher, and he flew into the air for the thrill of it, sometimes crashing and getting scratched up before trying again. I loved his bright spirit and sweet nature, the grace with which he took on the world.

28

ONE KIND OF LONELINESS is invisible pain. If a person breaks a leg and it's in a cast, others see the loss and empathize. But back pain is hidden. The person looks unbroken, healthy, able to do what others do, even if they can't. Their plight may be recognized for a day or two or even for a few weeks. But after that, they're made to feel ashamed, as if they're not pulling their own weight, as if they're malingering to get out of work, and are somehow guilty of bringing this on themselves, of not measuring up.

I'd had two brief episodes in my twenties—sharp pain in my lower back, an inability to stand up straight. The doctor had prescribed pain medication and bed rest which seemed to cure me. But after two pregnancies, pain persisted as a dull ache at the base of my spine. I assumed it was both from carrying children, and from labor, and would soon clear up, but a year later it still dogged me, so I made an appointment with an orthopedist who had me walk every day for five miles, had me wear lifts in my shoe, a back support. Finally, a year later, he recommended surgery. Two of the lower disks were fused with bone from my right hip. I had high hopes. My children were two and six, and I needed the energy and strength to care for them.

Within a year after surgery, the pain had sharpened and migrated down the left leg into my toes, alleviated only by lying down. In those days, orthopedists advised rest instead of the physical therapy we've come to learn is much more beneficial. I had more surgery to remove a bone spur that had cut three quarters of the way through a tendon. That helped slightly, but each day as I went about my work, the pain increased until, by mid-afternoon I was willing myself to cook dinner, clean up, give the children their baths, visit with George. I longed for night and the chance to lie down again. And during the day, whether I had five minutes or forty to myself, I used them to lie on the couch or outside on a foam pad under the sun's soothing heat.

If you've been there, you know. Your partner, your children, haven't a clue as to what you're going through, nor should they. Being a wife and mother was as essential to me as breathing, and having a family helped counter the pain. But not to be healthy and energetic for them frustrated and bewildered me. I seldom complained, practiced being brave, living as fully as I could. But I felt lonely and ragged, tattered by physical pain, so lost from who I was used to being. Robbed of mobility, energy, and freedom, I tried various doctors but without relief. Even poems eluded me; I was too busy taking care of my children to write.

Doctors, family members and friends became my skeptics and judges—probing, assessing, questioning and extrapolating, and I internalized their attitudes. Was I a malingerer? Was I causing my own pain? Only another swimmer, a stranger at the public pool, white-faced and walking gingerly, instantly validated how I felt, and empathized when we shared our stories. Back pain hobbled me for more than twenty years.

The Gould clan in Wilsonville, Alabama (top to bottom): Back row: Hailey from Louisville Kentucky, Mother, Dad, Charlotte, Uncle K, cousin Edward, Bill, Aunt Betty, cousin Lance. Front row: Frances Hailey, Aunt Edna (Grandfather Gould's sister), cousin Betsy, Grandfather (Alymer Gould), Grandmother (Cousin Carrie)

Lindsay, Kenneth (K), Stanley, their father Grandfather Gould

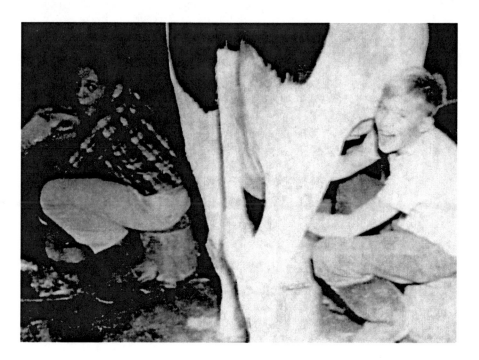

Bill and Edward milking

Edward teaching Charlotte to ride a horse

Florida: Charlotte, Aunt Betty, Uncle K, Bill, cousins Lance and Edward

Hiking the Cascades and Little Tahoma: Teena (dog), Bill, Charlotte, Aunt Sally, cousin

Bill and Charlotte in the Cascades

Charlotte with her first salmon, fishing Neah Bay with Lindsay and Sally Gould

Charlotte's senior year at Reed, 1959

29

As a child in Allahabad, when heat scorched the plains and defeated the crops, drying ponds and rivers, leaving animals to lie on their sides and pant; when clouds gathered only to evaporate, and people's tempers were edgy; when days dragged into famine, and hope flew from the human heart, no rescue in sight—just then the sky darkened and cracked open, and the first large drops spattered to earth. A surge of wind bent the trees, leaves clattered together under sheets of rain, rain fell and kept falling, everyone running outside to get wet. *Saris* stuck to women's legs, shirts to men's shoulders, and hairdos came undone, mud splattered freshly polished shoes as well as bare feet and the legs of cows and chickens. Rain stopped *tongas* and bicycles and buses, closed shops and schools, courts of law, restaurants. Children tipped back their heads to catch a taste of rain. Rain cooled the air, washed the trees, filled the wells. For a month, it rained. Bucketsful of rain. Days and days of rain. Sun caught its reflection in a trillion waterdrops. Hardened seeds split open. What was brown, turned green. Like the quick slapping wing beats of pigeons rising in a flock, rain sang its home-coming, and we survived.

On the game field around the banyan tree, water stood ten inches deep. As a girl I rode my bicycle into the grassy shallows, sloshing, standing on the pedals to push through the dense weight, toppling over instead, soaked and laughing.

1989. Now, AS I ride the bus to visit the Taj Mahal, that young girl still accompanies me. We lean out the window and watch the world together.

Occasionally beside the road, wild peacocks iridesce through the shadow and sun of newly-planted eucalyptus. As they come into view, I strain after glimpses of ibis, kingfisher, lapwing and hawk. Stopping to stretch or explore a crowded street scene, our group of American trekkers stare, and are in turn stared at, our privilege and plenty not always comfortable garments to wear.

The steady pace of water buffalo, camels, bullocks and cows soothes me. These animals seem timeless as they accommodate themselves to the press of traffic, the fumes and honking. Camels with bells around their ankles eye us balefully as we try to take pictures. A buffalo follows the lead of its nose-ring, head tipped back. Another lolls in fetid, comforting waters while a small boy scrubs it, splashing the back he can't reach, hooves and young toes sometimes touching.

All my life I had heard of the Taj Mahal, a catch-all for beauty, dulled to a cliché. I wasn't prepared for the power of its presence, its luminous marble, its forms intimate and metaphoric, full of resonance, surprise, inevitability. It floats beyond the red sandstone arches that introduce it, the procession of courtyards and reflecting pools, the lush trees and lawns surrounding it.

Because Indian shrines and temples are sacred, we step out of our shoes, leaving them with the hundreds of others flocking the entrance. I stand on the marble piazza to contemplate the Arabic script dancing around the border of the huge entrance arch, its milky marble alive with calligraphied strokes inscribing the first sixteen books of the Koran. Inside, I run my fingers over a lapis butterfly. Beneath the high-ceilinged dome over the crypt, an old man cups his hands to his mouth, tips his head back, and utters a call to prayer so haunting, it seems to unwind from his soul and gather us up.

Millions of feet have worn down these floors. I try to hold the glow of marble, the sensuous curve of dome and arch, the pressed flowers in memory. I don't want to leave, to relinquish this presence. I buy a book with the best photographs and text I can find, as if to keep what I must leave behind.

SHAH JAHAN, GRANDSON OF the great Mughal emperor, Akbar, shared his grandfather's passion for building and for bringing people of different faiths together. He encouraged respect, and even inter-marriage, between Muslims and Hindus, strengthening his kingdom in the process. When his third wife, the beloved Mumtaz Mahal, died during the birth of their fourteenth child, he ordered his court into two years of mourning, and never re-married. Jahan lived another quarter century, devoting himself to a memorial worthy of his love. Mumtaz's crypt lies in the center of the Taj and after his death Jahan was buried beside her.

At the time of its building, twenty thousand workmen labored over the Taj, master craftsmen, skilled engineers and architects from all over India, Persia, Turkey and west Asia, completing the task in 1654. Although professionals gave life to his dream, it was Jahan himself who envisioned the white marble exterior, the domed, arched and minaretted concert of forms that became the Taj. He borrowed the best features of Persian and Indian buildings without their distracting embellishments.

Because of his great wealth and power, Jahan was able to attract the best artists from many countries. A master calligrapher from Baghdad inscribed flowing verses from the Koran around the entrance way's great arch. Skilled Hindu stone-workers, whose ancestors had handed down the secrets of their craft one generation to the next, chipped away whole lifetimes with hammer and chisel. Goldsmiths, gem-cutters, masons worked in concert over the years. The entire building was first made of brick, formed and baked right there, the mortar hand-mixed from a special formula of flour, fruit juice and rock dust. Once set, the surface was overlaid with marble painstakingly cut and fitted with semi-precious stones.

In that hot, dry world, flowers, considered sacred by Muslims, occupied a central motif in the building's decorative features. And throughout the grounds, engineers fashioned ingenious canals to water real gardens, fragrant with fruit trees, flowering shrubs and every imaginable variety of rose, jasmine and lily. Finally, the long reflecting pool in front of the Taj mirrored the building the way a lover's eyes mirror the beloved.

Although Jahan proved a wise and benevolent ruler, he was also a warrior, his vast kingdom built on ruthless conquests whose treasure financed the Taj. That struggle for power spread to his sons, and one of them eventually captured and imprisoned the father to usurp his throne. Peering through an iron grate, Jahan spent the last ten years of his life in captivity watching Mumtaz's shrine emerge, floating up, as it seemed, over the river. Rumor has it that before he was imprisoned he had the right hand of the master mason cut off so that he could never create a building as beautiful as the Taj again.

Whenever I behold beauty, I think of the cost: the cut-off hands and the broken backs, the plundered treasure, the privilege granted a few, the dream and the shattering of dreams to dust and rubble. And yet, there it is, a beauty so pure, we cannot let it go. It infuses us with longing, the way truth does, or love.

30

AS WE CLIMB BACK into the bus and drive away, we watch the land gradually begin its rise to meet the great Himalayan foothills. Once in the hill town of Dehra Dun, the bus will go no farther, and we will move into Russian-built cars, hired for the final steep ascent into Landour. But first, we have a pre-arranged meeting with Mrs. Vijaya Lakshmi Pandit, former ambassador to the United States, Great Britain and Russia, past president of the United Nations' General Assembly, and sister to Jawaharlal Nehru. I knew her as a child, affectionately, as Aunt Nan, our house in Allahabad not far from Anand Bhawan, the gracefully-pillared two-storey Nehru family home with its sun-sheltered verandas and roof topped by a cupola.

Nehru was like a son to Gandhi, who chose him as his political heir. In the forties, when India was on the brink of Independence, our family, like so many others, was keenly involved in the movement. Besides passionate discussions with colleagues and friends, Dad attended many of the rallies that took place all over India. I went with him to one in Allahabad in which over a million people gathered. On a wooden platform wired with loudspeakers, Gandhi and other members of the Congress party addressed the sea of white-clad men listening attentively or cheering and chanting *Gandhi-ji ki jai!* Victory to Gandhi! *Inquala Zindabad!* Long live revolution!

Nehru was once at our house for dinner. He liked children, and before long, we were rough-housing on the rug. I was sitting on his chest pulling on his shirt while he made me laugh. Mother took a shine to him, to his beautiful dark eyes and attentive nature, his serious thoughtfulness and light-hearted banter.

We visited Aunt Nan at Anand Bhawan a few times for tea, her daughters playing tag with us children and enticing us with sweets while the grown-ups visited. Her daughters had attended Woodstock for several years, and when they went to Wellesley, our family took care of their little Cairn terrier.

During one of her speaking tours in America, Aunt Nan gave a talk at Bryn Mawr College. I was still a boarder at Shipley, and was given permission by Miss Speer to go and see her. In honor of the occasion, I dressed in a *sari* but neglected to gather the first row of pleats before wrapping the rest of the fabric around my waist. I had hobbled my stride, leaving me self-conscious as I minced my way along the half block to sit in the packed college auditorium.

Nan's impassioned speech thrilled me, as did her sparkling beauty. Later, led to a smaller room, I saw her face light up in greeting as she welcomed me, gathering me into her arms for a long hug. How quickly she put me at ease! A few weeks later, a package arrived in the mail containing a long, spring-green silk scarf richly bordered in gold lotus-blossoms. Still bright, it lies folded in tissue paper, and occasionally warms my shoulders.

Now, on this return trip to India forty-two years later, I don't expect her to remember me, but she does, and with such warmth, my eyes fill with tears. One of her daughters, Rita, is with her, affectionate and playful as she takes me in tow to help with tea, *samosas* and cookies. Before long, her sister, Tara, arrives with her steadying spirit. Rita and her mother reminisce about the long blond braids they remembered me by as a child, and the fun we had.

Aunt Nan, now in her nineties, sits in her soft green robe and slippers, recovering from illness, pushing her teeth in from time to time: *I'm sorry, but I'm having trouble with my teeth.* We trekkers sit around her, asking questions about family planning, the up-coming elections, foreign aid, women's rights, health care, the partition of India and Pakistan. Mentally quick, forthright as ever in her answers, she gives us a great deal to think about. Bob has arranged this meeting with her, and I'm especially grateful to him because within a year she is dead.

A small lawn and garden falls away from her house, and

when I admire it, she tells me that the week before, a black panther strolled across it in full daylight. Her pleasure in glimpsing the elusive, wild creature touches me. She, the panther and I share the startling vividness and brevity of our lives, and a longing to preserve the endangered wilderness that has sustained us.

WE'RE ON THE MOVE AGAIN. Upwards. First the winding roads, then the smudged valley below. First the whistling thrush, then sunlight on a ridge, the cool, still air, silhouettes of hills. This is the Gharwhal region of northwest India near the town of Mussoorie. During my childhood, the road hadn't yet reached the town or the school a mile beyond it. Students walked or rode a small horse up the zig-zagging trails. Woodstock—still perched at 7,500 feet in the Himalayan foothills—can now be reached by car. Leopard, bear, deer and game birds continue to roam freely. We arrive at the school mid-morning for tea, an introductory talk and a look around the old quadrangle.

I can't believe I'm here! Or that George is sharing this landscape with me! Unable to trek with the others because of my back, I'm content to stay at the boarding school, to see if the memories I've carried with me all these years ring true.

Soon the trekkers must leave, and I hug George goodbye, wave to the others, and busy myself unpacking and settling in. No schedule now. Ten days on my own while the trekkers are driven deep into the mountains on roads that didn't exist when I was a child. Once on foot, they'll be able to hike trails to some of the higher passes. I wish them good weather and safe return.

My room for the next ten days is over the principal's office. It's a corner room, spacious and letting in light from two side windows with a view of overlapping hills and the plains below the town of Dehra Dun. In the foreground, a long-needled pine—dubbed the lyre tree because of its harp-shaped outer branches—brushes needles against the sky. I feel as if I'd never left, and at the same time, as if I were a stranger looking in on the child who lived here long ago.

Before dinner, Saroj Kapadia comes to greet me, saying I'm to take my meals downstairs in the faculty dining room. She's an exuberant and lovely woman who serves as my guide and hostess. Head of the alumni office, she's been an active member of the school community for years.

That first morning, I'm awake at four, doze, then get up and wash my hair. I unpack a *sari* and a few cotton clothes to iron. Such a journey back in time! I'd forgotten how leaden the irons were, how massive the wooden boards, covered with flowered calico, pleated into skirts. I warm up the iron and the light goes on, then the three-pronged plug falls out, an overhead bulb in the ceiling falters, tap water stops. No need to iron. Slipping outside, I cut fresh flowers—one red, one pink geranium, a purple many-petaled climber. The little brass vase I find on a shelf brightens with its new bouquet. So do my spirits.

Sun on my back, I pull out my sketch book to study the Sansad-hara hills, listen as the sparrows wake, then the roosters and crows. The *chowkidar* moves as softly as his shadow to make the rounds, only his bunched keys talking, unlocking doors and hallways and hidden chambers of my heart.

Fifty years and there's still no heat in these damp and mil-dewed buildings. As children, we wore cotton dresses or corduroy jumpers over blouses, wool sweaters, socks that bunched up in our sturdy, leather, lace-up shoes. The *mochi*, or village cobbler, traced our feet on a piece of newspaper, and within a few days the shoes appeared. They always fit beautifully.

Over our dresses we usually wore pinafores sewn with pockets where a small hand could hide a piece of ribbon or a butterfly's lost wing. I was lost myself. Often late or in trouble, my six-year-old sobs were consoled by a classmates' narrow arm around my shoulder. Just as often, the two of us sat giggling unstoppably as we shared stories or sucked on the soft peppermints we'd just bought with the *paisas* dropped into our outstretched hands as allowance on Saturdays.

Today after breakfast, I meet Dohma, the diminutive Tibet-an nurse I admire and visit again later. Dohma, who fled across those numbing passes, losing everything to the Chinese butchers. Dohma, longing for home.

Each day, just at dawn and just at dusk outside my window, a whistling thrush sings its clear, piercing notes. Ponies necklaced in bells, their backs laden with burlap saddles carrying grain and milk to market, clop along the steep dirt road that wraps around the kitchen and administration building. The mountain folk wear soft, patched and layered clothes of cotton or wool that blend with the landscape.

Nature, unimpressed as always by our comings and goings, nevertheless lets me feel at home here, the lost child still looking back at me from gravel playgrounds and dank, peeling walls. I walk the trails, noticing again how pine trees freshen against the darker deodar, rhododendron and oak, dry moss fraying the branches of the oak. It's October, still summer in the mountains. Shy, masked *langur* monkeys plunge through treetops at my approach, bending branches to span the risk of space.

I try a watercolor of the overlapping hills I sketched earlier. In the courtyard someone practices the flute—lovely pure notes, breathy and halting.

Later this afternoon, I sit in on a Hindi class, wishing I could still speak the language. The students are bright, the teacher strict. When the customs inspector at the New Dehli airport looked over my passport, questioning me in the wooden voice of officialdom, he stamped and returned it and I thanked him in Hindi—*Dhan-yabad*. At the sound of my greeting his eyes, for the first time, widened into focus. I cherished the hint of a smile that escaped him as I walked away, and the sound in my own mouth reclaiming a bit of the past. Now I wish, also, for the fluency of childhood.

My next visit is with faculty and staff during their tea break on a walled patio overlooking the hills. Young men and women, Baptists, Methodists, Presbyterians, they come from the British Isles, Australia, the U.S. and other countries, to teach and serve, and to experience life in the Himalayas. Hard-working as teachers everywhere, they chat sociably in the brisk, sweet air.

Later I sit in on a student music performance—*cithar* and *tabla* with dancers. Two of the young girls are especially capable, but after the applause, one is in tears and still crying half an hour later. I try to console her with how beautifully she danced, but it doesn't counter the pressure students at Woodstock, as at most schools, still feel to excel. Hadn't I once played a piano solo for assembly, my feet barely reaching the pedals? And even though I played well, isn't all I remember fear?

I watch third and fourth graders at a game—*run, stop, fall down, get up, salute*—all on quick commands from the teacher. Clearly, if the teacher is not obeyed promptly, the once-eager-children are dropped from the game and their shoulders slump as they walk away. Collaboration and inventive play feel as absent in these games as they were when I attended Woodstock.

The path to Zig Zag robs my lungs. As I climb higher, the grey Presbyterian church rises rock-solid as ever. Fifty years ago I fidgeted in its pews. Now that I've reached the *chukkar*, or ridge road, the far-off Tibetan peaks once more reveal their splendor. I rest on the rock wall before circling the crest of the hill where a cow path leads me to the blackened houses of the very poor. Goats and chickens scatter, a few adults look up with unmasked hostility. I stare back at myself through their eyes.

No longer the child who spoke Hindi and was welcome anywhere—my platinum braids touched curiously by the women, the children crowding to pelt me with questions—I see now I'm a foreign tourist, and feel shame that my heavy, over-stuffed duffel was carried to my room by a bent-over old man.

31

THIS EVENING SAROJ INVITES me to a Hindi wedding. The bride hasn't arrived yet—she's still being dressed—but the reception has begun. Bob Alter drives us. He and Ellen are the last of the missionaries still serving in the community who knew my parents. In spite of their friendly manner, an edge of uneasiness creeps over me from childhood. What is it about missionaries?—the mix of humility and pride that surrounds them?—the coupling of Christian charity with entitlement? that sense of magnanimity toward their servants? How would they feel being the servants? As we rumble through the bazaar, Bob and Ellen wave at friends and acquaintances. We dodge foot traffic, cows, goats, horses, dogs, other cars.

MARIGOLDS! FOR THE WEDDING they've been strung across the entrance to the hotel. As a child I buried my nose in the cool thick petals, watched women thread the flowers for garlands, or heap them over corpses to be burned at the ghats. From trains hurtling across the double-decker bridge above the Jumna, men and women still throw marigolds and coins into the river. I wonder if six-year-olds continue to dive for the change tumbling like stars into the fathomless deep.

The father of the bride—a Westernized Indian attorney—welcomes us enthusiastically. He is a Rotarian friend of Saroj's husband, Ronnie. The women are dressed in their loveliest saris, deeply bordered in gold and silver to weight the billowing silks of magenta, saffron, lapis and jade. By contrast, the men wear dark Western-style suits as if to mimic their British colonizers.

The women assume their seats in a single file on one side of the room, men on the other. I catch a glimpse of the medieval kitchen, but the tables in front of us have been carefully prepared with hot hors d oeuvres, chili dips, plates of sweet, white fudge known as *burfi*, and kettles of tea. We are welcomed graciously (the only Westerners) and invited to please eat. I ask Saroj if the food is safe for my western stomach: *yes*, to the cooked items, *no*, to the candy. Delicious flavors—deep fried eggplant, cheese and cauliflower; hot sweet tea with heated milk. Sadly, we're never able to see the wedding. By the time it starts, over two hours later, we're due at Saroj's friend, Diana's, for dinner.

I finally get up enough nerve to take a few pictures. One woman in particular, stunningly bejewelled and saried, smiles broadly as I catch her in the frame, so I try for another, but the camera quits working. The mother-in-law of the bride comes over to say, I see you haven't eaten any sweets. I thank her for the delicious food, and go back for seconds. The woman I photographed stands serenely in a corner, smiling and watchful, but not eating anything. Saroj explains that as a family member of the wedding party, she's not allowed to eat.

Back at Woodstock, Diana serves a beautiful *Hindustani khana* complete with fresh *chapatis* still being made, and *hulva*. She, like her friends, entertains with graciousness and that touch of Raj dignity the Brits were fond of. The food couldn't be better. I am touched, especially because I know Diana does not have much money. She employs a shriveled-up, bent-over *ayah*—very sweet, with a toothless smile and cataracted eyes, a member of the family for decades. I learn later that the *ayah* has done all the cooking and serving, and a young boy has cleaned up. While we have drinks and conversation before dinner, this sweet *ayah* sits near us on a little settee. She is like a grandmother, moving slowly, but with a life-time of making in her hands—meals, children, clothing, conversation, community.

When I get back to my room, I have a stomach ache, and hope I haven't made some fatal mistake in eating, especially now that

I'm over my cold and want to stay well for George's return. Too uncomfortable to sleep, I stay up until midnight packing. Lights out. Just as I'm dozing, footsteps— soft and stealthy. Fear floods my body. I remember I didn't bolt the door as I'd been instructed to, and have visions of massacres and thefts. Getting up, I secure the bolt, turn on the light, and in the absolute silence, hear the faint shuffling of bare feet. But I'm wrong. It's a moth against the screen. How quickly I imagine the worst! I get to sleep eventually but wake at 5:30, insides still uneasy. My last day in the Himalayas.

Finish packing. Breakfast at 7:15. In my pockets fifty *rupees* (three dollars) for each of the servants, some pens and candy for the children. The usual toast and watery, gelatinous eggs. By the time I leave, only Darshan is there, the old man retired but not re-tired, who'd rather pad between kitchen and dining room than not. I will say final good-byes after lunch. Bitha has asked me at exactly what hour I'd take a cab down the mountain: 1:30 p.m.

After breakfast I walk up to the high school, greeting students and faculty along the way, return my books to the library—Karma-la Das' poems, a book on silviculture with marvelous pen and ink drawings of seeds in various stages of sprouting, leaves and grass-es, nuts and berries, and a book of short stories. I have enough time to attend a Hindi class or an assembly. Instead, I know I want to say goodbye to the mountains. Yesterday, tears. Today dry eyes, hungry to hold the image I cannot take with me. I let the pitch of the hill register, the flavors and textures be absorbed. Up the steep switchback by our old house, up through small groves of mountain oaks to the *chukkar*, and there, in the cool shade of evergreens, the far snows, their peaks coming close in the morning light. Then the tears fall and I let them.

These mountains: what is the kinship between us? Their steep sides taught my legs sturdiness; their oaks and deodars, hem-locks and rhododendrons provided a canopy for the hidden songs I carry with me, the radiant sunsets, the clatter and downpour of rain. Perhaps my children will see them, or my children's children. If not, they are loved by *those that dwell therein*. I know the icy granite chutes, the bitter stones and winds, the cold that pushes life away. But also that these foothills flutter with green, that war-blers and panthers flourish along the *khuds*, that human families call these mountains home. In spite of poor sanitation and simple conditions, life is lived richly and with great intensity. Small birds sing. The air is sweet and fresh. The distant snows hold.

Returning my *Namaste* as he passes, a milkman walks the steep hills as he has since childhood, his slim frame layered in the soft colors of the forest, his footfall rhythmic and steady, the heavy metal container on his back secure in its jute hammock. At dawn he or his wife have risen early to milk a few goats or the cow in its shed, the milk watered down to stretch its price for market.

Two hours. I know it's time to move back down the path— past the pair of monks in saffron robes walking a small dog; past the woman on a stone wall in the sun throwing rice into the air from a basket, blowing the chaff away, picking out bits of rock; past a ragged child bathing an even more ragged baby, the mother pouring water over a third child, cold water, dirty, from a bucket on the ground; past the slow cows, dung on their rumps, bells at their throats, the birds quieter now that the sun has heated up.

After putting my breakfast napkin and holder in its little box, closing the dining room door and stepping into the darker hall, I hear someone's soft call. It's Darshan. Hands together in Hindi greeting, his *Dhanyabad*, Thank you, falls like a blessing around me, kind face close, the spark of friendship between us, however awkwardly we've reached across the language barrier. I'm touched that he has made the effort to step out and offer me his own good-bye, wonder what his home life is like, his long history—wonder, too, about Bitha, knowing I won't see him again.

Packed bags ready, I hear a knock on the door and assume it's news of the taxi. But it's Bitha. I've never seen him in this remote section of the building, but he extends his hand and says goodbye in English. Will you write? he asks me again. I tell him I will, and am glad that he's bothered to stop by. It's amusing how he can't re-sist looking past me into my room to satisfy his curiosity. Earlier, he asked whether Americans had servants and how much a pass-port and an airline ticket cost: that hunger to escape, not present in the old man's eyes, but there in the young one's. Perhaps, too, he's looking for the parka I had him try on to see if it would fit. I want him to have it, but Saroj says no, it will leave the others out, and besides the school gives each person plenty of clothing.

We could be on opposite sides of the doorway, he the privi-leged traveler, me tethered by poverty and chance. He carries himself proudly, with no shortage of intelligence or skill. I continue to wish I knew Hindi and could talk freely with both men. Through the kitchen's swinging doors, I've often heard their animated voices, off-guard, with their friends. Or have seen one of them sitting on a bench out back, quietly smoking. Who am I to be served? To cross the barriers, we practice words: *Darwaza kholna*, open the door. *Darwaza bund kijiye*, close the door please.

Three women walking beyond the school grounds to the mountain road wish me goodbye. We hug, exchange looks, handshakes, laughter, the cost of even the slightest friendship a measure of loss.

My driver has a straight back and beautiful salt and pepper hair, long and carefully trimmed. He's uninterested in communicating but deftly maneuvers the Maruti through a crowded, bumpy bazaar. Faces pass by close to our open windows, young women in *purdha*, shop keepers, bunches of men, an occasional cow. The engine roars, gears grind, and once in Mussoorie where there isn't room for two cars to pass and he's forced under protest to back up, the car stalls several times. I have visions of never making it to Dehra Dun.

All the windows are down and a brisk wind cools us. I use a wet washcloth over my nose and mouth and hold my breath whenever an uphill bus spewing acrid black diesel fumes passes us. My driver careens downhill, honking the horn at every corner, just missing a cow, a mother and child, a bicycler, a throng of school children, women and men breaking rock by hand to build roads, carrying dung in baskets on their heads, laying brick, chewing *paan*, turning their backs to urinate beside the road. As I lean out the window, the hills are shaken with sunlight and wind, goldenrod among the grasses, two large *langurs* in a tree, birds flashing by.

All day I wipe away tears. I can't wait to see George, and I mourn the loss of the Himalayas.

School girls in uniforms, the motion constant and timeless—of people and animals, of dust and the landscape passing our car as it winds back and forth like a shuttle lowering itself through a tapestry, my heart not daring to imagine too freely that soon I'll see my husband—saying, instead, *grasses, gulleys, descent*—the sky farther up there as I crane my head at the corners to look back.

2:45 p.m. We arrive in Dehra Dun. I thank the driver and pay him ten rupees more than the one hundred thirty agreed on. He grins widely and is off. Now the long wait.

In my upstairs room, I wash, stretch out on the bed to write a few notes, and after an hour, walk in the back yard only to return to the balcony outside our room, looking for the trekkers. Finally, I'm content just to sit in the lobby, face the glass entrance doors, men coming and going, a light bulb replaced, Hindi over the phone, occasional cars, and at last, at 6 p.m., that car with red and blue knapsacks on its roof. I'm on my feet, and here they come!

Dusty, weather-beaten, the endless bus and car rides there and back, the days of trekking—overnights at Toppovan at 14,000 feet, hikes to 17,000, the land and its people, the pack animals and the soaring birds—the glory of it, and the fatigue, all, without their knowing it, clearly visible in their faces. Here's Bob, binoculared and knapsacked, both schoolmate and leader, hugging me warmly. Here are Tom and Gloria, smiling, and, heavens, Russel and Lorraine look sick. And where's Wendy?

There he is, at last, my love, my lost and found. Our eyes embrace before our arms reach out. And then the joy of perfect holding. I'm on my toes. He has brought back pictures, and reports excellent weather at the top of the world, a dazzle of peaks.

32

AS IT HAPPENS, WE start the return journey home on my fifty-fourth birthday, November 1, 1989. The lights of New Delhi, scattering into the dark, are behind us. We're flying at about 30,000 feet over the Karokorams, a part of the vast Himalayan range. I press my face to the glass, looking for K-2 against a ripening sky, see instead the great ridges and folds of lower mountains under a veil of blowing clouds.

India, like a dusty carpet rich in debris and jewels, sinks into memory. Drugged by Triaminic, overpowered by sleep, I fall under the spell of time-warps.

Sikh, Hindu, Christian, Jew, Agnostic, Jain, Buddhist, Moslem—all falling asleep in a stupor of fatigue and trust on the same plane, infants across their mother's bodies, turbaned men slack-jawed, silk-clad, braceleted women and young girls snoring quietly, trekkers in Kathmandu T-shirts and jeans, businessmen— British, German, American, Japanese—upright and comatose, or slumped against each other, the engine's steady drumming dulling us into oblivion. Dulling us to the passage of a spinning earth as mountain ranges and barren deserts move seawards, the heavens clear and endless over the cloud layer, the clouds' gossamer tops blowing off like crests of waves or the cornices of history, and we ourselves dispersed.

Last night, even though it made me feel conspicuous and shy, I wore my sari to our farewell dinner, as Wendy wore her Indian turquoise silk scarf over black slacks and sweater, all of us scrubbed and transformed. We sat at a long linen-clothed table holding three red roses, silver candelabra and the flame of camaraderie as fellow-travelers—Chinese soup in delicate bowls, entrees of Basmati rice, curried fish, chicken, beef and vegetables. Bob said goodbye to us and we to him, individual voices gathered like tinder.

Within hours, we dragged locked duffles, knapsacks, suitcases outside our doors to be picked up for transport on our journey home.

Bussed to the airport, slowly shuffled through lines of inspection, we faced customs, immigration, arms- and drug-searches; pried batteries out of clocks, radios, headlamps, cameras. People in uniform, as well as everyday travelers, sprawled across floors, over chairs, beside tables where strong tea or whiskey could be sipped.

A two-hour stop at Frankfurt. Nice to walk, even in a crowded, smoky place, to hear German, to catch the chorus of European languages. This time, seven out of ten stalls in the women's room are flooded and filthy. I complain to a female security guard whose rudeness turns surly. Raising my voice, I scold that if she can't help, she should find someone who can, that it's unfair to leave such a long line of women and children waiting. She finally sends me through several gates to an information booth where quickly and politely, a clean-up crew is summoned.

When we disembarked, the plane looked like a war zone—pillows, blankets, crushed paper everywhere. Now, inside again, the space is orderly. I'm sorry to lose the Indian faces, the courtesy and proud carriage of their flight attendants. On the other hand, it feels good to meet the American crew, brashly optimistic and at ease.

New York! A beautiful, sunny day, spring-warm. Things work! Even at the airport where we flag down a cab, we catch the cosmopolitan, melting-pot atmosphere of the city. The cabby's from Singapore, hoping to return there in a month. Mid-40's. Heavy accent. Squashed look to his head, his manner sturdy, animated, optimistic, expansive. He tells us about the high cost of owning versus renting a cab, about insurance rates and liabilities, about the city and how he's learned his way around (I try to imagine myself guiding travelers around Singapore!) all the while maneuvering smoothly through traffic. There's the Empire State building, Central Park, Riverside church that I visited as a teenager, the wonderful crush of people, their faces from all over the world, the battered, bumpy streets. In spite of the constant thunder of traffic, we're safely delivered to the Trump Towers where George's sister and her husband are temporarily housed on a business assignment.

When the doorman lets us in, I feel like I'm back in the city with a Shipley classmate who took me home for Thanksgiving. Florence's mother, sad-eyed and straight-backed, sits at one end of a mahogany table, the two of us on either side. A maid in starched white, frilled apron and cap serves lunch from a heavy silver platter. We eat in awkward silence. In the evening, we ride the elevator down to the dining room. Flo's mother slips some folded bills from her palm to the *maitre de's* while pretending not to, the murmur of voices and the glitter of beautifully gowned and suited couples drawing us in.

Soon a plate's before me, its slab of roast beef so big our whole family could have lived off of it for a week. *You must buy new shoes tomorrow,* Flo's mother intones, noticing her daughter's barely-scuffed patent leathers. The next morning the chauffeur opens and closes car doors for us high school girls, and I watch as Flo is fitted for a new pair of Mary-Janes. When the visit is over, I carry my treasured box of hand-me-down shoes and clothes back to school, knowing they'll sustain me for the coming year.

Here we are forty years later with another doorman opening the heavy polished glass that leads to a lobby quieted with carpeting. A bouquet of fresh flowers doubles in the mirror. The elevator operator, with the same courteous gestures, greets us as if he can't see our wrinkled Lands End clothes and unkempt hair, and we respond with small talk as if we don't notice the slight limp in his walk or that we're being ushered up to the fifty-first floor of some of the world's most expensive real estate. Our bags arrive simultaneously by the service elevator. George loosens the little brass key tied by a string to his belt-loop, and passes it to the doorman. Having flown in on an earlier plane, George's sister would have alerted him, and he lets us in.

We're greeted by the Swedish crystal and Chinese-blue silk carpet of a spacious living-dining area. At the other end of the living room a great wall of glass windows frames the distant trees of Central Park below us, and the buildings around it, the city itself becoming the room's work of art. Against a cerulean sky, the only visible movement is an American flag unfolding and folding itself serenely; beside it, an ancient, copper-celadone roof-spire catches the light. We stand like a caravan arrived at an oasis.

Tap water clean enough to drink. How sweet the taste of an orange!

After hours of trying, I finally get through to our sons, and fight back tears, hearing their voices. How I've missed them!

12:30 a.m.: We've been up for 50 hours! I'm still not in my own body which is traveling to catch up—or tugging at me to stay back with it at a slower pace.

After five hours of sleep, I'm wide awake again, enjoy reading a book I find on the coffee table: Benezir Bhuto's, *Daughter of the East.*

10:00 a.m. George and I take an hour's walk in Central Park. Bless the visionary who saved this space filled with beautiful trees!—Sycamores with dappled trunks, a great variety of hardwoods, among them the lovely ginkos with their fan-shaped, sunny foliage. As we crunch over fallen leaves, I'm reminded of boarding school, the trees around Shipley, their shuffle-around sounds, the aroma of autumn. A network of leafy branches crowds the sky. Squirrels in their silver-grey coats travel the aerial highway, or bound nimbly over the ground before scooting up trunks.

The new year looks promising—with word that Romania and East Germany might be free, and Russia opening up to the world.

We walk to the Metropolitan museum. Matisse. His poster of the dancers on the wall beside me—deep blue, turquoise and Sienna, the two figures beautifully in motion, reminding me of the Hindu lovers, Rama and Sitha, dancing together.

AN AMERICAN CHILD GROWING up in India, open to diversity and multiplicity, enriched by two cultures, I find myself claimed by neither, tumbled and shaped by opposing forces, the way waves work back and forth in fashioning the beach and its cargo of stones. The Pacific Northwest has long felt like home, but I remain, in some ways, a foreigner on both continents.

Memory: it constructs its own landscape. Why does it hold on to one experience and not to another? Perhaps the jolt of fear, the tug of surprise, of loss or joy with which an event originally registers, binds it to us, while the daily and familiar fall away. Does memory light the way, or does it blind me from seeing the truth? Do I wear the past like a talisman over my heart to keep me from danger? Or does the past contain the danger—prevent me from discovering who I can become? Whatever memory saves, seems to drift and shimmer in the light, as if with a life of its own. In the end, I like reaching back, drawing the past into the present, introducing the child to the adult she has become.

Now, when memory speaks, I write down what she says. Not to judge, but to enable—the way a wire enables electricity to travel through it, lighting up a room. Whatever wants to be carried or revealed rises out of the moth-dark shade, and I find space for it on the page. At certain times, the random scraps come together to illuminate a truth. That's what I'm after. That, and an on-going dialogue with the child who knew too much, but had no language with which to express it.

She tells me that sometimes she felt bleak inside, heavy as a rock. Or trapped and panicky as a bird flapping in a chimney. In the company of her peers, she often felt thin-skinned, her outer shell cracking in a thousand ways, the inner sheath shriveling as it pulled apart. Even after she grew tall, she felt at fault, unmendable, always hungry, always watchful.

But it wasn't just like that. Life still surged through her in a jumble of the daily. Little joys and victories, bits of beauty mixed in. Laughter. She loved the shapes and voices of the world—people, the burble of *hookas*, call of mourning doves, the pungence of wood smoke, curry and soap, the stateliness of trees and how they carried the sky. Water, stars, *saris*, mountains, cranes.

As a growing-up-girl, too close to pain and remembering, she learned forgetting, and later, numbness. Awkward and ashamed, she felt slow to comprehend, full of mistakes. Even though she was outwardly *happy* and excited by the world's possibilities, eager to find her way, she needed to be liked in order to feel safe, look pretty in order to be seen. Moving past that, she could become a warrior, championing the voiceless, fighting for equality between rich and poor, brown and white. *Why are they hungry and not us? What are we doing to help them? Why are cows sacred and children sacrificed, their bones broken so they can beg?* It was her father who talked over the questions with her, referring back to Jesus, Gandhi,

Schweitzer, calling for the formation of a United Nations, a World Bank, social justice, a more equitable distribution of wealth.

In high school I petitioned to have Blacks and Jews admitted to Shipley. One token Jewish girl was enrolled during the years I was a boarder. Could I invite a Black boy to one of our dances? No. Society wasn't yet ready to risk accepting Blacks in schools such as ours.

At least verbally, I became a mediator and an advocate for change. I encouraged others to think about social issues and ways we might promote justice and equal opportunity. In college I agreed to chair Reed's first Pacific Coast Arts Festival. We brought in painters, singers, poets, dancers from all over the country. I admired the Quakers, their non-violent, concensus-building principles, and considered myself a conscientious objector. At the Juvenile Home I was willing to take the heat for my co-workers when management threatened. Still, I regret not having freed myself enough from the damaging effects of childhood to feel secure, to become more pro-active, more subversive, better able to lead as well as to love and be loved.

BY APRIL, ON THE Olympic Peninsula, a few sandhill cranes will kettle up with the hawks to cross the Strait of Juan de Fuca, circling over Neah Bay as if to gather strength for the journey, their calls haunting reminders of that other world whose sultry heat vibrated with the same wooden flute notes ages ago.

Yesterday against a bank of darker clouds, or today after rain rinses the sky to transparent blue, the mountain range turns crisp, bringing far things near. Memory, too, holds up its field of flowering mustard against the greens of spring—both here at home in the American Northwest and on the hot plains of India.

For a moment, I stand at a window on this side of the world, and listen to a crow play the musical rattle I heard as a child. A second crow snaps off a twig high in the madrona and flies off to poke together a nest, as if time could be undone, and place constructed out of thin air, making something we call home. In India, I watched crows pumping their caws from the branch of a *neem* tree, or from Daddy's shoulder when he kept one as a pet. They gloss my thoughts, and catch the sheen of our passing lives.

33

WHEN MY FAMILY CAME to America to stay, America held out its hand to us, and many people helped. They still do. Recently, I listened to naturalist, Robert Pyle, read and talk passionately about the butterflies of Cascadia he's spent his life studying. Now, I think of him whenever a swallowtail or cabbage white sails over our deck or lands on a dandelion. His efforts in conservation, his writings, his quiet generosity imprint themselves on my life, guiding it as surely as Gandhi did, or the poet William Stafford. Stafford's reading was the first I heard by a live poet, marking me indelibly with the power of his unassuming presence and his quiet, listening-to-the-universe-voice. Beethoven still pours his heart into the emotional center of my world. So does Martin Luther King, finding shoes for dreams and leading us through the streets. Mary Cassatt catches the bond between mother and child I feel for my own. Yeats casts spells with the hidden music of his words, teaching me to listen.

I listen, too, to the Irish seamstress with brimming eyes who ripped seams and mended people's clothes when we shared lunch-breaks during my months at Peck and Pecks. To the local waitress putting three children through school as if it weren't a big deal. I'm in the faculty lounge packed full of Reed students listening to Roethke read "My Papa's Waltz," each of us touched by resemblances to our own lives. As a young housewife, Casals breaks my heart with his cello, Bird and Sachmo open it to the blues, a college professor coaxes me to read a few lines of Chaucer in Middle English out of love for its cadence. I'm handed on from one to the other, bringing me to my husband, steady as the north star for over forty years, my vibrant children who now have families of their own, my friend, writing partner and editorial soul mate, Alice Derry, who for decades has encouraged my work, and continues to probe the rough drafts with her swift and penetrating mind, her generous heart.

A child holds my hand, the same hand that has cradled other children. We have come this far; we will continue our journey together. Each of the countless mentors we've met along the way, like bright, separate beings, share their understanding of what it means to be human, helping us to survive, lighting up the dark.

D'ANJOU

All day
hunched over the table
trying to remember to breathe

I pencil in three pears.
Looking, drawing, looking.

When I stretch, when I
surface like a seal
lifting into the other world,

light douses me.
Out here
blue dragonflies

hover and sprint
rendering air visible.
Are we so different?

Plump and leaning against
each other sociably
the pears draw me to them,

draw what I never knew
out of myself—

the weight and sweetness
of what's hidden
freed.

—*Charlotte Gould Warren*

Charlotte Warren's poetry collection, *Gandhi's Lap*, won the Washington Prize and publication by Word Works in Washington, D. C. A second poetry manuscript was a finalist in both the Phillip Levine and Ashland national contests. Her memoir, *Jumna*, considers many of the same themes explored in the poems through the wider lens of prose.

Warren's poems have appeared on Seattle buses as well as in journals such as *Orion, Calyx, The Hawai'i Review, The Louisville Review*, and *Kansas Quarterly*. Anthologized poems may be found in *The Miller Cabin Poetry Anthology, Poetic Voices Without Borders*, and *15 Seattle Books*.

She received her MFA in Writing from Vermont College and taught part time at Peninsula College in Washington State. She and her husband have called the Olympic Peninsula home for over forty years, have two grown sons and two grandchildren.

CPSIA information can be obtained at www.ICGtesting.com
Printed in the USA
LVOW061213140712

290087LV00004B/5/P